TARGET FIVE

In the frozen wastes off Greenland's north-eastern coast, a grim battle is fought between highly professional representatives of the American and Russian secret services. An American team of three, led by the Anglo-Canadian, Beaumont, is attempting to ease the defection of a Russian scientist, though it is not so much the man himself they want as the information he carries: plans of the entire Russian submarine network. If the American President could attend the forthcoming Moscow summit meeting with these plans in his pocket he would be in a position of considerable strength. All this becomes clear to the Russians, whose own secret service, guided by that brilliant Siberian, Igor Papanin, quickly latches on to what is about to happen. . . . The defecting Russian is led across the ever-shifting icefield, and the protagonists grapple with appalling conditions on land and sea while desperately trying to out-manœuvre one another. This is a gripping and completely credible thriller, leaving the reader convinced that if it did not by chance happen last week then it must be happening now.

Also by
COLIN FORBES

★

TRAMP IN ARMOUR
THE HEIGHTS OF ZERVOS
THE PALERMO AMBUSH

TARGET FIVE

★

COLIN FORBES

THE
COMPANION BOOK CLUB
LONDON AND SYDNEY

THE COMPANION BOOK CLUB
The Club is not a library; all books are the
property of members. There is no entrance fee
or any payment beyond the low Club price of
each book. Details of membership will gladly
be sent on request.

Write to:
The Companion Book Club,
Odhams Books, Rushden, Northants.

Or, in Australia, write to:
The Companion Book Club,
C/- Hamlyn House Books, P.O. Box 252,
Dee Why, N.S.W. 2099

Made and printed in Great Britain
for the Companion Book Club
by Odhams (Watford) Ltd.
600871770
7.74/277

For Jane

'A crippled Soviet submarine wallowing in a North Atlantic gale . . . dashed by 50-foot waves in a 55-knot gale . . . was first spotted by reconnaissance aircraft from the American base at Keflavik . . .'

The Times, Wednesday, 1 March, 1972

Contents

The Arctic Chessboard, February 1972

As seen from Dawes' office (Washington) and Col. Papanin's (Leningrad)

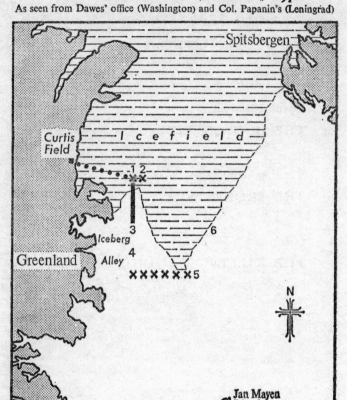

Spitsbergen

Icefield

Curtis Field

1 2

Iceberg Alley

Greenland

3

4

5

6

Jan Mayen Island

N

miles
0 50 100 200 300

0 100 200 300 400 500
kilometres

THE PIECES

1. Target 5 (American research base)
2. North Pole 17 (Soviet base)
3. American icebreaker *Elroy*
4. Soviet research ship *Revolution*
5. Soviet trawlers
6. Soviet helicopter carrier *Gorki*

●●●●●● Beaumont's escape route one

▬▬▬▬ Beaumont's escape route two

Opening Gambit

THE LOCOMOTIVE

Friday, 18 February, 1972: Midnight

EVEN IN THE YEAR 1972, a year which will hardly be noted in the calendar of history as a year of peace, it was not common for an express to be stopped in the middle of the night—in the middle of nowhere—while a passenger was dragged off it by armed men. Especially an American express.

And this traumatic experience was certainly something that Keith Beaumont had no inkling of as he relaxed in bed inside a sleeping-car aboard the Florida Express; for one thing, the thirty-two car train was roaring through the Carolinas at over ninety miles an hour, while outside the February storm beat at the curtained windows; for another thing, the next scheduled stop was over two hours away.

With the windows sealed tight against the rising storm, with the central heating turned up to God knew how many degrees, it was hot and steamy and airless inside the sleeping-car, so hot that the large Englishman was having trouble sleeping as he eased himself up on one elbow and checked his watch. Close to midnight. Behind the zipped curtain which shut him off from the corridor, he settled down again on his pillow and wrapped his hands behind his broad neck, dreaming with his eyes open.

By morning he'd be in Miami, thousands of miles away from Greenland—away from guiding frightened dogs through screaming blizzards, away from hauling bucking sleds over tumbled ice, above all away from endless darkness and cold that paralysed the brain. It was also wonderful to be dry again; Beaumont pressed his stockinged feet hard against the end of the bed and revelled in the warmth.

Twenty miles ahead of the express thundering through the storm-swept night three armed men were not so dry as they huddled in the pouring rain. Standing under the canopy of a whistle-stop station in the middle of nowhere, they waited for the oncoming express which wasn't scheduled to stop for another two hours. The signals were already changing against it, the driver of the huge diesel motor hauling the long, long train was already applying his massive brakes. The emergency was imminent.

'I hope to God he's on board,' one of the raincoated men mumbled as he clenched a sodden cigarette between his teeth.

'He's on board,' the forty-year-old leader of the group assured his companion. 'And we're taking him off it.'

'It could be tricky. . . .'

'This says it won't be tricky.' The older man extracted a ·45 Colt revolver from his pocket, checked the cylinder, put it away again. 'And don't forget, Jo, we have to make it look good—real good.'

Less than twenty miles up the track the driver of the Florida Express was staring anxiously into the night. The signal he had just passed had ordered a reduction of speed but the next stop was two hours away, so what the hell was happening? He went on cutting the speed, applying the great brakes slowly. Rain hammered his steel cab roof, trails of spume whipped off the roof and vanished in the dark. The next signal flashed by. Red for danger, for stop. What the devil was going on? He applied the brakes more strongly. They were close to Cedar Falls, an unscheduled stop.

Two minutes later the train ground to a halt as a thunder-clap burst and rain lashed the sides of the cars. Inside his roomette Beaumont settled down to sleep while the train was still, his large hands clasped outside the sheet. His eyes were closed when the curtains were torn open and a man with a sodden hat brim looked down at him while he checked a photograph in his left hand. 'It's him, Jo,' a quiet voice said. Beaumont opened his eyes and stared into the muzzle of a Colt ·45 revolver.

'Move that thing,' he murmured. 'It might go off—your hand's sticky.'

When he opened his eyes Beaumont registered several swift impressions—the sodden raincoat the man holding the gun wore, the steam rising off the man's sleeves, the scared look on the face of the passenger in the roomette across the corridor, the second raincoated man standing in the background with one hand inside his pocket. The older American, who was feeling the heat—there were sweat beads on his forehead—replied in a flat tone.

'Get dressed—you're getting off the train. . . .'

'And who the hell might you be?' Beaumont demanded.

Exhausted, tired out by his long trip from Greenland to Washington, he estimated his chances carefully. A hard chopping blow to knock the Colt out of the gunman's hand, a knee in the groin. . . . No, it was too dangerous—with other passengers in the sleeping-car.

'Dixon, F.B.I.,' the man with the sweaty forehead snapped. 'And hurry it up—this train can't wait all night. . . .'

'It doesn't have to—it can get moving now as far as I'm concerned. With me on board. And you've made a very bad mistake—I'm British. . . .' Beaumont reached towards his jacket hanging from a hook.

'Watch it. . . .' Dixon warned.

The Englishman stared at him over the width of his very broad shoulders and Dixon felt uncomfortable. 'I'm showing you my passport, for God's sake,' Beaumont rumbled. He took it from the inner jacket pocket carefully, extracted it with his fingertips and handed it to Dixon. The American opened the passport expertly with one hand, studied it for a moment, then showed it to the man behind him. 'It's as phoney as hell, Jo.'

Beaumont made no comment as he pushed back the bedclothes and showed that he was fully dressed except for tie, jacket and shoes. As the Englishman climbed out of bed and stood up, Dixon backed away and stared. Keith Beaumont, thirty-two years old, was six foot two tall, broad-shouldered and weighed over fourteen stone. Not that Dixon was too impressed as he watched the Englishman quietly getting dressed; a big ox was slow-moving. After a minute he checked his watch.

'Hurry it up,' Dixon repeated. He had been right: this man was slow in the reflexes.

'Get stuffed.'

The passenger in the roomette opposite was getting over his shock. 'I'm Andrew Phillipson from Minneapolis,' he informed Dixon in a glib voice. 'This guy said he was from Greenland—where all that ice is. I thought it was funny . . .'

'He'll be off the train in a minute,' Dixon broke in, 'then you can get back to sleep.' He looked at Beaumont who had finished dressing. 'That your bag? Good. Now, place both hands on the bed—close together.' There was a faint clink of metal as Dixon's companion took his hand out of his pocket. Beaumont shook his large head which was covered with thick dark hair and smiled grimly.

'So your friend can slip handcuffs on me? I'm not playing, Dixon, so you'd better make up your mind—do I come as I am or do you shoot me?'

They went down the corridor with Beaumont's hands still free, preceded by the man called Jo who carried the Englishman's suitcase while Dixon brought up the rear. Curtains screening the roomettes were pulled aside as passengers peered out at the little procession. Behind Dixon bare feet padded down the corridor as Phillipson hurried to catch him up. 'Who is the guy?' he called out excitedly. 'He talked to me so maybe I can help. . . .'

'Break-out from Folsom,' Dixon told him tersely.

Beaumont stumbled as he went down the steep steps at the end of the car, his shoulders sagging. Big, sleepy and clumsy, Dixon noted. At the bottom of the steps Beaumont paused on the track to button up his coat and pull his hat down over his ears. Cedar Falls was a small single-storey building, at the edge of a forest, with a side exit leading out into a road beyond. Beaumont saw this as lightning flashed, showing a brief, stark view of wind bending trees to the south, then a curtain of rain whooshed down the track and soaked him. A few yards away one of the train crew was watching with a mixture of nervousness and curiosity. A second railroad official stood under the station canopy. Dixon came down the steps behind him, nudged him with the Colt.

'Get moving—through that exit.'

They started walking with the other American still in front, carrying Beaumont's case. Then there was another flash which wasn't lightning at all: the railroad man under the canopy had just taken a picture of Beaumont with his Polaroid camera. 'Jo,' Dixon called out, 'get that picture.'

Jo cut away from them, heading for the station building as Beaumont plodded towards the exit. A second flash of lightning showed him the car beyond the exit they were moving towards, a big, red, expensive-looking car. Rain was bouncing off its roof. His shoulders sagged a little lower, he was careful not to alter pace, to show any reaction. But he was sure now—these men weren't F.B.I. agents.

They went through the exit into the dark, away from the blurred lights of the train, away from people, their feet tramping through pools of muddy water. Seen at close quarters the car was very big, very expensive-looking, and behind the wheel a third man had his head twisted round to watch them coming. Dixon opened the rear door for the Englishman as Beaumont fumbled inside his coat pocket, a coat Dixon had already checked before letting him put it on. Taking out a pack of cigarettes, Beaumont nodded towards the interior of the car.

'It's all right, Dixon,' he said amiably. 'I've got the message —I'm coming with you.' He cupped a hand to shield the match he had struck, still standing on the far side of the half-open door. The American hesitated, caught off guard by the sudden change of mood. A moment later he revised all his ideas about Beaumont's size and clumsiness, a moment too late. The Englishman rammed his large body hard and brutally against the car door which closed—closed on Dixon's hand and arm.

It was a reasonable risk, Beaumont had calculated—at the worst the gun would be fired harmlessly inside the car, at the best the Colt would drop into the mud in the gap between almost closed door and frame. He stooped so quickly Dixon saw the movement only as a blur, then he came up with the Colt in his hand, pulled the door open and hurled the injured man face down on the back seat. The muzzle of the Colt pointed at the man in the front seat who had had no time to move. 'Take it easy, sonny,' Beaumont warned. 'These things have been known to go bang.'

In the mirror he saw Jo coming through the exit, holding the suitcase. Still watching the man behind the wheel, he roared out a command which easily reached Jo. 'Stand perfectly still—if you want your partners to live. . . .'

'We're F.B.I., for God's sake,' the man behind the wheel said in a strained voice.

'That's right, Beaumont . . .' Dixon choked out the words as he stayed sprawled on the back seat and hugged his right wrist with the other hand.

'Prove it!' the Englishman snapped. 'And keep holding that bag—with both hands,' he shouted to Jo as he watched the third American in the rear-view mirror. Dixon repeated Beaumont's earlier performance, using his left hand to extract a card with his fingertips. 'Give me some light so I can see this thing,' Beaumont rasped. He watched the man behind the wheel press a switch and glanced quickly at the card. 'As phoney as hell,' he said cynically.

'For this you could go behind bars,' the thirty-year-old man behind the wheel informed him tightly.

'On what charge?' Beaumont inquired.

'Resisting Federal officers . . .'

'Federal codswallop!' Beaumont stared bleakly at the man lying on the back seat. 'You come aboard a train and point a gun in my face when I'm asleep. You don't show me a shred of damned identification. . . .'

'It had to be like that, Beaumont,' Dixon said wearily. 'It had to look good. . . .'

'I haven't finished yet and I'm not satisfied yet. Since when did the F.B.I. sport Lincoln Continentals—or have you all become millionaires suddenly?'

'Does the name of General Lemuel Quincey Dawes mean something to you?' Dixon asked. 'And can I show you something else?'

'I think I read the name in the paper once,' Beaumont informed him coldly, still holding the Colt pointed at the man behind the wheel, still keeping Jo standing with both hands clutching his suitcase. 'And you can show me something—if you're careful.'

The something was a folded sheet of paper which, unfolded and held by Dixon under the light, showed a brief letter written in a weird scrawl he recognized. *Keith—an emergency has come up, a real bad one. I need you back in Washington fast. As a personal favour. Yours. Lemuel.*

'Bugger,' Beaumont said simply. 'I'm not coming—except in here out of the rain.' He climbed inside the car and settled back cautiously against the soft leather as Dixon moved over and seated himself, still holding on to his right hand. 'Is that busted?' the Englishman inquired. He looked at the American behind the wheel, who was still twisted round in his seat, studying Beaumont like a butcher about to carve up a slaughtered animal.

'You're going to get a crick in your neck,' Beaumont remarked.

'I'd like to break yours,' the man behind the wheel replied calmly.

'O.K., O.K., Fred,' Dixon said irritably. 'But you know, Beaumont, you did a risky thing there. . . .'

'Risky?' the Englishman exploded. 'You wake me up with a gun in my teeth when my reflexes aren't functioning . . .'

'Then I just hope I'm not around when they are functioning,' Dixon said ruefully as he rubbed at his wrist. 'And I can see your point about the Lincoln Continental—my car broke down on the way from the airfield and this was the nearest one we could grab.' In the front seat Fred, who had turned his back on Beaumont, started the motor.

'He can switch that off,' Beaumont snapped. 'We're not going anywhere.'

'Switch her off, Fred.' Dixon sounded harassed. 'We're not going anywhere. Yet,' he added. 'Look, Mr Beaumont,' he said very politely, 'this was a bad night for us—even before we met you. We had to fly down from Washington through an electrical storm—no planes are flying tonight. . . .'

'I know,' Beaumont said crisply as he lit a fresh cigarette, 'I was all set to fly down to Miami when they told me everything was grounded—so I had to take the train.'

'We had one hell of a trip to get to an airfield ahead of the

15

train,' Dixon went on. 'Then we had to find a car to get us here in time to stop the express. That's how urgently they want you back in Washington. And another thing—in five years the Florida Express has never made an unscheduled stop before tonight . . .'

'We all make an unscheduled stop sometime,' Beaumont replied. 'I'm making one now. And what was that business about a break-out from Folsom?'

'It was cover,' Dixon sighed. 'The security on this thing is tighter than a steel trap. The other passengers will think we took a criminal off the train—just in case someone like that gabby Phillipson decides to contact the press. And I'm still holding that train,' Dixon added.

'That's your problem. The security on what is tighter than a steel trap? Dawes tells me less than nothing in his note.'

'I don't know anything about it. . . .'

'Good night!' Beaumont opened the door, then slammed it shut again as Dixon said something else. 'We know you've spent two years non-stop in the Arctic, that you were going on holiday, but I was told to tell you as a last resort that Sam Grayson and Horst Langer have agreed to help. I gather you know these men?'

Beaumont sat upright in his seat and stared ahead at the rain slashing across the windscreen. Dixon watched him curiously, noting the short nose, the firm mouth, the jawline which expressed energy and great determination. It was the eyes which disturbed him most, he thought, the large brown eyes which looked at a man with an unblinking stare and seemed to look inside him. The Englishman took off his dripping hat, turned his large head and smiled grimly at Dixon. 'You had a rough trip flying down here?' he inquired.

'We were all air-sick.'

'Pity. I'm afraid you're going to be air-sick again. I went through a lot with Grayson and Langer, so I suppose I'll have to go back to Washington. Let the train go—then get me to the airfield fast. It sounds as though Dawes has a little trouble on his hands.' As an afterthought he handed back the Colt.

*   *   *

At three o'clock in the morning of Saturday 19 February, lights were still burning on the top floor of the National Security Agency building in Washington. The N.S.A., which is far less well known to the public than the C.I.A., is one of the most effective intelligence-gathering organizations in the world, partly because it doesn't capture the limelight like its more notorious counterpart. But it spends more money more effectively.

General Dawes is a short, heavily-built man of fifty-three who looks like a company executive. He wears sober, grey business suits, has a fondness for tropical plants, and he hates cold weather. Which was probably why he was appointed to oversee operations in the Arctic zone. At three in the morning on 19 February he was pacing round his office in his shirt-sleeves, sweating a little from the temperature of eighty-three degrees which was kept constant by a sophisticated system of temperature control. Eighty-three degrees was obligatory to keep alive the tropical plants which festooned his office. It was also why less reverent members of his staff referred to the room as the Jungle Box.

'Beaumont just came in—they're driving him from the airport now, General. . . .'

Jerry Adams, Dawes's assistant, held a lean hand over the mouthpiece of the phone as he went on talking. 'The plane nearly flipped when it landed, but he's O.K. Any special instructions? The car bringing him in is on radio . . .'

'Just get him here—fast!'

'He could go to a hotel first, get freshened up,' Adams pressed. 'It would give us time to chew this around. . . .'

'We snatched him off that express,' Dawes growled. 'I know him—he'll be climbing walls already. It won't be easy to persuade him, and it will be a damned sight less easy if we park him—give him time to think. This one I'm rushing him into—so get him here!'

Adams, a thin, studious-looking man of thirty-five raised his dark eyebrows in silent disapproval and gave the instruction. He put down the phone and adjusted his rimless glasses. 'I still don't see why we need this Englishman. The way I see this thing developing it's a simple operation and we can do it with our own boys. When we know Gorov is heading for Target-5 we send in a plane, it takes him aboard, it flies him out. . . .'

'Simple?' Dawes completed one more circuit round the room with his bouncy walk and sat down behind his large bare desk. 'Simple?' he repeated softly. 'As simple as falling off the Pan-Am building—and you break your neck that way, too.'

'Given a little luck it could be a smooth run. . . .'

'A little luck?' Dawes' tone was deceptively quiet. 'You could be right there, Adams,' he went on genially. 'We have an important Russian coming over to us—maybe the most important Russian who ever left the Soviet Union. Agreed?'

'That's true,' Adams said innocently.

'He's going to make a run for it,' Dawes continued in the same even tone. 'He's starting from the Soviet ice island North Pole 17,* and he'll run for our nearest research base, Target-5, which at this moment in time happens to be twenty-five miles west of the Soviet island. As of now there are only three professors on Target-5 waiting to be evacuated before the island breaks up. Are you with me?' he inquired.

'All the way, sir. . . .'

'None of those three professors on Target-5 have any idea of what's going to happen—that Gorov will soon be on his way there over the polar pack.' Dawes was speaking faster now, holding Adams's gaze with his cold blue eyes. 'We can't tell them because they haven't got top security clearance. . . .'

'Maybe after all we should radio them,' Adams suggested, 'give them a hint. . . .'

'Hint hell! It's only recently we knew Gorov was coming. I can't send in a planeload of men too soon because that might alert the Russians. They might seal off their base—which would seal in Gorov. The whole guts of the thing at this stage is that conditions at Target-5 must appear totally normal.'

'I still don't see where Beaumont comes in.'

* All major Soviet floating bases in the Arctic are prefixed by the words 'North Pole', followed by a number. The base so named may, in fact, be drifting hundreds of miles from the Pole itself.

18

Dawes studied Adams before replying. At thirty-five Jerry Adams had more academic qualifications for his job than Dawes could remember. He was fluent in six languages, including Russian and Serbo-Croat. He was an expert cryptographer, a specialist in radio-communications, and he was reputed to be one of the six best interrogators inside the United States. There was only one Arctic qualification he lacked—the only ice he'd seen had been inside a cocktail shaker.

'Fog,' Dawes said.

'Fog?'

'Supposing Target-5* gets fogbound,' Dawes suggested with a grim note in his voice. 'How do we get in then to take out Gorov? We can't fly in—we can't sail in across solid polar pack—so we'll have to walk in, sled across the ice. That's why we could need Beaumont.'

'He's a piece of insurance?'

'Yes.' Dawes looked at the closed door to his office as though Beaumont might fill the doorway at any moment. 'The only trouble is he doesn't know he's just a piece of insurance—and I'm not telling him. Just to put your anxious brain at rest, Adams, I'll list his qualifications . . .'

'We have no one else who could take a sled across the pack?' Adams asked with a note of incredulity. 'Surely that's a simple enough operation?'

'Sometimes I wonder why I employ you,' Dawes said with a genuine tone of wonderment. 'Sledding is the roughest, toughest job on the face of God's earth.' He stood up and walked quickly over to a huge wall map. 'Come here and I'll teach you something they forgot to tell you at Harvard.'

He stared up at the map of the Arctic zone. At the top hovered the coast of Russia with Murmansk and Leningrad to the right. The centre point of the map was the North Pole with Spitsbergen, Greenland and the Canadian and Alaskan coasts below. The marker showing the present position of

---

* Very large ice islands drifting in the Arctic are called Targets by the Americans. T-1 (Target-1), the earliest known ice island, was first seen by the radar officer of a Superfortress off the Canadian Arctic coast on 14 August, 1946.

Target-5 was very low down, pinned just above Iceberg Alley, the dangerous funnel of moving ice between Greenland and Spitsbergen.

'Target-5 is now drifting a hundred and twenty miles off the Greenland coast,' Dawes said quietly. 'Twenty-five miles further east is the Soviet base, North Pole 17, where Gorov will make his run from. Every day those two slabs of ice supporting those bases are drifting with the pack closer to Iceberg Alley. Beaumont calls it the most dangerous place on earth—and I agree with him.'

'His qualifications?' Adams pressed.

'Unusual. His mother was Canadian, his father British—he was killed during the war. They're both dead now. Beaumont was brought to Canada as a child in 1943 and taken to Coppermine at the edge of the Arctic. He grew up among the ice—close to where the ice islands are born when they crack off the Canadian ice shelf. In 1952 he was sent back to Britain to complete his education and he became interested in aviation. He married in 1965—when he was twenty-five—and three weeks after the marriage a hit-and-run drunk killed his wife.'

'Traumatic,' Adams murmured.

'For the hit-and-run killer, yes. They found him, charged him, and Beaumont was in court when he was sentenced in London. Before they got him out of the witness box Beaumont got to him and half killed him. He was let off with a suspended sentence and came straight back to Canada.'

'That would be seven years ago?' Adams estimated.

'Nice to know you can add up,' Dawes commented. 'Since then he's spent most of his life in the Arctic—working part of the time for the Arctic Research Laboratory people at Point Barrow, part of the time for us. He's the man who brought us all that data on the Soviet submarine killer chopper when it first showed in the Arctic.' Dawes grunted at the memory. 'He's got top security classification and he speaks fluent Russian. If that isn't enough there was the Spitsbergen trip.'

'What was that, sir?'

'Our security must be better than I thought,' Dawes observed with a wintry smile. 'But you were in Saigon at the time. Last year three men set out across the pack to prove something we thought was impossible could be done—they crossed all the way from Greenland to Spitsbergen by sled. It didn't get into the papers because that trip has military implications. The three men were Sam Grayson and Horst Langer—now waiting at Thule—and their leader, Beaumont.'

'He sounds—promising,' Adams conceded. 'But we only use him if Target-5 becomes fogged in?'

'Correct! The trouble is Beaumont will only go straight back to Greenland if I tell him he's going there to bring out Michael Gorov. . . .'

'But you don't know that,' Adams protested. 'The latest met. report shows clear weather over the whole area. . . .'

'So I show him my latest met. report.' Dawes went back to his desk and extracted a typed form which he handed to Adams. 'He's just spent two bad years in the Arctic so it's going to be hell's teeth to persuade him to go back. That bit of forgery should help.'

Adams stared at the sheet of paper. It was an official met. report, dated and timed eight hours earlier. *Weather conditions vicinity Target-Five deteriorating rapidly. Dense fog. Visibility nil. Temperature forty-five below. Conditions expected to worsen.* Adams looked up from the report. 'What happens when he finds out you've fooled him?'

'He'll blow his top—but by then he'll be at Thule, Greenland, I hope.' Dawes took a short fat cigar out of a box and put it in his mouth without lighting it. He was trying to give up smoking for thirty days and so far he'd lasted out a fortnight. 'You've heard about the security leak at Thule?' he asked casually.

'No.' Adams straightened up in his chair. 'What leak?'

'Callard of the F.B.I. warned me two hours ago.' Dawes blew out the match he had absent-mindedly lit and his expression was grim. 'It appears a top Soviet agent has been sending out a stream of information for over two years. They know his code-name—Crocodile—and they expect to come up with his real identity soon.'

'That could jeopardize this whole operation,' Adams said.

'I don't think so—I'm going to warn Beaumont to deal only with the security chief up there, Tillotson.' Dawes checked his watch. 'And Beaumont should be here soon, so brace yourself, Adams.'

The moon was high, the night was clear, and the sky glittered with the spread of the Great Bear constellation above the polar pack. In the bitter cold of the long night Target-5 was besieged.

One hundred and twenty miles east of the Greenland coast, only twenty-five miles west of the Soviet ice island, North Pole 17, Target-5 was besieged by the pack grinding up against it, pressing against its cliff-like fringes, a constantly moving pack of billions of tons of ice which squeaked and gibbered as it tried to smash the island trapped inside its pressure.

It had been trying to smash the island for thirty years—ever since Target-5 had broken away from the Canadian ice shelf in 1942 when it started its spectacular orbits round the North Pole. But so far the pack had made no impression on the twenty-foot high cliffs which reared above it because it was salt-water ice—ice formed out of the sea. The massive island, a mile in diameter, was tougher.

Target-5 was made of freshwater ice, which is harder than its salt-water counterpart. And it had a long pedigree. For hundreds of years the ice shelf at the edge of the Canadian coast had been built up by the slow-moving flow of glaciers debouching into the frozen sea. Layer by layer the shelf had been formed until it was two hundred feet deep. Target-5 was a fragment of this shelf—a mile-wide fragment which had broken loose and drifted with the pack for thirty years.

It was starting its fourth ten-year orbit round the Pole, was heading once more for the Canadian Arctic coast, when the Greenland Current caught it. The huge slab of ice was dragged further south than it had ever moved before. Soon it was close to the funnel between Greenland and Spitsbergen, and then it reached the point of no return and continued heading south instead of west, south towards Iceberg Alley.

In far away Washington, Dawes was still waiting for Beaumont when Dr Matthew Conway, the fifty-year-old station leader on Target-5, came out of the headquarters hut to take another star-fix with his sextant. A normally placid man, Conway was edgy as he fiddled with the instrument, and his irritation wasn't helped by the fact that a second man joined him almost as soon as he was outside. Jeff Rickard, the thirty-two-year-old wireless operator, shut the door behind him quickly to keep in the warmth. 'Any sign of activity, Matt?' he inquired.

'Lots of it,' Conway replied with forced humour. 'A Greyhound bus for Omaha just went by.'

'Jesus, if that were only true! Any sign of the Russians, I meant.'

'I know what you meant.'

They stood in the middle of the twelve flat-roofed huts which formed the research base in the centre of the island. Across a narrow avenue of beaten snow six huts faced six more, and from a hut further down the avenue a wireless mast speared up into the moonlit night. In the distance all around them, at no point more than half a mile away, the enemy—the polar pack —was squeaking and gibbering like some huge beast in pain. It reminded them that the pack was alive, was moving and grinding up against the small cliffs which still held it back. A fresh sound came, a sharp report like a rifle crack.

'What the hell was that?' Rickard whispered.

'A piece of ice breaking off,' Conway said wearily. 'Get back inside with Sondeborg, would you, Jeff. I want to finish this job.'

'He's in one of his moods. I think he's getting worse, Matt.'

Conway, his face turned away from Rickard, tightened his mouth as he tried to concentrate on the star-fix. Sondeborg, twenty-six years old and the youngest of the three men, was on the verge of a nervous breakdown, whatever that might be. It was the isolation, of course, and it was near the end of their time on the island. In twelve days the plane would come to evacuate them from the doomed island and now the hours— even the minutes—were like years.

The research base was surrounded on all sides by a smooth snowbound plateau running away to the cliffs—on all sides except to the south where a small hill rose, its summit forty feet above the plateau. Here, over a hundred miles from the nearest coast, was a hill littered with giant, snow-covered boulders, real rocks, some of them the size of small bungalows. Ages ago they had been carried down inside a glacier and deposited on the Canadian ice shelf—and when the huge slab of ice had torn itself loose it had carried the hill with it.

The door behind Conway opened again and he felt his self-control going. Sondeborg was joining them. It was getting very difficult: no man wanted to be left on his own in this terrible solitude, even inside a warm hut, but when they were together they ground up against each other like the ice grinding against the nearby cliffs. 'Shut that door, Harvey,' Conway said as he pressed his eye to the instrument. The door slammed behind him.

'Those Russians have gone!' Sondeborg's voice was unsteady, close to hysteria. 'They've got more sense than we have —they've evacuated their bloody base while there was still time. Why the hell don't we wireless for our plane? Everything's packed. . . .'

'That's enough!' Conway lowered his sextant and swung round to face Sondeborg. 'Everything isn't packed yet—and you still have experiments to complete . . .'

'Damn the experiments!' Sondeborg blazed. 'There's a queer feeling about this place. . . .'

'You've been on Target-5 eleven months,' Conway interjected, 'it's still the same place.'

'It isn't in the same place,' Sondeborg rapped back. 'We're on the edge of Iceberg Alley. . . .'

'Get back inside and make some coffee,' Conway snapped. 'We could all do with something hot to drink.' The door slammed again as Sondeborg stormed back inside the hut. 'Better go with him, Jeff,' Conway advised, 'you know what he's like on his own. Then you can try and get through to Thule again—I want them to know our new position.'

'I'll try.' Rickard sounded doubtful. 'There's very bad static building up. I think we're cut off. It could be a weather change coming.'

Conway was frowning as he finished taking his star-fix. The reference to bad radio communication—or no communication at all—worried him more than he cared to show. He finished taking his star-fix and paused before going inside while he scanned the familiar wilderness of frozen sea and endless ice. For a reason he couldn't fathom, Conway felt afraid.

There was sub-tropical heat and tension inside Dawes's office, a heat and a tension which made the three men sweat. It was Beaumont who had introduced the tension. He sat in his shirt-sleeves, his hands clasped over his large knees as he stared up at Dawes. 'All right, you've given me the picture. Now—what makes this Russian, Michael Gorov, so damned important?'

'All you need to know is that he's important,' Adams intervened. 'The specifics are top secret.'

Beaumont swivelled his head briefly to give the assistant a hard bleak look, then he turned back to Dawes who answered quickly. 'Michael Gorov is the Soviet Union's number one oceanographer. He personally supervised the laying of their entire Sosus and Caesar* system along the Arctic seabed. And he's bringing with him the Catherine charts—the complete blueprint of that system which guides their subs under the Arctic ice to our shores. Does that tell you anything?'

'It suggests that Gorov is—important.'

'With those charts in our hands we could set about ripping up their whole offensive system—it could put them back ten years,' Dawes went on vehemently. 'It means even more than that—if the president goes to Moscow in May with the Catherine charts in his pocket he would be talking from a position of real strength. It's as big as that, Keith. So I need you in Greenland. . . .'

'You're going too fast—I haven't agreed to go anywhere yet.' Beaumont stood up and walked across the room to stare at the wall map. For a large man he walked with great economy of movement. 'This ship, the *Elroy* . . .' He pointed to a marker

---

* Sosus and Caesar: American term for the cable and sonar buoy underwater network which guides submarines along a predetermined course at great depth below the polar pack.

at the bottom of the map. 'Is she the icebreaker, the twin of the *Exodus*?'

'Yes. She's heading back for Milwaukee after a year in the Arctic.'

'I may want you to turn her round and send her straight back up to the icefield. . . .'

Adams's voice rippled with indignation. 'You seem to have forgotten that we're planning this operation, Beaumont.'

The Englishman turned round slowly and stared. Adams found the stare uncomfortable as Beaumont took his time about replying, 'Maybe you'd like to come with me—across the rough ice?' He turned back to Dawes. 'This thing is a mess—and I don't like the sound of that security leak up at Thule. I have to go there first to pick up Grayson and Langer and get equipment before we fly on to Curtis Field.' He stabbed a finger at the nearest airfield to Target-5. 'So that leak is dangerous.'

'The F.B.I. man, Callard, says they may have located Crocodile within hours. Any advance instructions we can radio direct to Tillotson—he's the security chief up there.'

'I still don't like it. Let me see that met. report again.' Dawes handed him the faked weather report with a wooden face while Adams studied his fingernails. Beaumont read the report and shook his head. 'It means the three of us have to fly in to the edge of the fog bank from Curtis Field. Then we sled our way to Target-5—if we can ever find it. We pick up Gorov—assuming he ever makes it across twenty-five miles of broken ice—then we have to sled our way back across one hundred and twenty miles of moving ice, probably with the Russian security people on our tails. . . .'

'We could pick you up off the ice once you get clear of the fog and fly you back,' Adams suggested.

'You could,' Beaumont agreed, 'if you ever found us, which you wouldn't. Have you any idea what it's like trying to find four men and two sled-teams from the air at this time of year? No, obviously you haven't. . . .'

'People do get rescued by air,' Adams persisted.

'That's right,' Beaumont growled, 'they do. Something else you obviously don't know is that usually it's by accident—a plane that wasn't looking for them just happens to see them. Another thing I don't like,' he continued, 'is that we don't yet know when he's coming.' He waved the met. report in Dawes's direction. 'Send an urgent signal to the *Elroy*—she's to turn round at once and head back due north for the icefield. This may be a rendezvous point . . .' Beaumont took out a pencil and marked a thick cross on the wall map.

'That's deep inside the ice,' Adams protested.

'So she has to ram her way in. I want to be on a plane for Greenland within two hours,' he told Dawes, 'a fast machine that can get me there non-stop.'

'There's a Boeing waiting for you now,' Dawes said.

Beaumont raised an eyebrow. 'You were confident, weren't you? American organization—sometimes it frightens me. Now, let's go quickly over this dangerous business of when we'll know Michael Gorov is coming.'

Adams began talking in a quick competent voice. 'We're waiting for a man to come back from Leningrad—to Helsinki. He's contacting a relative of Michael Gorov's and he'll bring out the date when Michael Gorov is leaving North Pole 17. We do know that it will be within the next few days—and when our man gets out we'll know the exact day.'

'Supposing he never leaves Leningrad alive?' Beaumont demanded.

'He should make it,' Adams said confidently. 'He's never been behind the Iron Curtain before—that's why he was chosen. But he's a very experienced man. When he reaches Helsinki he goes straight to our embassy and they'll signal us.'

'The whole thing depends on one man inside Russia,' Beaumont said grimly.

'A first-class man,' Adams assured him. 'We'll know at the latest by one o'clock Sunday morning, our time. As soon as we hear we'll signal you at Curtis Field.' Adams's optimism was carrying him along on a cloud. 'You don't have to worry. You'll see—it will be a very simple operation.'

'It won't,' Beaumont rumbled. 'That's the one and only thing I can predict—it won't be a simple operation.'

27

Friday, 18 February

A MAN WAS KILLED on Nevsky Prospekt in Leningrad at exactly five minutes past three in the afternoon of Friday, 18 February.

At three in the afternoon in Leningrad it is still only 7 a.m. in Washington. Beaumont had not yet even boarded the Florida Express he was to be taken off so unceremoniously seventeen hours later. But it was almost three in the afternoon when an American tourist, Harvey Winthrop, walked carefully down the five icy steps which led from the Hotel Europa to street level.

A tall, serious-faced man of thirty-eight, Winthrop was described in his passport as a writer, but writing can hardly have been on his mind as he checked his watch and walked out of the Hotel Europa. 2.55 p.m. Reaching street level, he turned left and began trudging through the snow towards Nevsky Prospekt.

Overhead the sky was swollen with the threat of more snow to come and there were very few people about; in this northern latitude it would be dark within thirty minutes. In fact, the street lamps were already glowing, their light reflecting weirdly off the snow as Winthrop arrived on Nevsky Prospekt and glanced cautiously along the broad avenue in both directions. He gave the impression of a man unsure whether it was safe to cross, but really he was checking three cars parked on the far side of the avenue.

The Intourist guide, Madame Vollin, who had accompanied him on each trip to the Hermitage since he had arrived from Helsinki five days ago, was nowhere to be seen—not inside one of the parked cars, not gazing into any of the dimly-lit shop windows behind the vehicles, so she must have accepted his word that he wouldn't be going back to the Hermitage today, that he was too tired to look at any more Rubens. He hesitated, waited until a trolley-bus was close, which gave him another excuse to wait a little longer, to double check.

On the far side of the almost-deserted avenue a youth in a black leather jacket rushed round a corner, rammed a key into a car door, opened it and then waited as a girl followed him round the corner. A red-haired girl, she wore a tight-fitting mini coat, and she began punching the youth as soon as she got close to him. Winthrop smiled dryly as the trolley-bus rumbled past, the traction flashing blue sparks off the ice-coated wire: even the Russians had a juvenile problem, especially when the juveniles were offspring of high-up party officials. He began to cross the wide street.

Not by chance, Winthrop could easily have been mistaken for a Russian: he was wearing a fur coat, a fur hat and knee-length boots purchased from the GUM store three days after his arrival. 'I didn't realize it would be as cold as this,' he explained to Madame Vollin. As he reached the far side and walked past the young couple who were still arguing, he checked his watch.

2.58 p.m. Two minutes to the meeting-place he could see as he walked, the little tree-lined park further down the Nevsky. He trudged along the avenue with his gloved hands thrust deep inside his coat pockets, the art catalogue tucked under his arm, taking the same route to the Hermitage Museum at the Winter Palace he had followed for five days with Madame Vollin at his side. The little tree-lined park came closer. He could see the statue of Lenin by the path and in the distance a short, stocky figure had turned off the Nevsky, was already inside the park. Was this the seaman? Winthrop entered the park.

Winthrop had never met Peter Gorov, the brother of Michael Gorov, the oceanographer, and he strained his eyes to check three details before the man reached him. The duffel bag—carried under the arm instead of over the shoulder, the normal way Soviet seamen carried it. Check. A red scarf wrapped round his neck. Check. But there was one further detail and the light was fading badly. Winthrop kept his slow, casual pace.

The third detail was a button, a single white button at the top of the coat while the other buttons would be dark-coloured. Jesus, he couldn't see that at all. A militiaman—a policeman—trudged into the park from the far end and started walking up behind the seaman.

Winthrop's heart skipped a beat but he maintained the same pace. It had happened—the unforeseen factor which could ruin everything, make the contact impossible. A fresh fear tingled Winthrop's nerves—was the policeman following Gorov? It didn't seem likely: it was too open a tag. Get a grip on yourself, man! Helsinki, Finland—safety—is only a hundred miles away. It wasn't a thought that gave Harvey Winthrop any comfort as he walked steadily towards the seaman approaching him: he might just as well be in Kiev, in the heart of the Ukraine where Gorov had just come from after meeting his brother, Michael.

It was getting darker every minute. The seaman came closer, trailed by the policeman who wore a dark blue greatcoat and kept an even distance of fifty yards behind the seaman. Was this another coincidence—that the policeman was maintaining exactly the same walking pace as Peter Gorov? If this was Gorov—Winthrop still couldn't see the button. He could see the red band on the policeman's peaked cap but he couldn't see Gorov's goddamned button. The seaman, less than thirty years old, was staring straight ahead and Winthrop fancied he saw strain in the stiffened jaw muscles. The poor devil must be close to screaming point: he hadn't been trained for this kind of tension. Then Winthrop saw the lighter-coloured button at the top of the coat.

Winthrop slipped on the ice in front of the Lenin statue, slipped while the seaman was only feet away with the policeman fifty yards to his rear. As the American fell, the coloured catalogue dropped to the ground and an illustration of a Rubens painting stood out on the darkened snow like a blood stain. The catalogue was his positive identification. In the most natural way the seaman paused while Winthrop was trying to get back on his feet and spoke swiftly and softly in Russian.

'He is coming out on 20 February . . . to the American

research base Target Number Five . . . 20 February . . .' He repeated the date in an even lower tone and Winthrop knew he was terrified about two things—that the American might not have heard the vital date, that the policeman might overhear him.

Winthrop was on his feet now, brushing snow from his coat. The seaman shrugged his shoulders as though people were always slipping in this weather and continued through the park towards the Nevsky Prospekt and the docks beyond. Winthrop picked up his catalogue, tried to walk, limped badly, then leaned against the railings round the statue. The policeman reached Winthrop and asked his question in Russian. 'Can you walk? Have you far to go?'

'I'm O.K. I reckon I twisted my ankle a bit—but I'm O.K.' Winthrop had carefully replied in English—no one knew that he understood any Russian, no one except Gorov who was already outside the park. The policeman stared at him without understanding as Winthrop smiled painfully—he really had twisted his ankle. 'I'm from the Europa Hotel,' Winthrop went on, anxious to get rid of the man. He waved a hand. 'Not far to go.' He smiled again and began walking slowly back the way he had come.

Winthrop limped painfully through the park, really worried now about slipping. He simply had to make it back to the hotel, and even in his pain the American's brain was working. Maybe this twisted ankle could be used to get him out of Russia.

Winthrop was due to leave for Helsinki the day after tomorrow—on the early Sunday morning flight. But that was the day Michael Gorov was starting his run for Target-5. The Soviet authorities knew his exit date, knew that he was in Leningrad to view the wonderful collection of Rubens paintings in the Hermitage in his capacity as a writer on art, so normally they might think his early departure strange. The genuinely-sprained ankle gave him his reason for catching Saturday's Finnair flight to Helsinki—then the signal could be sent to Dawes in Washington a day before Gorov fled from North Pole 17.

As Winthrop limped out on to the Nevsky Prospekt it began

to snow. He observed the situation along the street automatically, noticed that the leather-jacketed youth was still arguing with his red-haired girl. They must be in love, he thought ironically. No traffic was coming. He still hadn't glanced back to see if the policeman was following. He stepped off the kerb.

It was probably the fresh fall of snow which caused it to happen. The leather-jacketed youth must have been frozen and the snow broke up the argument. He climbed in behind the wheel of his car and the red-haired girl got into the front passenger seat beside him. The youth switched on the ignition, gunned the motor, pulled away from the kerb with an exhaust burst like a bomb detonating, accelerated, then remembered to switch on his lights.

Even then Winthrop might have jumped clear had he been faking the limp, but the car was screaming towards him as the lights flashed on, blinding him. In the headlight glare Winthrop's limping figure hurtled towards the car, filled the windscreen, then the radiator lifted him and hurled him a dozen yards. He crashed down on the kerb with the impact of a man falling from a great height. He was dead before the car swept away round a corner as a woman on the sidewalk began screaming.

A hundred yards further down Nevsky Prospekt the seaman, Gorov, had stopped to cross the avenue. He saw Winthrop limping over the highway, saw the car strike him, saw the body curving through the air before it dropped and he knew that the American was dead. He crossed the avenue and went on towards the docks where the trawler *Girolog* was waiting to depart in three hours.

Gorov walked like a man in a dream, hardly able to grasp what had just happened. It was a total disaster: the message would never get through to Washington and now there was no way of warning his brother. Michael would start out across the ice and the Americans wouldn't know he was coming. Crushed, Gorov walked on through the snow, his feet leading him along the familiar route. God, what could he do?

Saturday, 19 February

IT WAS EIGHT O'CLOCK on Saturday morning inside the Leningrad headquarters of the Special Security Service.

'This American, Winthrop, who was killed on the Nevsky yesterday—I smell something funny about him. . . .'

The Locomotive—this was the nickname they used in Leningrad for Colonel Igor Papanin, chief of Special Security for the Arctic Military Zone. The dictionary definition of the word is '. . . having power . . . not stationary . . . constantly travelling . . .' It is as good a description as any of Col. Papanin. For many the word suggests a huge engine dragging hundreds of people behind it at speed—this also describes the Siberian.

'Get me a full report, Kramer! Bring in that damned Intourist nursemaid, Vollin, or whatever her name is! Bring in the policeman who saw it happen. Find any other witnesses and parade them here by noon. I'll question them myself!'

Strictly speaking, the headquarters of the Special Security Service for the Arctic should have been at the port of Murmansk, but when Leonid Brezhnev, First Secretary, appointed Papanin to the post he ordered that the headquarters must be in Leningrad. And this was a matter of power, too.

Like Hamburg in Germany, like Quebec in Canada, Leningrad is a maverick city. It was in Leningrad that Communism was born when the cruiser *Aurora* fired the gun which signalled revolution. It was to Leningrad that Stalin, fearing the city's independence, sent his most trusted oppressor, Kirov—and Kirov died from an assassin's bullet. So Brezhnev sent Papanin to Leningrad.

'And, Kramer, contact the airport where Winthrop came in. They will have made a note of this man's arrival. Did he come in alone?—that's what I want to know. By noon!'

Unlike Kirov, the bloody-minded citizens of Leningrad didn't try to shoot Papanin—they nicknamed him the Locomotive instead. A familiar figure striding down the Nevsky Prospekt, no Russian could miss him in the densest crowd—Papanin towered above the crowd. Six foot four tall, wide-shouldered, heavily-built, his large Siberian head was shaved almost bald and he had a mouth as wide as a carp's. And when he raised his drill-sergeant's voice they swore you could hear him in Murmansk.

'Get down to police headquarters and fetch me Winthrop's personal possessions, Kramer. Go yourself! An American tourist in Leningrad in February? I tell you, Kramer, I smell stinking fish. . . .'

Walther Kramer, forty-five years old, a short, stout Communist Balt from Lithuania who moved with the agility and silence of a cat, didn't believe a word of it. As Papanin's assistant he had a certain latitude in talking to his chief, a latitude about as wide as the edge of a razor blade. He voiced his disbelief cautiously.

'There's no evidence that this American was anything but what his passport says. . . .'

'Haven't you gone yet?'

As the Balt left the second-floor room Papanin stood up and went over to the window, then he took out a pocket chess set from his jacket and stared at it. The window a foot from his smooth-skinned, hard-boned face was rimed with frost as he studied the tiny board. At eight in the morning it was still dark outside and he could hear below the shuffle of footsteps on the cobbled street as people hurried to work. An ancient green-tiled stove he had recently lit stood in a corner behind him and its warmth hadn't yet penetrated the chilled room. Only one wall away the most modern American teleprinter was chattering non-stop, but Papanin warmed himself with a stove as old as the revolution itself.

It was the Jewish problem which had aroused Papanin's suspicion of Winthrop, and the Jewish problem was another reason why Leonid Brezhnev was glad he had put Papanin inside Leningrad. On top of all his other duties it was now

34

Papanin's responsibility to find out how finance was being smuggled in to help Jews emigrate to Israel.

As he stared at the chess board Papanin grunted to punctuate his thoughts. Winthrop could have been a courier, a contact man with the Jewish underground, so Winthrop—even though he was dead—was going to be investigated up to his eyeteeth. Literally. The Siberian had already ordered an intimate examination of the naked corpse. He frowned, decided on his move, shifted a pawn. He was sure he was right: there was something very odd indeed about Mr Harvey J. Winthrop.

At eight o'clock on Saturday morning Papanin still had no idea that he was engaged in a race against time—to solve the Winthrop mystery before Michael Gorov fled from North Pole 17 at midnight on Sunday.

In Washington it was still only midnight, Friday. Beaumont was still inside the sleeping-car aboard the Florida Express. At the Soviet base North Pole 17 it was four in the morning and Michael Gorov had only recently arrived from Murmansk.

Michael Gorov, forty years old, a member of the Soviet Academy of Science and the Soviet Union's most distinguished oceanographer, was almost ill with the strain, sick with the tension of waiting, of counting away the hours to Sunday.

At four in the morning he stood in the moonlight at the edge of the recently-swept airstrip which bisected the ice island, North Pole 17. He was very carefully gazing towards the east, not to the west where the American research base, Target-5, lay twenty-five miles away. Beyond the island the tumbled pack glittered in the moonlight like a vast endless heap of frosted glass, smashed frosted glass. Behind him lay the huts which formed the base, their flat roofs deep with snow. It was from that direction that he heard the footsteps coming, the steps of Nikolai Marov, the security man. Marov came close, stopped and watched the stooped back of the oceanographer. 'Are you feeling all right, Academician Gorov?' he inquired.

'Never felt better.'

'You're up early,' the security man persisted.

'I'm always up early—you should know that by now.'

Gorov deliberately let his irritation show and the stratagem worked. Marov mumbled something and padded back towards the base. Inside his coat pocket Gorov's gloved hands clenched: Marov was going to be a problem—because Marov always came with him when he ventured out on the pack. And there was another reason why Gorov had allowed his irritation to show: he had reached the stage where he couldn't stand the sight of a security man. It was Col. Papanin's Security Service which had killed Rachel Levitzer six months ago.

Gorov's eyes filled with tears as he thought of her. They had been unofficially engaged, but because she was Jewish, because he was an eminent Academician, they had kept their relationship secret. Then the news had come through in August 1971: Rachel had died in Leningrad.

The Security Service had come to her flat to arrest her: something to do with the Jewish underground—Gorov had never been clear on the details—but Rachel had attempted to escape, fleeing down a long staircase. A security man had tripped her and Rachel had gone down—down a flight of thirty stone steps. When they had reached her she was dead, her neck broken.

Gorov checked his watch. 4.10 a.m., local time. Twenty more hours to wait before he started out across the polar pack in his desperate bid to reach Target-5. Timing was everything: he had been warned by the Americans that he must fix his own departure date—and then stick to it. Gorov's plan was to leave North Pole 17 at exactly midnight and he wondered how he was going to get through the next twenty hours while he pretended to be absorbed in his depth-sounding experiments. But at least there was one consolation: his brother, Peter, would by now have passed on the message. The Americans knew already when he was coming.

The Locomotive was building up a head of steam. By eleven o'clock on Saturday morning all witnesses had been interrogated at security headquarters—interrogated by Papanin himself. He had seen the Intourist guide, Madame Vollin—'a cow of a woman, Kramer. And she has bad breath. I don't know how Winthrop stood it. . . .' He had spent far longer with the policeman who had seen Winthrop die. He had interviewed staff from the Hotel Europa and the airport official who had noted down Winthrop's arrival five days earlier from Helsinki. And he had found nothing remotely suspicious.

'I think we are looking down a large hole with nothing in it,' Kramer remarked as the airport official left. 'There is not one piece of evidence to connect this man Winthrop with the Jews.'

'Someone is bringing in money to them—we know that. And Winthrop still smells.' The Siberian bounded up from behind his desk and started striding round the room. 'For five days he behaves himself—he goes to the Hermitage and stares at the Rubens, always with his nursemaid, the Vollin woman. Then, what happens yesterday? Papanin bent down, picked up a poker and began to attack the interior of the stove, stirring up the glowing coals the way he stirred up people.

'He dies in a street accident. . . .'

'Before that! He breaks routine, Kramer—he tells the guide he is tired and will not be going out.' He rammed the poker in deep. 'The moment her back is turned he slips out again on his own—when it is nearly dark. Why, Kramer, why?'

'He is feeling better. He is going back to the Hermitage. . . .'

'When the museum closes at four? He'd get there just in time to come back. Why did he go out on his own?'

'To meet someone. . . .' Kramer made the reply casually, for something to say. The Siberian's grip tightened on the poker. He withdrew the weapon from the stove, straightened up slowly and stared at his assistant. 'I don't really believe that,' Kramer said quickly.

'To meet someone?' Papanin repeated. 'You know, you could be right. But who? He didn't meet anyone—he didn't have time before he was killed.' Papanin prodded the poker in Kramer's direction. 'Let's use our heads—by which I mean let's use my head. The American goes out, walks to the park . . .'

'Twists his ankle . . .'

'Appears to twist his ankle, Kramer.' Papanin had his eyes closed as he tried to visualize the scene the policeman had described. 'He slips close to the seaman, then he starts back again. I wonder who that seaman was, Kramer?'

'Could have been anyone.'

'No—we can narrow it down! The seaman was carrying his duffel bag and was walking towards the docks. . . .' Papanin put the poker back on the stove and took a file out of a drawer. Each day he received a report on events in the city, including a police report, but he was looking for the docks report. 'The only ship which sailed yesterday was the *Girolog*, a trawler, and the ice-breaker which took it out. He must have been going to embark on the *Girolog*.'

'With a crew of about thirty. . . .'

'True. So now I want you to drive immediately to the docks to get me the list of all personnel who sailed on the *Girolog* last night. I want it by noon.'

'There isn't time. . . .' Kramer protested.

'That's your problem!' Papanin sat down behind his desk and waited until Kramer had reached the door. 'Incidentally, while I was away in Moscow this week I see you signed a movement order for Michael Gorov to go back to North Pole 17. I thought he'd finished his work there.'

'That is correct.' Kramer paused near the door, vaguely worried by this sudden change of topic. 'He wanted to take some final depth-soundings before we evacuate the base. He gave me the impression that you knew about it.'

'That's all right, Kramer. It just struck me that he hadn't planned to go there again. And get me the *Girolog* list by noon!'

Alone in his room, Papanin put one booted leg on top of his desk and stared moodily at the green-tiled stove which was now emanating great waves of heat. Without knowing it, he now had exactly seventeen hours to find out why Winthrop had come to Leningrad before Michael Gorov started his run for Target-5.

It was a six-hour flight at forty thousand feet from Washington to Thule, Greenland, and it was eleven o'clock on Saturday morning when Beaumont woke up and saw the huge runway coming up to meet the Boeing 707. It didn't feel like Saturday

38

—by now Beaumont was so bemused that he had to think to remember the day of the week. And it didn't look like eleven o'clock in the morning as the Boeing dropped out of a moonlit night towards the wilderness of snow and ice below.

'Seems like only five minutes since we left Washington,' he called out to Callard, the F.B.I. man who sat across the gangway from him.

The man in the neat blue suit, freshly shaven, looked back at the big Englishman as though wondering whether to reply. 'Seems more like five years to me,' he said eventually. He turned away and looked out of the window on his side.

Beaumont smiled to himself. At five in the morning Callard had jumped aboard the plane at Washington minutes before its departure for Greenland; obviously he had been driving the plane every mile of the way while Beaumont had slept. He looked out of his own window, staring down at the desolate snowbound plain on the Greenland icecap. In the distance the thousand-foot high radar mast sheered up into the moonlit sky, the warning light at the summit flashing red. The tallest mast in the world, it had a range of three thousand miles over the roof of the world. It was the key station in the Distant Early Warning system.

'I'll see you in Vandenberg's office,' Callard suddenly called out. 'Sometime this evening, maybe.'

Beaumont nodded and he thought the suggestion significant. As the Boeing continued its descent he was certain that Callard had cracked the case, that he now knew the identity of Crocodile, that he was on his way to arrest the Soviet agent. They went down below the level of the radar mast tip and the grim panorama of the icecap slid up closer. Beaumont had a tilted view of flat-topped buildings on either side of Main Street, the snow-covered road which ran down the middle of the camp, then they were landing.

Tillotson was waiting for Beaumont when he disembarked from the plane, wrapped in a fur parka they had supplied before he left Washington. It was forty below and the still air hit him like a physical blow, taking his breath away as he stood at the foot of the steps. Tillotson, a tall, tough-looking

39

man with a face like one of the heads carved out of Mount Rushmore, shook Beaumont's gloved hand with his own. 'I have everything ready for this trip of yours . . .'

He stopped speaking and stared at Callard who had come down the steps behind Beaumont, brushed past the two men and walked quickly across to Colonel Vandenberg, the camp commander. 'Who was that?' he asked.

'No idea,' Beaumont said instantly. 'He wasn't very talkative and I slept most of the way. Maybe there's been a complaint about the hamburgers.'

Tillotson looked back at the plane where the chief pilot was coming down the steps. 'Excuse me,' he said and intercepted the pilot. 'That second passenger—who is he? Only Beaumont was reported as coming on this flight.'

The pilot, carrying his flying helmet, pulled the hood of his parka over his head. 'Every time I make this trip it gets colder up here. The guy jumped aboard at the last minute just before we left Washington. He came in a government car. . . .'

'I'll check him later.' Tillotson led Beaumont to a covered jeep and started talking as he turned on the ignition. 'As I said, everything is ready for your trip. Two Sikorskys have been sent to Curtis Field on the east Greenland coast. Grayson and Langer are waiting for you at headquarters—Grayson was here but we had to scoop up Langer from Ellesmere Island.' He drove the jeep slowly along a track towards the camp, keeping well behind the car which was taking Col. Vandenberg and Callard ahead of them. 'Two Norwegian-type sleds are being sent on to Curtis . . .'

'They're useless,' Beaumont interjected. 'I specified Eskimo sleds—they're heavier and won't break up on rough ice. Your sleds will.'

Tillotson looked surprised. 'We use Norwegian-type sleds ourselves. We haven't any Eskimo sleds. . . .'

'I think you have. When I was last here you had two of them stowed away at the back of the big helicopter hangar.'

'Like to check now? I could turn off and we could go straight over.'

'Now?'

'No time like the present. And I gather that for you every-thing is hurry-hurry.'

Tillotson changed direction as they came to a fork in the beaten snow-track, heading away from the encampment of huts as he drove towards a large hangar in the distance. A quarter of a mile ahead the wire surrounding the military airfield glittered in the moonlight—it was sheathed in solid ice. Beyond the wire a stationary orange snow-plough stood close to the hangar. Tillotson pulled a folded sheet of paper from his pocket and handed it to Beaumont. 'Met. reports on the whole area—I don't know which area you're interested in. Rough ice, you said?'

'Rough ice, I said.'

Beaumont hadn't yet acclimatized to the bitter Arctic air which was streaming inside the jeep, freezing his face and making him feel short of breath. The car carrying Vandenberg and Callard was disappearing along the main track, its red light growing smaller as another jeep came tearing in the opposite direction, driving towards the Boeing 707.

'Any fog about?' Beaumont asked casually as he began reading the report.

'No fog anywhere, thank God. According to the latest report —and that's what you're reading—there's clear weather all the way from here to Norway.'

'You mean you've had it and it's cleared recently?' Beau-mont pressed. He was thinking of the report Dawes had shown him in Washington concerning weather conditions round Target-5. *Dense fog . . . visibility nil.*

'We just haven't had any fog, period. Not for the past three weeks.'

Tillotson slowed down, glanced at Beaumont who was still reading the report while the anger grew inside him. Dawes had fooled him, had shown him a faked weather report to get him to Greenland. Tillotson pulled up, left the engine ticking over. 'Mitten's slipped inside my glove,' he explained. 'I'll just fix it.' He fiddled with the glove, took it off, put it inside his coat pocket. When he withdrew his hand it was holding a .38 Smith & Wesson. He turned sideways and with one swift movement

41

smashed the barrel against Beaumont's temple. Instinctively Beaumont shifted a second before the gun hit him and the barrel grazed rather than clubbed him, but he was hurt. He grabbed at the ignition key, tore it loose, threw it sideways out of the window into the snow. Tillotson smashed the revolver down a second time. A flash of light exploded inside Beaumont's head, a blinding flash, then a horrible wave of blackness engulfed him.

Saturday, 19 February

BEAUMONT lay half-conscious in the snow, fighting to get a grip on himself as Sam Grayson's cheerful face bent over him, but there was anxiety in the American's expression as he eased the brandy flask close to Beaumont's lips. 'Take it easy, Keith. . . .'

Beaumont forced himself up on his elbows, took the flask in one hand, helped himself to a drink. His head was pounding, his vision was blurred, then the strong spirit reached his stomach and he could see clearly. He took a slow, deep breath of the bitter night air. That seemed more potent than the brandy. 'Get me on my feet,' he said between his teeth.

'Better wait a bit. . . .'

Beaumont swore, clambered unsteadily to his feet, swayed, nearly fell over as Grayson grabbed for his arm. Tillotson's jeep stood a few yards away and Beaumont remembered he had thrown the ignition key into the snow. Another jeep stood a few yards away, its windscreen shattered, the front right tyre flat. 'Tillotson shot at you?'

'Tillotson . . . ?'

'Yes, Tillotson,' Beaumont rasped impatiently. 'He's Crocodile—the security leak. But you wouldn't know about that. We've got to get after him—where's he gone?' Beaumont looked towards the airfield and there was nothing in sight— only the guard-post by the gate in the wire, the orange snowplough in the distance and the hangar beyond. Where the hell had Tillotson vanished to? 'Which way did he go?' Beaumont snapped.

Grayson, a short, wiry man of thirty-five with sand-coloured hair, was still recovering from the shock: he had thought Beaumont was dead. 'We've heard rumours about a security

43

leak. I was late coming out to meet you off the plane and the pilot said you'd driven off in a jeep. I couldn't believe it was Tillotson when he started shooting. He ran off towards the airfield. . . .' Grayson was talking to himself—Beaumont had started running towards the guard-post.

'He can't get away,' Grayson shouted as he followed Beaumont. 'Vandenberg declared a state of alert just before your plane came in. The base is sealed off. . . .'

'I think Tillotson can fly a helicopter,' Beaumont shouted back. He was getting into his stride now, his legs carrying him over the snow with surprising speed for so large a man. It was will-power which kept him going; his head was aching horribly, the blood at the side of his face had congealed in the bitter cold, his stomach was on the verge of nausea. The bitter air helped his recovery as he ran and took in great gulps of it. Close to the strangely deserted guard-post he stopped and waited for Grayson to catch him up.

'Sam, have you a gun? Good—give it to me and keep back.'

He took the Colt .45 from the American and approached the guard-post. Something was lying in the snow just outside the concrete blockhouse. An American soldier still clutching his carbine, swathed in his parka, lay on his back staring up at the Arctic sky. Beaumont bent down, checked the man's pulse, then heaved him over on his stomach. He was dead and the blood patch which surrounded a rip high up in the back of the parka was already frozen. It couldn't have been difficult; after all, Tillotson was the security chief. The alert meant that no one could get on to the airfield, so Tillotson had removed the obstacle in his escape route.

'He's already on the airfield,' he told Grayson grimly as the American reached him.

'I've never heard that Tillotson can fly,' Grayson objected.

'I think he can fly a helicopter—and there are helicopters inside that hangar.' Beaumont stared beyond the wire where there was no sign of movement. 'I once saw him inside a machine. That's how he's going to try and get out—by helicopter. Come on!'

'There are two guards inside that hangar,' Grayson said

44

quickly. 'There's a phone inside the guard-post—we must warn the men inside the hangar. . . .'

Beaumont was half-way inside the guard-post doorway when he saw phone-cord slashed and dangling. 'It's no use, Sam—he thought of that. But where the hell is he?' Beaumont ran to the open gateway and stared across the white desert of the airfield.

The snow-plough.

It was smaller now, like an orange bug as it crept up to the hangar where the helicopters were housed. Tillotson had grabbed the nearest available transport to get him inside the hangar fast. Beaumont would have shouted—anything to warn the men guarding the machines—but he was too far away. He took a deep breath and began running again while Grayson followed. Unlike the American, who wore boots, Beaumont was still wearing the rubber-soled shoes he had come in from Washington, but the snow was a hard crust and again he was covering the ground with astonishing speed. He had run for several minutes, was near the hangar when he stumbled and sprawled head first in the snow. He clambered to his feet, his head aching, his face stinging, and had to search for the revolver which had jumped out of his hand. He found it half-buried in the snow and at that moment heard a sound which chilled his mind: the throbbing beat of a helicopter's motor. With the gun in his hand he ran the last two hundred yards.

'Keep back!' he shouted to Grayson.

The orange plough was parked close to the hangar entrance and the huge, power-operated doors were open now. The mouth of the hangar was a dark cave as his tired legs carried him forward on sheer will-power, and he was within ten yards of the entrance when the machine appeared, an H-19 Sikorsky, its blades whirling at speed as it emerged from the dark shadow. Snow was whipped from the ground, thrown across the airfield, and the machine came forward through the disturbed snow, advancing towards Beaumont, its size enormous in the moonlight.

Beaumont stood quite still, braced himself, hoisted the revolver, gripping the butt with both hands to steady his aim as the machine came on. In ten seconds it would grind over him. The gunsight was aimed for the cockpit, for the blurred helmeted head-and-shoulders behind the ice-rimed perspex. He took a deep breath, aimed carefully, squeezed. The hammer clicked. He felt rather than heard the click as the helicopter roar hammered at his ear-drums. The firing mechanism was choked. The gun wouldn't fire.

'Look out!' Grayson shouted, his warning lost in the roar.

Tillotson drove the machine straight at him and Beaumont dived sideways and downwards. As he hit the snow he rolled, took the impact on his shoulders, kept rolling over and over while the hideous roar enveloped him. The motor coughed, changed, the roar became a steady, purposeful beat, and when Beaumont looked up the machine was ascending, was already the height of the hangar roof. He climbed to his knees, wiped snow scuffed up by the rotating blades off his face as Grayson reached him.

'We've got to get after him,' Beaumont snapped. 'He mustn't get clear—our lives depend on it. . . .'

He hardly glanced at the crumpled form lying half under the terrible blades of the snow-plough. One of the guards. It had been so easy, so coldly brutal. The snow-plough was a familiar sight on the airfield—the soldier had come out to meet it—Tillotson had driven straight over him. Inside the hangar entrance Beaumont stumbled again, nearly fell over the body of the second guard. He grasped instantly how this had happened. Tillotson had simply shouted for his victim. 'There's been a horrible accident. . . .' The knife had gone in before the youngster recovered from the shock, the knife showing in Beaumont's torch beam where a handle protruded from the dead man's back.

Beaumont dropped the useless Colt, picked up the carbine the soldier had never had a chance to use and ran inside the hangar. A second Sikorsky was standing at the rear of the hangar under a hooded lamp. An electric cable plugged in to keep the motor from freezing ran from the machine to the wall. Beaumont unplugged the cable, climbed up to the machine, opened the door and went inside the cabin as Grayson came up behind him. 'He's gone,' the American warned. 'We'll never find him. . . .'

'We'll find him. . . .' Beaumont was fixing on the pilot's helmet and headset which was always left in the pilot's seat. Stripping off his parka, he settled himself behind the controls. 'Shut the door, Sam—we're going up.' The instrument panel faced him—radar-altimeter, fuel gauge, rev. counter, other instruments. The collective stick—controlling ascent—was on his left. The cyclic control stick—which changed flight direction—was on his right. A twist-grip throttle, rather like a motor-cycle's throttle, was ringed round the collective stick. Beaumont started the motor.

The whole cabin shuddered. Sound blasted across the inside of the hangar. The rotor blades above swivelled sluggishly, start-stop-start. Then the machine burst into power. In the ghostly light from the instrument panel Beaumont's expression was grim as he built up more power. The helicopter edged forward, drummed across the concrete, emerged from the hangar.

The radar mast which reached almost to the stars came into view and Beaumont used the throttle. The fifty-foot rotor blades tore through their ellipse, whipped through the Arctic air, sounded as though at any second they would rip loose from the machine. The rev. counter climbed on the dial. The machine quivered like a great bird, tethered and desperate to leave the ground, then they were going up.

Beyond the perspex dome which vaulted above them they saw the hangar wall descending like a lift. The snow-covered roof appeared, disappeared as a glow-worm of vehicle lights drove close to the guard-post at the airfield entrance. 'They've tumbled to it!' Beaumont spoke the words into the mike hanging from the headset under his chin. Grayson heard him through the earphones of his own headset as he sat alongside Beaumont in the observer's seat. The helicopter gained altitude as the vehicles rushed across the snow below and Beaumont swore as he heard reports above the muffled roar of the motor. 'They're shooting at us,' he said.

'For God's sake, why?'

47

'Because Vandenburg and Callard think Tillotson's aboard this machine. . . .'

To escape the gunfire Beaumont was ascending vertically as the altimeter needle climbed. In the pale glowing night there was no sign of another helicopter: Tillotson had vanished again. Beaumont turned east, the direction he assumed Crocodile would take. 'And who is Callard?' Grayson asked.

'The F.B.I. man who came up here to arrest Tillotson. Everything was beautifully laid on—the alert you mentioned put into operation just before the Boeing landed—which sealed off the base. Callard gets off the plane, drives to the camp with Col. Vandenberg, then when Tillotson arrives they confront him.' Beaumont was maintaining an easterly course as he peered ahead: nothing but the flattened-out icecap in view. 'Nice and neat, Mr Callard's plan,' Beaumont went on. 'It merely failed to take account of Crocodile.'

'What happened?'

'I imagine Tillotson had a vague notion they might be on to him—he was the security chief, remember. Then he'd wonder about the alert. Next thing he finds out from the pilot that Callard came aboard at Washington at the last minute—without anyone telling Tillotson. So he decides it's time to catch the first plane out—I don't think anyone else suspected he knew how to pilot a Sikorsky. . . .'

'Over there! To the north. . . .' Grayson pointed and Beaumont looked to his left. More icecap, desolate, cold, hideously barren. Then he saw it. Tillotson's machine was, at a guess, ten miles away. A shadow, a swift-moving blip of darkness scudding over the snow. Seconds later he saw the machine which was casting the shadow. He began to change direction.

'Why may our lives depend on stopping Tillotson?' Grayson asked quietly.

Beaumont grunted as he aimed his machine along the same course Tillotson was following. 'This could be a savage one, Sam, so you don't have to come. We have to lift a Soviet scientist out of Target-5. He's coming across the ice from North Pole 17—that's about twenty-five miles east across the pack from Target-5 at the moment. We go in if fog closes Target-5 and they can't send a plane in. It means going by chopper with sleds aboard to the edge of the fog, then it's sledding the rest of the way.'

'And sledding back—all the way to Greenland?'

'I think so. Dawes doesn't—he hopes to pick us up again when we come out of the fog. I don't think they'll find us— so we'll have to sled all the way back to the coast. At least that's the official version—I've got another idea. And the Russian security forces will be on our tails. A very savage one, Sam.'

'But there's no fog.'

'So we just sit around eating American army rations. The key date could be Sunday—tomorrow. I've arranged for two Sikorskys to be ready for us at Curtis Field on the Greenland coast.'

'Tillotson's heading due north,' Grayson commented.

The American was using a pair of night-glasses he had found in the cabin and the shadow of the Soviet agent's machine was still more visible than the machine itself. Without that shadow, Grayson reckoned they would have lost him. Beaumont glanced at the compass. Due north as Sam had said.

'I think he's heading for the Humboldt Glacier,' Beaumont replied. 'I wonder why? If he'd gone due east he'd have made the coast—they keep these machines tanked up when they're on the ground so there'd be enough fuel. What the devil can there be for him on the Humboldt Glacier?'

'Why is he so important?' Grayson asked again.

'Because he knows too much about us,' Beaumont said tersely. 'He doesn't know about Gorov—the man we have to lift out. No one up here knew about him until I arrived. But he does know about the preparations for a trip. He knows Curtis Field is involved—the nearest airfield to Target-5. He had to know that because we needed those machines sending there. I'm just hoping to God he hasn't got a transmitter hidden away up here—that if we don't get to him in time he'll transmit to Leningrad. If that happens, Sam, none of us will qualify as very good insurance risks.'

* * *

49

The awesome sight of the Humboldt Glacier unfolded itself as they flew closer. From high up on the icecap a massive river of ice stretched down to a fiord far below, a half-mile wide river of ice glistening like a sheet of fractured crystal in the moonlight. It sheered down from the icecap until it reached an icefall where it plunged over a monstrous cliff down to the fiord hundreds of feet below. As they came closer they could see, at the bottom of the steep-sided fiord, great icebergs marooned on the snowbound foreshore. Tillotson's Sikorsky had already landed, was perched on a knoll at the side of the glacier. For the third time Tillotson had vanished.

'He's the bloody invisible man,' Beaumont grumbled as he circled above the stationary helicopter.

'Maybe he's still inside his machine—he waits for us to land and then starts shooting before we can get out,' Grayson suggested shrewdly.

'Maybe. . . .' Beaumont continued circling at about two hundred feet. It made him almost dizzy to look down the sheer of the glacier, and then he banked the machine slightly. 'He's down there! See that smaller knoll further down the glacier— look, you can see him moving now.'

'Land on that knoll.'

'Too small—we could go over the edge. I'm bringing us down alongside Tillotson's machine, then he can't get away. You stay with it in case he gives me the slip—and keep trying to raise Thule.'

Five times Grayson had used the radio to try and get through and five times he had failed. 'Damned thing never works when you need it,' Beaumont had commented. He hovered the machine, dropped it slowly and landed on the knoll fifty yards away from the stationary machine. It had a dead look, as though Tillotson never expected to return to it. He switched off his motor. 'I should be back in an hour, Sam,' he said casually as he put on his parka with difficulty.

Grayson nodded, knowing that if Tillotson was armed with a rifle the Englishman could be dead in a good deal less than an hour. But in the long dangerous trip to Spitsbergen, the three men—Beaumont, Grayson and Horst Langer—had learned

50

never to waste words or energy. You just got on with the next job. And Beaumont's next job was capturing or eliminating Tillotson.

The atmosphere inside the cabin was very warm and he tensed himself as he opened the door and picked up the carbine. The temperature dropped—from forty above to forty below. 'Get on with it,' Beaumont muttered to himself. He dropped out of the machine and the iron-hard ground hit his feet like a blow from a hammer. The paralysing cold choked him. He fastened the parka up to his neck, pulled the hood over his head.

Behind him Grayson slammed the cabin door shut quickly without so much as a word of farewell. Again no wasted words. Above him the blades had stopped whirling and an incredible silence descended, the silence of the Arctic night.

He tried to take short breaths as he trudged past Tillotson's Sikorsky to the edge of the knoll, then he stood looking down the vast sweep of the glacier slope. The second knoll further down the glacier was clearly visible in the moonlight, a small cap of rock surmounted by a crude wooden cross. Tillotson was stooping over something perched on an Eskimo grave, a sacred place in Greenland which couldn't be disturbed under any circumstances by edict of the Danish authorities. The some-thing was a box-like object with a small mast protruding above it. Beaumont's face tightened: Tillotson did have a transmitter.

The rock side above the glacier was too steep to make his way down, so he was forced on to the glacier itself. Tentatively, he began moving down the ice with the carbine trailed in his hand: the light was too difficult to try a shot at this range. He found the surface horribly treacherous and it was rather like climbing down the side of a skating rink inclined at an angle, a skating rink corrugated with ridges and gullies. His rubber-soled shoes were not ideal footwear and he was worried that if he started to slide he might never stop before he reached the brink of the icefall. Grimly, he kept moving as fast as he dared because Tillotson might already be transmitting. And the Soviet agent, hidden behind the knoll, was completely out of sight now.

Lower down it became much more dangerous because frequently the glacier was split open, exposing crevasses of unknown depth, dark gashes which disappeared in the shadows. He had to move more slowly, using the carbine as an improvized support, treading from one rib of ice to another, crossing the narrow crevasses between. And all the time he was waiting for the first slither. The intense cold didn't help: Beaumont, whose resistance to low temperatures was phenomenal, probably because of his boyhood spent at Coppermine, wasn't properly clothed for Arctic work. The cold was penetrating his gloves, infiltrating his parka, creeping up his legs.

He was very close to the knoll, no longer using the carbine as a support, holding the weapon ready for instant use, when he looked up for the third time in a minute. Tillotson had appeared from the far side of the knoll, a tall fur-clad figure holding something in his right hand. Perched about twenty feet above the Englishman, Tillotson whipped back his hand in a throwing position. For one terrible, drawn-out moment Beaumont thought he was hurling a grenade. He jerked up the carbine and then the missile was hurtling towards him. It hit the ice, bounced, ricocheted. A rock. The realization flashed through Beaumont's mind that Tillotson no longer had a gun.

The aim was astonishingly good—or damned lucky. The rock ricocheted off the ice, flew towards Beaumont's right leg. He jumped sideways, the rock missed him, then he was off-balance, falling, sliding down the glacier like a toboggan, rushing towards the icefall brink.

The carbine was gone, slithering away under its own momentum, preceding him over the icefall brink as Beaumont, tobogganning on his stomach, desperately tried to halt the slide, to grab for any projection, to jam his foot in a gulley. And all the time as the bitter air hit his face and the glacier whipped past under him he was expecting to halt, to go down instead of forward, to drop inside a crevasse. The slide went on, he was shooting over the ice down a smooth slope of polished surface tilted at an angle of thirty degrees. The parka saved his body from the friction and the grazing, but he was still plunging downwards at increasing speed. His gloves hammered at the ice, the toes of his shoes pressed in hard, but he couldn't stop the diabolical momentum.

The brink of the icefall, a hard line with nothing beyond it—nothing but a sheer drop of hundreds of feet—rushed towards him, and he still couldn't slow down, let alone stop. He was in a perfect position to swallow-dive over the abyss. He rammed his forearms down hard, reached the brink, was going over. Endless space, depth, yawned below him and something spiky. His left arm felt the boulder, a rock embedded in the glacier.

It was pure reflex—his arm crooked, got a hold on the rock. The brief anchor point merely served as a fulcrum to shoot him over the drop. His prone body swivelled to the left, went over the brink. His left hand felt a projection on the rock, his gloved fingers closed, held on. The weight of his body, the momentum, nearly tore his arm off, or so it felt. Then he was still, hanging over the drop, held by only one hand, one curved arm, his body suspended in space.

Below he caught a brief glimpse of nothing, of the sheer ice cliff going down and down, at the bottom the splay of the glacier, huge spiked ice pinnacles. He made himself look up, concentrated his remaining energy on holding on, on levering himself back up over the brink. He wrapped his right arm round the boulder, felt his exploring fingers contact his other hand. He clamped one hand over the other. Only then did he look up the glacier past the boulder. Tillotson was coming down the glacier.

It was terribly silent—except for the crunch of spiked boots driving into the ice. Beaumont's face twisted: Tillotson was wearing crampon boots, which made his descent much safer. Where the devil had he got hold of them? He must have had the boots ready in the jeep, must have planned his departure from Thule even before the Boeing 707 had landed. And it was going to take the American less than half a minute to reach him.

Too late to try and clamber back over the edge. Beaumont was having trouble with his vision now—the oncoming Tillotson looked like two men. Beaumont blinked. The vision dissolved into one man, a man with a knife in his right hand.

Tillotson was very close when Beaumont's head flopped, when his right hand lost its grip.

Beaumont's right arm went limp, flopped out of sight behind the boulder. The strain on his left arm was appalling, almost unbearable, and under the parka his clothes were clammy with sweat. Tillotson paused about three feet from the boulder, decided he couldn't reach with the knife. Taking two more careful paces, he lowered himself to a sitting position behind the rock, raised his right foot, aimed the crampon spikes at the Englishman's left hand. The spikes were half an inch long, rimed with ice from the glacier. He lunged to spike the gloved hand.

As he drove the boot down hard, Beaumont's right hand whipped up over the boulder, locked round Tillotson's ankle, heaved savagely sideways. The spikes grazed Beaumont's other hand as Tillotson lost his balance. He started sliding. His body skidded round the far side of the boulder, his hands flailed desperately for something to grip on. His fingers clutched the boulder, gained a hold, and he thought he had saved himself. Beaumont's right hand struck again, struck this time as a clubbed fist, smashing down with brutal force on the bridge of the American's nose. Tillotson yelped, lost his grip, went over. The scream travelled back up the icefall, a long-drawn-out scream which ended abruptly. Beaumont began hauling himself back over the edge.

He collapsed when he reached the far side of the boulder, still conscious but hardly able to move as he propped himself against the rock and massaged his left arm slowly. Clambering to his knees, he peered over the boulder into the depths. Tillotson had died in a macabre way—his body was perched at the summit of one of the numerous ice pinnacles, speared through his middle.

'You can fly us back, Sam.'

Beaumont sagged in the observer's seat as Grayson watched him. 'He did have a radio transmitter,' he went on, 'a pretty powerful one. Made by Radio Corporation of America, of course, in case anyone found it. Not that it was likely—he had it hidden in an Eskimo grave and no one goes poking about in that. We'd better get started,' he added. 'Vandenberg can send someone to collect the transmitter.'

'Had he transmitted?' Grayson asked.

'He transmitted something, I'm sure. He may not have had all that much time, the message could have been garbled—he must have encoded it before he left Thule.'

'Probably we'll never know.'

Beaumont looked at Grayson. 'Probably we will know—when the Russian security people are waiting to meet us out on the ice.'

Saturday, 19 February

'I KNOW why Winthrop came to Leningrad. I can see clear down to the bottom of your large empty hole, Kramer!'

At eight o'clock on Saturday night—eight hours before Michael Gorov planned to escape from North Pole 17—Papanin was still in his office. The room was like an inferno, the green-tiled stove was roasting the office—and its occupants. The Siberian loved extremes of temperature, had loved them since his childhood in Omsk when the terrible winter cold stimulated him while it obliterated everyone else, but then he had also luxuriated in the warmth of Siberian stoves when he came indoors. Kramer, on the other hand, was gasping for air.

'I don't see why you're suddenly interested in Michael Gorov,' he said hoarsely. 'Why should he be mixed up in this Jewish business?'

'Like the rest of them, you'll see it next year. That's why I'm sitting in this chair—because I can see things before they happen.' Papanin leaned back in the chair, put his hands behind his neck. 'It was the shipping list which tipped me off.'

'You mean the deputy mate, Peter Gorov?'

'You'll see down this hole yet.' Papanin regarded the Balt with an unblinking stare. 'If you don't fall head first into it. Do you remember the case of Rachel Levitzer, that Jewish girl who made a run for it last August and fell down a staircase?'

'She broke her neck. . . .'

'She also broke Michael Gorov's heart. Did you know that?'

'I heard a rumour. . . .'

'It was hushed up—their relationship—because of the position Michael Gorov occupies. We've been looking for a grubby little courier bringing in large sums from America— someone who might at any time be searched at the airport

56

when he comes in. I think they've been cleverer than that. . . .'
Papanin paused to give his bombshell maximum impact. 'I
think Michael Gorov, our eminent oceanographer, is bringing
in the money.'

Kramer was astounded, appalled. He stared back at Papanin,
trying to guess what he was up to, always an impossible task.
'You can't mean it,' he said eventually. 'Where would he get
the money from?'

'That's the clever part! He spent three years in the Arctic
planning and laying the Catherine system of cables and sonar
buoys along the seabed. He often visited American ice islands
to see what they were up to.' Papanin hammered his huge fist
down on the desk. 'And that's when they gave him the money
to bring in—during those visits to American bases! He's never
been searched when he came back—no one would dream of it.'

'But why?' Kramer was bewildered. 'Why would he do it?'

'That damned Jewish mistress of his persuaded him. He was
going with her for three years before she died—and he's still
doing it, for the sake of her memory or some such lunatic
sentiment!'

'It's fantastic. . . .'

'It's logical!' Papanin shouted. 'He met his brother, the
deputy mate, Peter, in Kiev this month while they were both
on leave. Peter comes back here to board his ship—and on the
way he meets this American, Winthrop, in the park. He was
passing a verbal message to Winthrop—from his brother,
Michael.'

'We'll have to be careful,' Kramer warned. 'Michael Gorov
is a friend of Marshal Grechko.'*

'Grechko is an arrogant hog. If I'm right about Gorov you'll
find that Grechko hardly knew him.'

'It's still dangerous. . . .'

'Maybe, but there's someone else we can get at—Peter
Gorov, a mere seaman. You found out the present position of
the *Girolog*?'

'She's five hours' sailing time from Tallinn. . . .'

'Send a plane immediately to Tallinn airport to wait for

---

* Soviet Minister of Defence.

Gorov. Radio the ship's master to sail straight for Tallinn. Five hours to port, half an hour to and from airports at either end, one hour's flight to here. Peter Gorov should be in my office in seven hours' time—by three o'clock Sunday morning! What are you hanging about for, Kramer?'

Alone again in his overheated office, Papanin took out his little pocket chess set and stared at the board. The Siberian, a man of many talents, was a Soviet grandmaster of chess. In July he would be in Iceland for the coming Spassky–Fischer chess match. Officially he would attend as one of Spassky's advisers; unofficially he would be chief Soviet representative to keep an eye on security.

Outwardly a flamboyant and extrovert personality, Igor Papanin had a cold, detached brain which regarded the whole Arctic as a gigantic chess board. There were Soviet pieces and American pieces on the board and in any contest of wills you had to get the opening gambit right. Curiously enough, considering the role Keith Beaumont was to play in the coming battle of wills, the Siberian was studying the English Opening.

'A message has just come through from Crocodile.'

Kramer reported the news casually when he came back into the Siberian's office half an hour later, as though it were of no great importance. 'They are just decoding it,' he added. He paused as Papanin went on reading the personal file on Michael Gorov.

'Anything else?' Papanin grunted without looking up.

'Who is Crocodile?'

'A person. Identity known only to General Syrtov and myself.' Having delivered the snub, Papanin looked up. 'I want to see that message the moment it's decoded.'

It was 9 p.m. before Kramer returned with the message. The *Girolog* had already changed course and was heading slowly south through the ice for the port of Tallinn. The plane Kramer had sent was due to land at Tallinn airport within ten minutes.

In Washington, where they were eight hours behind Leningrad, Dawes and Adams were waiting with growing impatience for a signal from a man who was dead. In Greenland, also eight hours behind Leningrad, Beaumont and Grayson were flying back to Thule from the Humboldt Glacier. One message —from Winthrop—would never arrive. Another signal—from Tillotson—was just being handed to Papanin.

'They had trouble with it,' Kramer explained. 'It's rather garbled. The operator says it was transmitted very erratically and he's sure it isn't complete.'

Papanin read the message. 'What a brilliant deduction,' he commented. He stroked the top of his close-shaven head while he read the message a second time. *Americans preparing . . . over polar pack . . . general area Target Five . . . Beaumont going in over ice to meet target . . . American planes Curtis Field . . . Beaumont force . . .*

Without a word the Siberian stood up, strode out of his room into the office next door where the American teleprinter was still chattering away, spewing out a stream of reports from Soviet bases spread out across the Arctic. Behind chromium-leg desks four men were working away on reports and answering telephones. Papanin took a small curved pipe from his tunic pocket and started filling it from an old pouch as he stared up at the wall map.

It was not unlike the huge wall map in Gen. Dawes's office, but here the Arctic was seen from a different angle: the Russian coast low down, near the floor, the distant coasts of Greenland and Canada and Alaska high up near the ceiling. 'There is Curtis Field,' he said to Kramer, pointing with his pipe-stem to the airfield on the Greenland coast nearest to Target-5. He called to one of the men behind the desks. 'Petrov, fill me in on the position of the ships in this area. . . .'

'The trawler fleet k.49, sir?'

'That will do for a start.'

'As you see, it's a long way north of Iceland at the moment, but it's heading south now—to watch the NATO sea exercise *Sea Lion*. There are twelve ships—all equipped with the normal electronic gear. . . .'

'Including wireless-jamming apparatus?'

'Yes, sir. The helicopter carrier *Gorki* west of Spitsbergen has also turned south with the same mission. . . .'

'What about the *Revolution*? It's the closest vessel to Iceberg Alley.'

'She'll be there for several weeks—she's tracking American satellites.'

'This American vessel . . .' Papanin's pipe-stem stabbed at a marker higher up.

'The American icebreaker *Elroy*, sir. We've just moved her position, less than an hour ago. She was heading south and now she's turned due north again—a helicopter from the *Gorki* saw her.'

'Thank you.' Papanin was always polite to junior members of his staff: the more senior men like Kramer could look after themselves. He marched straight back inside his office and went behind his desk. His normally explosive manner had gone and when he issued the dramatic order to the Balt his voice was quiet and calm.

'Order a state of alert throughout the entire Arctic Zone. Every coastal base, every airfield, every ice island—including those off the Alaska coast. Radio Murmansk that I want a Bison bomber standing by night and day, fully tanked up. Warn Leningrad airport to have a plane ready to fly me to Murmansk at one hour's notice. . . .'

'I clear this with Moscow first, of course. . . .'

'Send Vronsky and his special security detachment to Murmansk—they must be in the air in thirty minutes. . . .'

'Surely we must refer this to Moscow?'

'The detachment will wear civilian clothes and will be fully armed with personal weapons. Bring me the latest met. reports of the Target-5 area. . . .'

'Without reference to Moscow, sir? Operations on this scale need General Syrtov's approval.'

Papanin removed the pipe he had just placed in his wide mouth. 'You don't understand any of this, do you, Comrade? You can't stand the pressure of having two large holes to look into at the same time, can you?'

'Crocodile's message doesn't make sense. . . .'

'It does, if you know Crocodile. The Americans are planning some big operation near their floating base, Target-5. They are using the code-word Beaumont for the operation. We have to get in our opening gambit first.'

'You still want Peter Gorov brought here from Tallinn?'

'Of course.' Papanin relit his pipe, watching Kramer. 'That is a separate problem. And now,' he went on without any change of tone, 'get the bloody lead out of your boots.'

Curtis Field stands on the top of a 300-foot-high cliff that rises sheer from the east Greenland coast. It is debatable whether flying in or out is the more chilling experience—but probably the latter is worse. The plane takes off along a runway which ends at the brink of a cliff; as Beaumont put it, 'When you see nothing ahead you'll go either up or down. . . .'

At nine in the evening of Saturday, Washington time, Beaumont was ready to go, a feat of organization which was little short of miraculous. In the past sixteen hours he had flown from Washington to Thule; in pursuit of Tillotson he had flown to the Humboldt Glacier and back again; since then he had flown the breadth of Greenland to Curtis Field. And by nine in the evening everything was ready—and Curtis Field knew that a whirlwind had hit them.

'I need those two Sikorskys fully serviced, fully tanked up within two hours. . . .'

'Not possible,' Fuller, the airfield controller had snapped.

'Put more men on the job! Do I have to phone Dawes in Washington? It's your damned emergency. . . .'

The helicopters were ready to fly by 9.5 p.m. A plane had flown out to check weather conditions near Target-5—and came back to report no sign of fog. The two Eskimo-type sleds had been brought from Camp Century, had been packed with food, a powerful radio transceiver, rifles, ammunition—and an Elliott homing beacon.

'What's that for?' Fuller had asked.

'Insurance.'

Beaumont's reply had been abrupt and totally non-informative. Restlessly, he had prowled round the hangar where icicles hung from the girders, poking his nose into everything, checking the controls of a Sikorsky, giving a hand with packing the sleds, frequently striding into the radio room to ask whether a message had come in from Washington. His energy, which seemed boundless, injected urgency into the airfield staff, made them work twice as fast as normal. Had Colonel Igor Papanin been able to witness the performance it would have made him thoughtful.

But Beaumont would never have achieved the impossible without the aid of the short, wiry, thirty-five year old American, Sam Grayson. It was Grayson who spent nerve-racking hours on the phone calling Thule, the huge American air base at the top of Baffin Bay. 'I want those dogs sent here now. No plane available? Only a Hercules just taking off for Point Barrow? Then drag yourself out of that arm-chair and stop it. Listen! If it takes off I'll get on to Dawes and have it turned round in mid-air. . . .'

'Those dogs were due here one hour ago,' Beaumont rumbled behind him.

Grayson twisted round in his seat. 'Keith, do you want them now or when they arrive?' he demanded.

Beaumont grinned bleakly. 'Both—and sooner!'

Most Arctic teams function in one of two ways. A British team has a leader and the rest do what he tells them to; other nationalities work differently—Americans and Norwegians work democratically, they exchange opinions. Beaumont's three-man team was unique. As he put it with a dry smile, 'They do what I tell them because they know I'm right.' Grayson's version was different. 'In a crisis we follow Beaumont, then argue it afterwards.' Horst Langer's version was different again. 'We have three bosses—and it works. Don't ask me how!'

Sam Grayson, brilliant navigator, marine biologist, and a first-rate marksman, came from Minneapolis. Before going with Beaumont and Langer on the epic Spitsbergen crossing he worked for the U.S. Geological Survey and the Lamont Geological Observatory of Columbia University. An old Arctic hand, he assured his wife before each trip, 'Maybe this will be my last crack at the ice—could be I'm getting sick of it. . . .' That was until the next trip came up.

'The dogs just came in,' he informed Beaumont two hours after calling Thule.

'Horst had better check them right away. . . .'

Beaumont swung round as the third member of the team, Horst Langer, came into the tiny room Grayson was using as his headquarters. 'The dogs are here—and what's that sinister bit of paper you're waving about?'

'An urgent signal just came through from Dawes—we're to stand by ready for instant departure.'

Because it was unprecedented, the depression caught all the met. experts off balance, the vast filling depression gathering over northern Greenland in late February 1972. This was the depression which affected the whole of north America and western Europe later in the year, which turned summer into something like winter, which sent icebergs farther south than they had ever reached before, which invaded transatlantic shipping lanes and caused great liners to change course. And this was the depression which brought the fog.

The Soviet met. people on Novaya Zemlya didn't see it coming. The U.S. weather plane which flies daily across the roof of the world from Mildenhall in East Anglia to Alaska missed it. The U.S. Weather Bureau failed to foresee it. But as Beaumont prowled restlessly round the ice-cold hangar at Curtis Field, a great bank of fog half a mile high, many miles wide, a bank of freezing black fog, appeared north of Target-5 and began to drift steadily south.

Sunday, 20 February

YOU CAN ONLY DIE ONCE, but sometimes it seems you are dying a hundred times over.

For Peter Gorov the flight from Tallinn to Leningrad was a nightmare. No one would give him a reason for his recall, no one would tell him who he was going to see in Leningrad, but he was treated like royalty when he disembarked from the *Girolog* at one in the morning.

A black Zil limousine with chains on the wheels took him through a snowstorm to the airport. When he went aboard the waiting plane the two pilots shook hands with him. He was invited to travel in the control cabin and was given a seat behind the co-pilot. The nightmare started from the moment the plane moved off down the runway.

It almost crashed as it was taking off—they were heading direct for the airport control tower, still on the ground, when the co-pilot shouted, 'You'll never make it!' He threw up a hand as though to ward off the collision when metal struck steel, then the pilot lifted the machine and it cleared the tower by feet, so it seemed to the petrified Gorov.

But this was only the beginning. As the plane gained altitude and turned east away from the ice-laden Baltic, a fierce, long-drawn argument broke out between the two pilots, each accusing the other. 'You fool, Serge, there was not enough power. . . .'

'Idiot! There was too much power! Would you sooner take over yourself?'

The argument raged on, the technical terms beyond Gorov. The plane suddenly side-slipped, started to drop at an alarming rate. With an oath the pilot regained control, then continued arguing at the top of his voice. Gorov watched from behind, fearfully: it seemed they were more intent on their quarrel than on flying the plane. His fear was intensified when the machine climbed abruptly, heading up at an acute angle. Pressed back against his seat, Gorov was terrified. It was his first experience of flying. Half-way to Leningrad they began drinking.

The quarrel subsided suddenly and the pilots made it up with each other with a bottle of vodka. But their consideration for their honoured guest stopped short of offering him a drink; instead they emptied the bottle themselves. Gorov watched with growing horror as the effect of the vodka made itself felt in their flying performance. The machine was thrown all over the sky as they fell like a lift into air pockets, then shot upwards at an almost vertical angle. 'The met. report was terrible,' Serge explained in a slurred voice. 'If you hadn't been so important we wouldn't have flown.'

'Important to who?' asked the bewildered seaman.

'Maybe the First Secretary. How the hell would I know?'

Twice Gorov had to move swiftly to the small, cramped toilet where he was violently ill, but when he returned to his seat after the second visit his head was clearer for a few minutes. He calculated roughly that wherever they were taking him to in Leningrad he would arrive about three in the morning. It would then be eleven in the evening at North Pole 17, which was four hours behind Leningrad time. He was sure now that they had found out about the American, that they were going to question him. He had to hold out until after midnight, North Pole 17 time, which was four in the morning in Leningrad. He would have to hold out for over an hour.

As they came in to land at Leningrad his stomach muscles felt tighter than the strap which Serge ordered him to fasten. They were gliding down through the snow when the first motor cut out. Seconds later the second engine failed. Could they land on only two engines? Gorov had no idea. The pilot spoke to airport control with a note of hysteria. 'Emergency situation, emergency situation . . .'

Gorov closed his eyes, felt his head starting to spin, opened them and saw the glare of the landing lights coming up. The plane wobbled badly. The co-pilot cursed, waved the empty vodka bottle at Serge. 'You're coming in too fast . . . you're going to kill us. . . .' Gorov sat in his seat bathed in sweat, unable to take his eyes off the incoming lights which tilted as the plane wobbled. His clothes were soaked but his mouth was parched, his throat constricted. They were drunk, both of them, the criminals. He was going to burn to death, horribly.

At the last moment the two dead motors burst into action, the wheels bumped the runway, the machine cruised between the lights, made a perfect landing. The pilots waited until Gorov had disembarked without speaking to them, then Serge burst into laughter as he waved the empty bottle. 'I don't like mineral water—next time ask them to put the real stuff in it. . . .'

Gorov would never know it, but he had been flown to Leningrad by the two most experienced pilots in the Baltic Command. They were probably the only men who could have handled the plane in such an appalling manner and survived. It was Papanin himself who had phoned the airport controller at Tallinn and given him the instructions. 'I want you to play a little game with your passenger—scare the guts out of him. When he lands he must be a jelly.'

The man in the chair was sweating and the spotlight shining on his face reflected off the sweat globules. Fear—and the green-tiled stove—were responsible. Papanin sat behind his desk in the gloom. The other men were shadows behind the chair, unnerving presences Peter Gorov couldn't see. One of them coughed—to remind Gorov he was there. The watch on Gorov's left wrist registered 3.20 a.m.

Papanin, who was completely on the wrong track, who still believed he was close to identifying the money courier financing the Jewish underground—whereas Michael Gorov had never had the slightest connection with that shadowy organization—had exactly forty minutes left to break Gorov. In forty minutes it would be 4 a.m. in Leningrad and only midnight at North Pole 17. In forty minutes Michael Gorov would have disappeared on to the polar pack.

'We'll go over it again,' Papanin said. 'Just to make sure I've got it right. Start with when you went into the park.'

Go over it again. . . . Gorov's head was reeling. He had been driven from the airport in a battered old Volga. Kramer had made him travel without his coat and with the windows open, so during the drive Gorov had become steadily frozen. It was a detail which Papanin had planned: sudden violent changes of temperature reduce a man's resistance. He had visualized the overheated control cabin in the plane, had frozen Gorov during the journey from the airport, now he was roasting him again. Gorov's stomach was empty, his nerves shattered, and he could hardly think straight as Papanin repeated, 'Go over it again.'

Gorov had lost count of how many times he had explained it. He tried to repeat it as a catechism as the heat of the stove burned his back. 'I went into the park. . . .'

'Why?'

'I was on my way to the docks.'

'So you went straight along the Nevsky Prospekt—it's the direct route.'

'I went along the Nevsky Prospekt. . . .' The voice was a monotone, like a child repeating its rote.

'You didn't—you went into the park. Why?'

They came to the part where the pedestrian had tripped on the ice, and Papanin went on asking the same questions he had asked ever since Gorov had come in. 'We want to know his name,' the Siberian repeated. 'That's what it's all about. We want to know his name.'

'I don't know the American's name. . . .'

Gorov stopped speaking. He knew instantly that he had made a fatal blunder. Papanin let him sweat it out for a minute. They hadn't said anything to Gorov about Winthrop being American, and Winthrop had worn clothes which made him look like a Russian. And Winthrop hadn't spoken to the seaman: Gorov had stated this time and again. 'Take him downstairs,' Papanin said, and then waited until he was alone with Kramer. 'Find out what he knows—quickly.'

*　　　*　　　*

Because their suspect was a seaman, and because a seaman's nightmare is drowning, they used the water treatment.

In the basement cellar—which was as cold as Papanin's room had been torrid—they strapped Gorov to an adjustable couch and blindfolded him. He was stretched flat on his back, strapped by his neck and his wrists and his legs to the couch. Somewhere out of sight water slopped in a container.

'What message did the American pass you?' Kramer asked.

'No message. . . .'

One man gripped Gorov's jaw, another man thrust a huge rubber funnel into Gorov's mouth, the third man started pouring water down the funnel. The choking sensation began immediately, the drowning sensation came later. On a stool beside his patient, a doctor sat with a stethoscope pressed against Gorov's naked chest.

For Gorov, flat on his back, blindfolded and unable to move, the world was water—water flooding into his mouth, water pouring down his throat, water surging into his lungs. Desperately he tried to lift his arms, his chest, to hold his breath, and then he was spluttering, choking, retching painfully, and his whole body seemed to swell up, to be on the point of bursting. His eyes bulged, his neck muscles tautened, collapsed. He tried to scream and the scream was strangled and he knew he was dying, drowning. They kept on pouring in water until the doctor looked quickly at Kramer. The Balt nodded. A foot pedal under the couch was pressed and hands lifted the rear of the couch swiftly, elevating Gorov to a sitting position. The seaman choked, spewed, gasped for air. Then he lolled, head down, panting irregularly. Kramer pulled up the blindfold, lifted Gorov's head under the chin.

'What message did the American pass to you?'

Blurred eyes stared back at Kramer, eyes full of hate. He tried to speak twice, looked down at his left wrist, and twice only a hoarse crackle emerged, a hardly human sound. They had taken away his wrist-watch. For Gorov this was the worst ordeal: now he had no idea of the time, nothing to tell him how long he must hold out. The third time he managed to get the words out, glaring at Kramer. 'No message. . . .' Eyes full of hate, the Balt noted, so resistance was high. It would take half an hour, he estimated, maybe less. When the hate vanished, was replaced by agony, they would be getting somewhere. He nodded and they renewed the treatment. Gorov guessed that a good twenty minutes had gone. In fact, it was less than five minutes since they had brought him to the cellar.

The Locomotive moved into action, driving people as though he had only got up an hour ago—whereas in fact he had been twenty-two hours without sleep. It was not the information which Kramer burst into his room with which generated this explosive activity, and once again he deflated the fat Balt.

'Michael Gorov is defecting to the Americans. . . .'

'It took you two hours, Kramer.' Papanin looked at the clock on the wall which registered 5.30 a.m. 'That deputy mate is a courageous man—and you're too late with your news—this signal has just come in from North Pole 17.' He handed the signal form to the Balt who was already sweating from the temperature change as he read it. *Michael Gorov left North Pole 17 with dog team midnight. Security man Marov found dead on the ice. Search parties have been sent out. Please advise. Minsky.*

It took Papanin less than a minute to scribble a reply in his own hand which Petrov rushed to the signals room. *Send all available helicopters farther west than Gorov can have gone. Then sweep back towards North Pole 17. Report immediately any signs of American activity near Target-Five. Papanin.*

He ordered Kramer to contact Murmansk, to check that the Bison bomber was ready for instant departure, to confirm with Leningrad airport that a plane was standing by, to signal trawler fleet k.49 and the *Revolution*, requesting information on any American activity in the area, to signal the helicopter-carrier *Gorki* asking for an immediate check on the present position of the American icebreaker *Elroy*.

He phoned General Boris Syrtov, chief of Special Security in Moscow, but Syrtov had been on the verge of calling the Siberian and the conversation opened with a battle.

'Papanin!' Syrtov's tone was sharp. 'Murmansk tells me you have ordered an Arctic alert. It isn't true, of course?'

'It is true, General. . . .'

'Without my authority?'

'It was a precaution. . . .'

'Brezhnev has heard about it—I have to go to the Kremlin at once.'

'Good. . . .'

'What did you say?' Syrtov roared.

'The precaution was justified,' Papanin snapped. He fired his big gun. 'Michael Gorov has fled across the ice. . . . He's taking more than his brains to the Americans. I've just found out he spent two hours inside the security room while I was away in Moscow—I think he photographed the Catherine charts. He's taking them a blueprint of our entire underwater system.'

Syrtov's anger was replaced by chronic anxiety. He asked what resources Papanin needed—the answer staggered him.

'Personal control of the carrier *Gorki*, trawler fleet k.49, and the research ship *Revolution*. . . .'

'You know that's unprecedented.'

'It's an unprecedented situation. The First Secretary can sanction it—which is why I'm glad you're going to see him.'

'I'll come back to you,' Syrtov said tersely. 'Meantime continue your preparations.'

'I've made them—including ordering an alert nine hours ago without your authority, which has gained us nine hours of invaluable time. . . .' Papanin heard the click of the receiver at the Moscow end with satisfaction. He looked up as Kramer came in, eager for news. 'Pack your hot-water bottle, Kramer —we'll be in the Arctic within twenty-four hours.'

At precisely one o'clock on Sunday morning in Washington Lemuel Dawes switched on the light over the camp bed he had set up in his office and checked the time. As usual, his internal alarm clock had woken him punctually. And he had a headache, which was hardly surprising—the heat, the lack of air and the tropical plants banked up against two walls were building an atmosphere which could only be described as nauseous. Ten minutes later Adams knocked on his door and came in.

'No news from Helsinki,' he said grimly. 'But the plane might have been delayed—he may still get through.'

'So we wait?'

'We wait. . . .'

'Which could be a mistake.' Dawes scratched at his rumpled hair. 'But we can't do a damned thing about it. Gorov could be on the ice already, we could fly a plane into Target-5 now, but I daren't do it—if Gorov hasn't left yet any sign of unusual activity at Target-5 could alert the Russians.'

So while Beaumont was climbing the walls at distant Curtis Field at the edge of the Greenland icecap, while Dawes waited for a signal from a man who had died forty hours earlier, Papanin's far-reaching preparations were gaining momentum and looked like winning him the game before it had even started.

Leonid Brezhnev, First Secretary of the Communist Party of the Union of Soviet Socialist Republics, walked briskly into Colonel Papanin's office at noon on Sunday accompanied by General Boris Syrtov.

As always, when he removed his fur coat, Brezhnev was smartly dressed in a dark business suit, his thick hair was neatly brushed, and in Detroit he could easily have been taken for a Ford executive. No one helped him to disrobe; the First Secretary intensely disliked fuss. And as always he came straight to the point.

'Papanin, you have control of six vessels of the trawler fleet, the helicopter carrier *Gorki* and the research ship *Revolution*. None of these will make it look like a military operation—they are civilian vessels, so to speak. You see the point?'

'There must be no international incident.'

'No international incident,' Brezhnev agreed. 'In May the American president is coming to Moscow for a summit meeting and I want him to come—so be careful.'

'But there could be an international accident,' Papanin said bluntly. 'I know that area—anything can happen there. Men can fall into an open lead, they can get lost for ever in a a blizzard. . . .'

Brezhnev held up a well-kept hand. 'No details, please! There is, I agree, a world of difference between an incident and an accident—that is your sphere.' His thick eyebrows lifted as he spoke with great emphasis. 'But you must bring back Gorov —neither he nor the Catherine charts must ever reach Washington. I have flown here personally to stress how vital this thing is.'

'We are three moves ahead of the Americans already,' Papanin replied. 'That's what counts. . . .'

'But we must keep ahead of them.' Brezhnev glanced at Syrtov, a small, lean-faced man with irritable eyes who was holding a leather folder. 'The general has the codes and wavelengths for you to communicate with these ships. They have already been ordered to proceed to the area involved.'

'I'd like to leave at once.' Papanin took the folder from Syrtov. 'I think we may just be in time. . . .'

Brezhnev grasped the Siberian's arm. 'Igor, you have to be in time. You have to be.'

It was 3 p.m. in Murmansk when Papanin went aboard the crowded Bison bomber. At 3 p.m. on Sunday, 20 February, it was night at Murmansk, a clear moonlit night. The four jets were tuning up to screaming pitch as the Siberian settled into an improvised seat near the pilot's cabin while he studied a map and marked the latest position of the American ice-breaker, *Elroy*. Behind him, spread out across the bare deck, a large body of fur-clad men were packed in close as they nursed their rifles. The enormous power of the jets increased, bursts of snow bounced up from the recently-ploughed runway, then the control tower gave the go-ahead and the throbbing machine began to move.

From the control tower they could see the fiery glow from the rear of the jet pods as the machine taxied forward, turned, moved on to the main runway. Then the machine really came alive, the jets ejected the growl peculiar to the Bison, the wheels whipped down the runway, left the earth. As the bomber climbed steeply its jet ejection hit the runway like gunfire, scouring snow from the concrete, hurling up clouds of whiteness. Five minutes later it was only a vapour trail in the night, thirty thousand feet high. Colonel Igor Papanin was on his way. Destination: North Pole 17.

'Still no word from Helsinki.' Adams handed Dawes the message form as he sat down. 'That just came in—I'm beginning to think something's happened to Winthrop. . . .'

'I guessed that, hours ago.' Dawes glanced at the form. 'My bet is you won't have heard from your boy come Christmas.'

It was ironical that Papanin was the man who alerted Dawes. For hours with growing alarm he had received a stream of reports coming in from ships, from weather planes, from satellites orbiting high above the Arctic—and all the reports indicated that something very big was on the move.

First Dawes heard that the Soviet carrier *Gorki* had changed course, that she was now steaming north at top speed towards the icefield. An hour later the report came through that six vessels of the trawler fleet k.49, ships crammed with electronic gear, had also turned due north, abandoning their obvious spying rendezvous with the NATO naval exercise *Sea Lion*. Finally he had heard that the huge new Soviet research ship *Revolution*, on its maiden spying exercise from the Nikolayev shipyard on the Black Sea coast, had also changed course. 'She's heading into the gullet of Iceberg Alley,' he had told Adams. Then he had made his urgent phone call.

Only thirty minutes later a quietly dressed man wearing horn-rimmed glasses had arrived at Dawes's office. The president's assistant, his closest confidant, he had listened intently for a quarter of an hour before he spoke.

'Lemuel, this is the position. If the president goes to the Moscow summit with the Catherine charts in his pocket, then he'd be talking from a position of great strength—and we may get the concessions we want from the Russians. . . .'

So Dawes had been given permission to take his own decisions without further reference back to Washington. 'Provided you don't stir up an international incident,' the brilliant, German-born assistant had warned him. 'That might spoil the summit meeting. . . .'

Dawes was thinking of this proviso when he took a piece of paper out of his pocket and handed it to Adams. 'I didn't show you the met. report which came in at the last minute. Dense fog has come in out of nowhere and blanketed Target-5. Looks like this is going to be Operation Beaumont after all.'

Adams said nothing as he read the report and then fastened his seat-strap. The Boeing they were travelling aboard was descending and in the distance twin chains of landing lights glowed in the whiteness of the night. Dawes had taken the first of his decisions—he was flying to the edge of the chess board to see for himself. Destination: Curtis Field.

THE FROZEN SEA

Sunday, 20 February

THE MEAGRE AIRSTRIP on North Pole 17 rushed towards the Bison, the Soviet pilot pointed its nose between the rows of lights now blurring into continuous bands, throttled back and prayed. The strip was too short for the Bison.

The ice flew up at him, sped away below, the wheels touched down, the bomber lurched. The pilot gritted his teeth, braked. Snow clouds stormed up, splashed over the windows like white fog. Fragmented ice bombarded the undercarriage, struck it like a million machine-gun bullets. The plane hurtled on, running out of airstrip . . .

'Exciting, isn't it, Kramer?' Papanin remarked.

In the seat beside him Kramer was rigid with fear, almost in a muscular spasm as his gloved hands grasped the seat arms. The Siberian watched with interest as the Balt stared straight ahead without replying; and this, Papanin thought, is a trained interrogator, the man who goes down into the cellar and screws information out of poor broken-down suspects. Sweat it out, my little Balt, sweat it out. The bomber halted fifteen metres from disaster. 'Now you can relax, Kramer,' Papanin said genially.

He glanced out of the window, stared out for a moment, then tore off his seat-strap. He was at the door before the fifty-odd security men lying on the deck behind him had stirred. He had the door open before the ground staff outside had time to perch a metal ladder against the fuselage, then he was hanging half-out of the machine as he stared up into the moonlit night.

'Has it gone? Bloody hell!'

Papanin asked the question, fired the expletive as he stood at the foot of the ladder propped against the Bison, hands thrust deep inside his parka as he stared down at the base leader, Dr Alexei Minsky. Like Kramer, the base leader was short and stocky and he wore snow-goggles which, because the moonlight reflected off them, gave him a sinister appearance. He immediately infuriated Papanin.

'Has what gone, Colonel?'

'For God's sake! That plane I saw when we were coming in.'

'It has flown off to the west. . . .'

'The radar? You've checked the radar?'

'No, Colonel. One moment—I will be back. . . .'

'He's shit-scared,' Papanin snapped to Kramer who had come down the ladder behind him. 'He's more dangerous than a polar bear—he's an idiot! From now on Minsky must be kept inside.'* He stood with his hands in his parka looking round, observing everything. The bleakness of the Soviet base impressed him: for a quarter of a mile in every direction the ice was reasonably level, but beyond it lay the frozen maelstrom of the pack, a hellish jumble of heaped-up ice which looked to be on the verge of lapping over the island.

'This place isn't going to last long,' he remarked.

Unlike American research bases—where the airstrip is always well clear of the camp area—the prefabricated huts on North Pole 17, their flat roofs layered with snow, were barely thirty metres from the improvised runway. A radar mast dominated the little colony, spearing one hundred feet up to a wing-like ear which revolved to face any point of the compass. The Siberian gave brief instructions to Kramer and then faced Minsky who had run back over the ice.

'Hardly a pinpoint on the radar,' Minsky panted, his goggles steamed up. 'When the American plane saw you he flew straight back to Greenland!' He made it sound like a triumph.

Papanin reached out a hand, pushed the goggles up over Minsky's forehead.

'You don't need these on a night like this—or did you think you were in a blizzard? Have the helicopters found Gorov?

---

* Soviet security jargon for must not be allowed outside the borders of the Soviet Union under any circumstances. Presumably two hundred million Soviet citizens are members of this exclusive club.

Have you brought him back? Have you sent out the Sno-Cats? Have you done anything worth while?'

'Gorov hasn't been found. . . .' Minsky sounded nervous. 'They are still searching. . . .'

'Disembark!'

Papanin roared the command up to the aircraft exit and strode long-legged across the airstrip towards the camp. Now there was no danger of an American aircraft observing what came out of the Bison he didn't even bother to look back at the armed men filing down the ladder. And now he was outside Russia the Siberian was feeling free again: he had full control, could take instant decisions without Syrtov peering over his shoulder and making damnfool suggestions.

The precise date when the Special Security Service was formed is not known, but, some time in 1968, Brezhnev decided that for overseas work the K.G.B. was a broken reed. Demoralization set in with the death of Stalin—the most repressive organization in the world, the K.G.B., found itself repressed. Physical torture was banned, was replaced by such devices as the Serbsky Institute in Moscow,* and soon top K.G.B. officials were vying with each other to keep within the law. This change of heart fitted in beautifully with Khrushchev's new liberal policy inside Russia, but it didn't work overseas. A terrorist organization without terror is like an impotent man trying to make love. So a new organization was formed.

The Special Security Service can operate only outside Soviet Russia—it has no power within its own borders. It can use any method to attain its objectives, and because it is confined to overseas operations there is no danger that it may grow into the Frankenstein monster the K.G.B. once became. Brezhnev made only one exception to this rule—because of the Jewish problem Papanin had certain powers inside the city limits of Leningrad. But once he left Murmansk the Siberian controlled the game.

---

* The Serbsky Institute specializes in certifying those who don't conform as insane. The threat of a visit to this place is enough to make many people toe the party line.

'Those machines—why aren't they in the air?' Papanin snapped. He gestured towards six helicopters standing beyond the airstrip where they had been parked to let the Bison come in. Beside him the short-legged Minsky was dog-trotting to keep up.

'They have just arrived from the *Gorki*. . . .'

'They should be in the air—searching! What about the latest met. report?'

'The fog over Target-5 is expected to continue. It is making the search more difficult. . . .'

'That's where you're wrong again! While the fog lasts the Americans can't airlift Gorov back to the States.' They were coming close to the group of huts where metre-long icicles hung from the rooftops, icicles which wouldn't melt again until spring. 'They'll try and get him out over the ice—make for the Greenland coast,' Papanin said, half thinking aloud. 'We'll scatter a screen of men over the ice west of Target-5. We'll keep a screen of helicopters in the air above them. We'll grab him whoever is there to protect him.'

'Might that not be dangerous?'

'We have the perfect excuse. Gorov is a madman, a murderer—he killed Marov, one of our oceanographers. Gorov has been in the Arctic so long he's gone round the bend.'

'I don't understand,' Minsky began. 'Marov was a security man. . . .'

'You're so thick it's hardly credible,' Papanin barked. 'Marov has just become an oceanographer—Gorov is a criminal who killed one of his own colleagues and we have to apprehend him. That changes it from a political case into a police affair.' There was a savage, jaunty note in Papanin's voice. Here, out in the open, he was in his element. This was the Siberian who, ten years ago, had been told to speed up the removal of the Russian missiles from Cuba. His method had been characteristically direct: he had threatened to explode the missiles over the island if the Cubans didn't co-operate. Ten years older, he had not lost his quick, savage touch.

'A police affair?' Minsky said thoughtfully as they came up to the huts. 'That makes a difference?'

'Yes! It means that if we want to we are justified in shooting at Gorov and anyone with him—after all, Michael Gorov is a dangerous maniac.' Papanin smashed an icicle from the roof with his gloved hand. 'You see, Minsky, we are starting a manhunt.'

Within minutes of meeting Beaumont at Curtis Field, Dawes was in the air again, this time as a passenger aboard a two-man Cessna aircraft which took off along the runway ending at the cliff brink. The pilot, Arnold Schumacher, who hated flying top brass, wheeled the plane away from Greenland and headed out to sea. The icecap below merged with the polar pack glued to the mainland as the plane flew like a dart due east.

'You're not expected to find Target-5,' Dawes growled, 'so just pretend you're looking for it. I'm checking conditions.'

'Terrible.' The pilot paused. 'Sir,' he added. 'I can't see anyone getting to the base over the ice. When the fog clears we'll have to fly in. The usual way.' He transferred his chewing gum to the other cheek, the cheek away from Dawes.

'That's the trouble with you people up here. All you think of is engines and machines. You can't imagine anyone fighting their way in over the pack. We're getting soft, Schumacher— if Pan Am can't take us we don't go.'

'I'm not Pan Am. . . .'

'And take that gum out of your mouth when you're talking to me.'

Screw you, chum. But the pilot preferred this type: at least they didn't try to fraternize, kidding you up they were just one of the boys—with their pay ten times your own. The plane flew on through the cold, moonlit night at two thousand feet, a wisp of metal over the Arctic. The altitude flattened out the pressure ridges, made the pack look like a sheet of opaque glass, crazed and splintered glass. Conditions were really terrible. Thirty minutes later Dawes was half out of his seat, peering down into the grey murk below, a solid sea of rolling fog which masked the solid ice under it. A squat globular bug with a whizz of rotor-driven air above it was cruising towards them, barely skimming the fog bank. 'See that?' Dawes rapped out.

79

'Chopper. Russian.' The pilot was thinking about the pad of gum stuck under his seat.

'Submarine killer?'

'Yes,' said Schumacher.

'Must be off that Soviet carrier south of the ice. I want a closer look. Dive!'

Schumacher was irked about his lost chewing gum. Screw all generals: they ought to be abolished. Like state taxes. So he dived, dropped like a bomb. But Dawes, braced in his seat, was ready. The Russian helicopter was no more than half a mile away, floating towards them on the fog sea as the Cessna went down and down and the fog swept up. Schumacher pulled out of the dive with a jerk which could have knocked out Dawes, but again he was ready for the impact. They were now about three hundred feet above the helicopter. Then it vanished, fell into the fog.

'Hell!' Dawes was annoyed. 'I wonder why she's such a shy girl? Seen any of them about here before, Schumacher?'

'Never this far west—not that model. We've passed over Target-5,' the pilot added, 'somewhere down there in the oatmeal.' The edge of the fog bank was in sight and the polar pack loomed as a mellow crystal sheen beyond. 'Coming close to the Russian base, North Pole 17, sir.'

Schumacher's access of politeness intrigued Dawes. 'I want to see what they're up to. Does it worry you?'

'They buzz us—send a machine up and fly close. I nearly collided with one somewhere about here. They don't like us playing good neighbours with them. So we still keep on, sir? There they are.'

Twinkles of green phosphorescence glowing on the ice showed the landing strip on the ice island, showed that the airstrip was in imminent use. The buildings couldn't be seen yet, but something else could be seen, was just coming into view. Dawes leaned forward, his eyes narrowed. 'Perfect timing! You almost deserve a medal. . . .' A small—at that range—Satanic-looking shadow was drifting down out of the sky, trailing pencil-thin vapour as it pointed its nose down. A Bison bomber was landing at North Pole 17.

80

'Go back, sir?'

'Not yet!'

A Bison bomber. That was interesting. The Russians didn't use the Bison as an Arctic taxi, but they might in an emergency use it to get here fast from Murmansk, to bring in a man—or a lot of men. The Bison swept down to ground level, swept along between the lights, and Dawes could see the buildings now, a tiny cluster of dark smudges. The moving smudge between the lights came to a stop, the green pinpoints faded, vanished.

'They've hooked us on their radar,' Schumacher warned. 'Now they'll send up a plane.'

'Not with their lights doused. Look below us.'

From seven hundred feet they could see them clearly, tiny turtles crawling over the ice. Sno-Cats, six of them, and they were west of the Soviet ice island—heading direct towards Target-5. They scarcely seemed to move, but behind them their caterpillar tracks left tell-tale furrows in the snow, furrows leading from North Pole 17. That—and the Bison bomber—decided Dawes.

'Home,' he said, and Schumacher reacted instantly, turning at speed as he gained altitude. 'Get through on your radio to Curtis Field. . . .'

'There's bad static. . . .'

'Get through. Go on until you do get through. Send one word time and time again. Nitrogen. Got it? Nitrogen. . . .' It was the code-signal Beaumont was waiting for, the signal for him to leave for Target-5.

Sunday, 20 February: 4 p.m., to
Monday, 21 February: Midnight

THE TWO SIKORSKY HELICOPTERS came down vertically as though suspended from a cable, dropping towards the ice over a hundred miles from the Greenland coast. It was a critical moment—any landing on unknown ice is critical. For one thing you can never be sure from the air that you are coming down on firm ice; it may look quite solid and then the skids land, the ice cracks and you are going down into the ocean. For another thing, if the machine doesn't settle on a flat surface it can keel over, topple, and the whirling rotors hit the ice first. One moment the men inside are preparing to disembark, the next moment steel blades are mincing them to pieces—unless the fuel tanks detonate, in which case they are incinerated.

So it was with a certain tension that Beaumont waited for the bump which would tell them they had touched down.

Seated in the observer's position beside the pilot, he watched with professional interest the hand holding the collective pitch stick controlling their descent. The hand seemed steady enough. He glanced at the pilot's face—what he could see of it under helmet, goggles and headset. The face seemed steady, too, but the mouth was tight. Pilot Rainer was, in fact, clenching his teeth while he waited for the bump.

Behind Beaumont, Sam Grayson was perched on a flap seat and there were also nine dogs aboard, nine whimpering dogs who didn't like the sudden descent. A sled completed the congestion. Horst Langer, with a second sled and more dogs, was coming down in the other machine Beaumont could see beyond the perspex dome. Beaumont checked his watch. They would hit the pack in thirty seconds Rainer had said. Twenty seconds to go.

'Would you normally risk a landing here?' Beaumont had asked a few minutes earlier.

'No!' Rainer had been uncomfortably direct in his reply. 'But I have orders to get you down if humanly possible. So we've got to risk it, haven't we?'

Beaumont adjusted his ear-pads. Everything was shuddering —the floor under his feet, the dome, the controls Rainer was handling. Beaumont rested a hand on the dog by his side and felt the vibrations through the poor beast's fur. Transport planes the dogs minded not at all: helicopters they hated. The descent went on. Rainer adjusted the twist-grip throttle on his stick. Ten seconds to go. Maybe only ten seconds left to live.

They were now low enough to see the ice beyond the dome. It was a churned-up mess, like a blurred sea which had frozen suddenly—blurred because the dome was steamed up inside the cabin. And the grim wilderness of tumbled ice was shuddering unpleasantly, dithering giddily because of the cabin's shuddering. When they opened the door the temperature would drop eighty or ninety degrees within seconds, taking their breath away. If the machine landed steady, if it didn't topple. There were skids—skis—under this Sikorsky and that should help stability. Unless one ski skidded while the other sank. Rainer glanced at Beaumont, who winked at him. The wink was not returned and Beaumont saw the blank eyes behind the goggles. Rainer was scared stiff. Then the skids touched the ice.

The machine wobbled. Beaumont felt it going down on his side. Soft ice to port, hard to starboard. Rainer's hand was welded to the stick. Bugger this trip—he should have gone sick. The dogs sensed disaster, began whimpering pathetically. The blades were still whirling, whipping the air as the sinking sensation went on. The tension inside the cabin was a physical presence as the three men sweated out their terror. Then the machine settled, the sinking stopped. Rainer switched off, lifted his goggles and his face was seamed with sweat.

'Nice landing,' Beaumont said, as he pulled off his headset and reached for the door.

'Wait . . . !'

'I am waiting—for the rotors to stop.'

It wasn't necessary—if you kept your head down when you went out—but Rainer didn't know that Beaumont had flown helicopters all over the Arctic. Beaumont opened the door and the Arctic came in like a knife. He dropped to the ice and walked away from the machine stiffly as he looked round for Langer's Sikorsky, then frowned as he saw it was coming down on to pressure ridge terrain. It was going to crash.

Behind him Grayson was sending the dogs out and they came out joyously, barking and scampering round the machine with sheer delight at being free again. A quarter of a mile away to the east the fog bank hovered in the moonlight, a grey curtain like a dirty cloud anchored to the ice. Then Langer's machine dropped out of sight behind a pressure ridge, a twisted wall of ice ten feet high. The machine hit the ice and the blur of the rotor disc steadied above the crest. 'He's O.K.' Grayson's voice was husky behind the Englishman. 'For a moment I wondered. . . .'

'He isn't—he's toppling!'

Beaumont started running across the ice, his boots crunching into soft crust which crumbled under him. The whole area had only recently frozen over, was dangerously unstable. Beaumont ran as fast as he could without slipping and his heart was in his mouth—the rotor disc above the crest was no longer horizontal, it was canting sideways. He ran through a gap in the pressure wall and saw that Langer's quick reflexes had already reacted to the emergency—the door was open, dogs were spilling out on to the soft ice and running towards the gap, their legs smeared with the dark ooze they had plunged into.

The Sikorsky was an extraordinary sight—with its port skid sinking, already below the surface, its strut still going down, the machine was heeling over while its rotors still whirled at speed. The situation couldn't have been more dangerous and as he ran close Beaumont wondered what the hell the pilot was doing, why the hell he hadn't switched off. Langer appeared, heaving one end of the sled close to the aperture, getting ready to push it out. 'Leave it!' Beaumont shouted and his warning was lost in the hideous roar. He jumped up, hauled himself inside the cabin where the pilot, Jacowski, was sitting behind the controls, reached across and cut the motor.

'I'm taking off,' the pilot yelled.

'Start that motor again and I'll brain you,' Beaumont rasped. 'Our lives depend on that sled—give a hand to get it out. The machine's expendable—we're not.' He went back to help Langer. 'Take it easy, Horst—the ground's like a sponge out there. . . .' He saw Grayson arrive below the aperture. 'Sam, watch it as it comes down—it could sink. . . .'

'Hurry it up—I'm sinking,' the American called out.

They wrestled with the heavily-laden sled, balanced it on the brink, and then Beaumont dropped out to help Grayson take its weight. The Sikorsky seemed temporarily stable but was tilted at an acute angle as they lowered the sled carefully and rested it on the ice. It started sinking at once and then Grayson and Langer grabbed hold of the harness and began hauling it away towards firmer ground near the gap. Beaumont looked at Jacowski who was still sitting behind his controls.

'If you stay there that's going to make a nice coffin for you —it's gone in deeper.'

'I'm going to try and take her out.'

'Better have a look first—unless you want someone to collect your insurance.'

Jacowski climbed gingerly to the ground, felt his boots sinking, moved quickly to join Beaumont where the ice was firmer. The helicopter had almost righted itself, was almost horizontal again—because the starboard skid had now sunk to the depth of the port skid. It was knee-deep in black ooze. 'The next problem is how to get rid of it,' Beaumont said roughly. 'It has to go either up or down—it can't stay here as a landmark to show some Russian chopper where we went into the fog. If we start the motor I think the vibration will take it down.'

'That's government property,' the pilot said nastily. 'It belongs to the Arctic Research Laboratory at Point Barrow. We can bring a team to dig it out. . . .'

'It goes up or down,' Beaumont informed him, 'so you'd better get clear before I start her up.'

'Keith, that's damned dangerous,' Grayson protested as he came back to see what was happening. 'If it goes down too quickly while you're inside it. . . .'

Beaumont was already climbing up carefully into the cabin, testing it with his weight to see the effect. Nothing happened so he sat down in the pilot's seat and looked out to make sure the others were clear. Jacowski had gone all the way back to the gap but Grayson was waiting just beyond the span of the rotor blades. Starting up the motor in these circumstances wasn't a course of action Beaumont would have recommended to anyone, but the machine had to disappear—either into the sky or under the Arctic.

It was just possible that when he started the motor he'd be able to drag her free, to take her up and land the machine close to the other Sikorsky; it all depended on the strength of the drag of the ooze gripping the skids. The more likely outcome was that the vibration would shiver the skids, open up the ooze and force her down. When that happened he'd have to take rather quick evasive action to avoid being carried down with her. Beaumont started the motor.

For a moment he thought he'd managed it, that he was going to lift her out. The machine wobbled and he could feel the power trying to haul her out, then she started going down and going over to port all at once and quickly. He dived for the doorway, went out, slipped on the ice and sprawled under the toppling, dropping machine. He was caught in a kind of closing press—between the ice under him and the descending whirling blades coming down on top of him. He scrambled to his knees, felt the ooze sucking at his boots, holding him in. The beat of the descending rotors deafened him, the ooze clamped round his boots, his hands clawed at firmer ground to drag himself loose.

Other hands grabbed his own as Grayson tugged ferociously and between them they got him out. He curled his toes upwards to stop his boots sliding off and then, crouched low, they ran in a shambling trot. The racing blades were only feet above them and Beaumont felt their wind-force beating down on his neck as they ran together, still stooped low when they were yards beyond the reach of the flailing metal. At the gap they turned to look back as the motor coughed, choked and died. The fuselage was sitting on the ooze and the motor had sucked a churning mass of the filth into its innards while the rotors whirled on their own momentum. 'Get ready to get behind the ridge,' Beaumont warned. He was foreseeing the moment when the blades broke free and started flying across the ice, but the warning was unnecessary. As the fuselage sank more slowly the rotors slowed and were hardly moving when they reached the ground. They flicked great gouts of blackness across the ice and then settled. The ooze opened up, the Sikorsky went down with a dreadful sucking sound, the ooze closed over it.

'That was government property,' Jacowski repeated peevishly.

'Tell them to take another gold bar out of Fort Knox,' Beaumont suggested.

There was a reaction after the crisis, a tendency to move slowly, but Beaumont dispelled it as he urged everyone to move faster, to get the other sled out of the surviving Sikorsky, to harness up the dog teams, to get moving before a Russian plane arrived. 'I want us inside that fog bank in fifteen minutes —there we're invisible. . . .' And there was another confrontation with the pilots before they left.

'We'll have to report what happened to that helicopter,' Rainer called down from his machine.

'In triplicate,' Grayson shouted back at him. 'Don't forget they like it in triplicate!'

Jacowski slammed the door in his face as Rainer started his machine. Five minutes later the two sled-teams were assembled, the dogs were hitched up, ready to go. The Sikorsky had vanished, fading into the night on its way home. The feeling of isolation descended on the three men the moment the machine had gone, and the terrible silence of the Arctic wilderness was overwhelming.

They were alone on the ice, a hundred miles from Greenland, a pinhead on the frozen sea—three men, eighteen dogs

87

and two sleds. The ice under their feet was possibly twelve inches deep, except where it had no depth at all, where the weight of a single dog could fracture it, taking the living weight down into the freezing black water they were floating on. And even though the ice seemed still it was moving all the time; caught up in the powerful Greenland Current it was drifting south towards Iceberg Alley at the rate of over ten miles a day, and under the smear of ice which coated the ocean the water plunged down ten thousand feet. Beaumont took over the leading team from Grayson. 'Let's get moving,' he said. 'I shan't be happy until we're inside the fog.'

'It looks extremely inviting,' Langer said with a dry smile. The twenty-eight-year-old German had spent two years in London, and Beaumont often remarked that his English was more idiomatic than his own. 'In fact, it looks very much like one of your famous pea-soupers.'

'It won't be so bad when we get inside it,' Beaumont replied, and they started off. It was always the initial start which called for an effort—to get the dog teams moving, to get your own reluctant legs moving in the bitter Arctic night. And Horst was right he thought as he held the whip in one hand and gripped the sled's handlebar with the other: the fog looked damned uninviting.

The fog bank hung over the ice like a threat, a threat of grey vapour which rose high above the ice and clung to the ground. It was bitterly cold but there was no wind, so the fog was almost motionless, like a cloud hovering above an icy plateau, a cloud which could hide any number of dangers. The danger Beaumont feared most was movement—that while they were inside the fog the ice might stir afresh, opening up leads of water, bringing them together again, heaving up pressure ridges which could crush a man, even bury a whole dog team in seconds. He cracked his whip, shouted at the team, and the dogs moved faster, hauling the sled, their legs stretched, their bodies straining at the harness.

And now the deathly silence of the ice was broken by man-made sounds—by the creak of harness, the hiss of runners coursing over the ice, the crackle of snow-crust giving way, by the crack of whips and the thump of boots treading harder ice. They were under way, heading for the fog bank, heading towards Target-5 lost somewhere inside the dense pall. Beaumont drove the lead team with Langer controlling the second team behind, while a few paces ahead Grayson moved across the ice staring down at his compass. 'It's nervous already,' he called out. Which was another problem—in this part of the world compasses were notoriously unreliable.

Langer easily kept up with Beaumont's hard-driving pace —his lead dog, Bismarck, was a big, tough-minded animal who kept the other dogs moving, the Beaumont of the dog teams. Horst Langer, five feet ten inches tall, dark-haired and clean-shaven, was a Rhinelander, a cheerful, easy-going man with a sense of humour which concealed great resilience. An expert with explosives—essential knowledge for depth-sounding work—he was also a brilliant dog-handler. As Beaumont said, 'They'll fly over thin ice with Horst when other dogs would cringe.' Born in Düsseldorf, still a bachelor—'With so many attractive women about how can you choose just one?' —he had spent four years in the Arctic working on American bases. And like the other two men he had top security clearance from Washington.

'Something wrong, Keith?' he called out.

Beaumont had halted his team, was standing with his head turned to one side. 'Thought I heard something. Keep very quiet for a minute.'

They waited. The dogs twisted in their harness to see what was happening. There seemed to be nothing but the ton-weight of the Arctic silence pressing down on them. Beaumont, in his fur parka and fur hood, was huge and still in the moonlight as he swivelled his head like a radar wing towards the east. The fog bank was close now, only a few hundred yards away, a dirty cloud like motionless smoke. Then Beaumont heard it again, the faint beat-beat of a large helicopter growing louder, coming closer by the second.

'Run for it! Inside the fog before they see us. . . .'

The urgency in his shout communicated itself to the dogs as the whips cracked, the sled teams surged forward and the helicopter's motor sped towards them. They were actually racing towards it, expecting at any moment to see it come over the top of the fog bank. Bismarck exerted all his strength, his paws flying over the ice at Beaumont's heels as the sleds lurched over uneven ground and the men behind them fought to keep them upright. A spill now would be disaster, would anchor them in the open until it was too late. Grayson ran alongside Beaumont, ready to grab at the handlebar. The helicopter beat was very close. Rat-tat-tat . . . Beaumont cracked his whip, urged the dogs to move faster while he struggled with the bucking sled.

'Thin ice!'

Beaumont was turning the sled as Grayson shouted, turning it away from a depression where something dark showed below treacherously smooth ice. The helicopter sound had become a drumbeat which meant it was coming in very low, only a few hundred feet up. The sled caught an ice rib, was heeling over to port when Grayson steadied it and behind them Langer swerved widely to avoid the obstacle. To keep them moving, Beaumont cracked his whip a third time over their heads and they went forward in a spurt. He thought he saw something above him as they plunged into the fog, then his team was swallowed up, followed by Langer's sled, and it was like diving into moonless night as the fog closed round them. It enveloped them, drifted clammily over their faces, blurred the shapes of the dogs only feet away from their drivers. Beaumont pulled at the handlebar, called out for the dogs to halt, then turned his head upwards and stared into the murk. The engine beat was muffled and sounded to be directly overhead.

'I think it's Russian,' Grayson said breathlessly.

'Could be a routine patrol,' Langer suggested. 'North Pole 17 isn't far away—for a chopper. They're always checking on what we're doing.' The engine beat was still above them and it gave them the eerie feeling it could see the men below it, which was impossible.

'It's circling,' Beaumont snapped.

'So it could still be routine,' Langer insisted. 'Or maybe it's looking for Gorov.'

'Or maybe it's looking for us,' Beaumont replied, 'if Tillotson got through to Leningrad.'

'Fifteen killers. . . .'

Papanin stood outside the headquarters hut as the last helicopter landed on the moonlit airstrip, its twin rotors spinning giddily as the jet power died. They were lined up in a row—squat, bulbous silhouettes in the moonlight, like big-bellied crows; submarine killers just flown in off the Soviet carrier *Gorki*. The sonar devices under the domes looked like pus sacs, and each of them sagged on a quadruple support of two-wheel carriages. A jet pod like a bomb was slung to port and starboard of each machine.

'I want them airborne in thirty minutes,' Papanin told Kramer. 'And then they stay up—until they've found Gorov. They can come down to refuel,' he added.

'There's only one pilot per machine,' the Balt pointed out.

'Very economical,' was the Siberian's only comment.

Thirty minutes later the fleet of submarine killers started taking off from the airstrip and Papanin watched them go. It was one of these fifteen machines which Beaumont heard coming when he rushed the sled teams inside the fog bank. And it was one of these machines which photographed them just before they disappeared, photographed them with a telephoto lens of great range and power.

The first few hours inside the fog bank were uneventful hell for the three men and their dog teams—if uneventful is a true description of a time when they constantly expected to lose their lives. For one thing they couldn't see where they were going; under any other circumstance Beaumont would have called a halt, would have pitched camp and waited for the fog to move. Instead they drove themselves on, stumbling through the icy dampness, often only able to see the lead dog beyond their sled, and when it disappeared Grayson went in front to test the ground, walking slowly with the dogs coming up close behind.

If their calculations were correct, if the star-fix Grayson had taken with his sextant soon after he left the Sikorsky was any-thing like accurate, the ice island Target-5 was only a few miles due east when they landed. But navigation in an Arctic winter is not always an exact science and privately Beaumont had his doubts.

The tension rose as they heard another helicopter coming at the moment the fog was thinning. Suddenly it was lighter, the fog above them drifted away, a faint glow which was the moon began to percolate the mistiness. The machine came closer. 'Halt!' Beaumont tugged at the sled. 'Try and keep the dogs still. Sam, take over here a minute.' Beaumont took his night glasses out of the case strapped to the handlebar and walked a few yards away from the sled teams. Above him a hole was opening up in the fog; he couldn't see the moon but its light was all around him as he raised the glasses. The helicopter drummed in, swept into view, a blurred, huge shape flying very low indeed.

It went over quickly, so quickly he couldn't catch it in his glasses but he was sure it was Russian. Then he heard another one coming. This time he was ready for it as it flew in on the same course as its predecessor. In the lenses he caught a glimpse of a jet pod, the blur of a pilot's helmet, then it swept past out of sight. 'Submarine killer,' he told Grayson when he went back to the sled teams. 'And there's another one up there in the distance. 'I think they're covering the fringe of the fog bank to see what goes into it.'

'Or what comes out of it.'

'It's promising in a way,' Beaumont pointed out as he took over the sled. I think Dawes was right—Gorov is making his run. You don't get that number of Soviet machines down here normally.'

'Promising for us, too—if they're looking for us.'

They moved on again, often with the sound of a helicopter somewhere overhead, but the fog closed in again so they were hidden. Their progress would have been difficult in clear weather—in the fog it was dangerous. The ice was broken up, pitted with gulleys, so the sleds constantly lurched from side to side, always on the verge of overturning, and soon

Beaumont's arm ached with the strain of holding on to the jerking handlebar. Horst Langer suffered equally and Sam Grayson suffered also, but in a different way. The strain of moving just ahead of the dogs when the fog became really dense was appalling. Every step he took he expected to be his last, to land in icy water where a lead had opened up, exposing the black Arctic ocean.

It would have been uncomfortable in summer—when the temperature hovers at freezing point or a degree or two above. In February with a temperature of forty below it was diabolical. Despite their clothing. They wore long woollen underwear, two pairs of socks apiece inside fur-lined boots, two woollen pullovers, a fur-lined jacket, and over all this a wolfskin parka made by an Alaskan fur trader Beaumont knew in Fairbanks. But they were still frozen, their hands and feet numbed beyond feeling, the small portion of their faces exposed under their fur hoods aching and damp—always damp—with the clinging fog which pressed against them as they struggled forward.

Because they had left Curtis Field so quickly they stopped after five hours for food and drink, thankful that the dogs ate only every forty-eight hours. With the fog creeping around them they sat on the sleds to eat their pemmican, a nourishing form of dried meat which tastes rather like old leather. The nerve-racking beat of a nearby helicopter stayed with them all through the meal and it put their tempers on edge.

'Why doesn't the damn thing break down, run out of fuel, get lost?' Langer demanded.

'Because it tanked up at North Pole 17,' Beaumont snapped.

'That thought had occurred to me.'

'Then why ask the question?'

The horror occurred while they were eating and they didn't know it had happened because of the row the Soviet machine was making. At the end of the meal Beaumont took the compass off Grayson and tried to get the needle to steady. The helicopter stopped circling suddenly and flew away towards the east. He was standing up, holding the compass, when he looked up and stared into the distance. It was very faint even in the sudden quiet after the helicopter's departure, and

Beaumont was the only one who heard it, a sound which shouldn't have been there. The lapping of water, a gentle swishing sound.

'I'll be back in a minute,' he said casually. 'Stay exactly where you are and don't move around.'

He was back again in five minutes and the other two men obviously had no inkling that anything was wrong. Langer had interpreted his instruction as a warning not to go wandering around in the fog; he was actually standing behind his sled ready to move off. Beaumont handed the compass back to Grayson. 'You won't need that for a while,' he said quietly. 'There's nowhere to go. We're now drifting on a small floe away from the icefield. . . .'

'That's impossible,' Langer burst out. 'We'd have heard the ice cracking, making a hell of a row.'

'You've forgotten the din that helicopter was kicking up— and this time when it cracked it didn't make too much row, not enough for us to hear it above the hammering of that Russian's motor.' Beaumont gestured into the fog. 'Walk in any direction and you'll fall off before you've gone thirty yards. We're marooned on a slab of ice drifting down a huge lead. We'd better get used to the idea—we're no longer on the polar pack—we're at sea.'

The worst had happened. The icefield had opened up one of its vast leads, an expanding lane of sea which could be many miles wide. Sometimes it is the wind, sometimes the current always flowing under the ice which cracks the ice open, snapping it apart—in this case they may have been close to the brink of the lead when they had stopped to eat and a fragment, the floe they were marooned on, had broken free. Sooner or later the lead comes together again—unless the lane was close to open sea, in which case they would drift on the ocean until they froze to death.

It was the coming together of the ice which worried Beaumont, which made him issue the warning to stay constantly alert. It is not a gentle process, this coming together. The ice closes like a vice, like the impact of two steel-plated

94

vessels steaming towards each other on collision course. When two ice edges meet, the sound is like the thunder of a thousand artillery salvoes, a terrifying crash which can be heard many miles away, and like the steel plates of a ship the ice buckles in collision. It buckles and it heaves up huge pressure ridges to displace the smashed ice, moving ridges which can climb as high as thirty feet above the ice while over their crests shiver massive chunks of ice which topple down, flattening everything in their path. And when the ice edges met, the floating raft would be caught between them, would be cracked open like a nut. This was why they had to stay alert.

In an attempt to see the danger in time Beaumont posted both Grayson and Langer at opposite ends of the little island. A rope was attached to one of the sleds and extended to both lookout points—so that the moment they saw the icefield coming back at them they could find their way through the fog quickly. While the two men took up position, posted like lookouts aboard a ship, Beaumont fed the dogs. He cut up walrus meat at a distance from the animals and then threw the meat to them; they devoured it with their usual lack of table manners. They weren't due for a meal but he wanted to keep them quiet.

The floe continued its eerie drift into nothingness. There was no sensation of movement—the floe was large, it was a windless night—but the current was carrying it steadily further south, away from Target-5. Perched at the edge of the ice, squatting on his haunches, Langer strained to see through the fog. It was a bloody hopeless task he was thinking: he could barely see six feet before the grey pall blocked his view. But it wasn't quite as hopeless as it seemed. The advance of the ice edge, which would come through the fog like a moving platform, a platform of hard, solid ice, might well be preceded by a disturbance, a small wave being pushed in front of it. The first warning should be when water lapped over the ice beyond his boots.

In front of the fog the black water was like oil, oil covered here and there with a dirty sheen as thin patches of ice formed on its surface. The temperature was almost fifty below and the water was trying to freeze all the time, to form a fresh layer of ice. Only the movement of the current prevented it succeeding. He was out of sight of the sleds and the dogs; when he glanced over his shoulder all he could see was dirty vapour. A terrible sense of isolation descended on him—he couldn't get rid of the feeling that he was on his own, that he was floating on a fragment which had split off from the main floe, a fragment hardly larger than a table-top.

Fear tingled his nerve ends. He listened with all his ears. If the ice he was crouched on split off from the floe he should hear a warning crack. It might be very slight—they had no way of knowing the thickness of the raft they were floating on —but there should be a sharp crack when the ice splintered. With his hood pulled well down, crouching at the brink of the ice, Langer looked like a furry animal in the fog, and despite the layers of clothing, the two mittens under his heavy gloves, his body felt like the block of ice he floated on. His hands were numb, his feet ached with the pain, his face was cruelly frozen—but fear kept him alert. Then he heard a cracking sound.

Trembling, he forced himself upright, his leg muscles taut with tension. He was alone. His piece of ice had broken off from the floe. If he took two steps in any direction he would go down into the freezing water which would kill him inside three minutes. In a panic he swung round. The fog pall came up to his face. He was absolutely alone, he had lost his two companions, he would never see anyone again. Blind, horrible panic welled up. He shivered, clenched his teeth. Get a grip on yourself for Christ's sake! He stood quite still, shivering, forcing the panic down. Then he felt the rope he had forgotten, the rope end he was still holding in his right glove. He was still attached to the floe: he had imagined the horror. Wearily he sank down on his haunches and his ice-coated boots creaked again, made the same cracking sound he had heard before. He felt weak with relief and very foolish. The strain was already telling and they had been adrift for less than an hour. Twenty-four hours later the lead closed.

*　　　　　*　　　　　*

Beaumont's watch registered 10.30 p.m. The floe was wobbling, turning slowly, caught up in a cross-current. And to the east the fog was thinning. 'It's clearing over there,' Langer said, standing up and pointing. 'Dear God, it's clearing. We may see something. . . .'

'I can see something now,' Beaumont said grimly. 'It looks like land.'

He used the word land automatically, although the blurred line he was staring at could only be more ice—if he was seeing anything at all. When you stared into the fog for a long time your eyes played you tricks, showed you trees and mountains and other impossible things where you knew there was only fog. He closed his eyes, opened them again. The fog was thinning out rapidly as moonlight percolated through and globules of moisture caught its reflection. Yes, he could still see the blurred line, but was the damned thing stationary? Were they—he hoped to God they were—being carried by a change in the current gently towards static ice?

'I think it's coming this way,' Horst said tersely.

It was less than a quarter of a mile away across the water, a white platform like the edge of a continent. In front of it was a shadowed ripple as the sea was thrust back by the immense icefield moving westward, westward towards the fragment of ice floating in its path. 'Horst, stay here and keep an eye on it. I'll warn Sam.'

Beaumont moved across the floe, looping up the rope which was no longer needed—the fog had dispersed enough for him to see Grayson who was staring in the opposite direction. And it was continuing to thin out, so he could see across several hundred yards of calm water beyond the western brink of the ice raft. Beyond that the fog was as thick as ever. 'The icefield's coming up behind you, Sam, coming up fast from the east.'

'That means trouble.'

'It means trouble. The dogs are ready and it looks as though we'll have to jump for it. You'd better stay here—just in case something else happens. When I call you, come like a bat out of hell.'

Just in case. . . . There was no need to elaborate. Beaumont's great fear now was that the whole lead was closing up—with jaws of ice closing on them from both east and west. It was the fresh movement of the floe he didn't like—it was revolving slowly, which indicated more than one current was on the move. He spent a moment with the dogs and then went back to where Langer was staring fixedly to the east.

'Look at the wave,' the German said.

The ripple of black water had become a wave, only a small wave but it was a warning of the tremendous force pushing up behind it as the icefield cruised towards them with the power of millions of tons of polar pack behind it. The fog had thinned even more, although further back on the icefield it was as dense as ever, and the platform was like a whole coast advancing, a low coast of tumbled ice and frozen pressure ridges.

'Keith . . . !'

Beaumont swung round at Grayson's shout, and for seconds his mind froze with his body. A wave was almost on top of the floe, a wave from the other direction. Behind it the second jaw of the ice was sliding towards them, shooting the wave ahead of its slide. He shouted to Grayson and the American was running towards him as Beaumont swung round again to check the position to the east. It was going to be disaster—he saw this instantly. The western jaw was going to catch them just before the eastern jaw reached them—and they had to go east. 'Get to the dogs, Horst!' He heard a noise behind him and looked back. The wave was breaking against the floe, sending black water skidding over the floe The water caught up with Grayson and washed over his boots. The dogs, water swirling round their legs, were going mad as they reached the animals and grabbed the harness.

'It may push us—the ice behind us . . .' Beaumont shouted.

While Horst wrestled with his team Beaumont fought for control of his own, one hand on the sled's handlebar, the other holding the whip. Water swirled round them; for seconds the floe disappeared and they seemed to be standing on the sea. The dogs were terrified, thought they were on the verge of drowning. They might all be drowning within seconds—it depended on the strength and depth of the invisible ice they were standing on. If the massive blow of the ice sheet coming up behind them caught a weak point, fractured the floe, they would be in the sea with nothing under them, struggling in icy water until the two jaws met and pulverized them to thin layers of flesh.

The eastern jaw was still a hundred yards away, its wave hadn't reached them, when the impact came, a shattering blow which quivered the ice under them. The dogs stopped going berserk, stood quite still in sheer terror. The sea had flowed off the raft, leaving pools behind in depressions, but it was still intact. And now they could feel the raft moving, being carried forward towards the advancing sheet heading towards it for collision. Beaumont glanced back, saw the ice sheet behind, a foot higher than the floe, like a giant step. 'Get to the other edge,' he shouted.

They used the whips, drove the demoralized dogs forward the short distance until they were almost at the brink. Really, they hadn't a chance in hell. Beaumont wished now that he had turned round, taken the teams back on to the jaw behind them, but it was too late. The wave from the east splashed down on the floe, threw water round their legs, and the dogs tried to go berserk a second time. Beaumont tightened his grip, held the whip ready for one sharp crack. The water was still around their feet when the gap closed. The sleds were alongside each other when the whips cracked, the men shouted, the dogs leapt forward seconds before the point of impact. Under them the sea flooded the raft, surged knee-high, submerged it totally.

The dogs leapt forward, took the sleds with them over the gap before the ice met in thunderous collision. Something reared up under Beaumont's right leg but the momentum of the sled took him forward with the boom of the ice in his ears. The icefield was smooth near its brink and the sleds scudded forward, the friction breaking off the newly-formed ice on the runners where the sea had frozen. They were deafened by the boom, deafened so they hardly heard the monstrous smashing sound as both jaws of the ice sheets broke off and heaved up a pressure ridge, heaved it up twenty feet high, shot up a wall of jostling ice with great blocks wobbling on its crest. Then Grayson, dog-trotting beside Beaumont, slipped and went down. Behind him the pressure ridge came forward like a lava wall, toppling the blocks in front of it.

Beaumont saw him falling, held on to whip and sled with one hand while he grabbed. Grayson was on his knees when Beaumont grasped one arm, jerked it up savagely. The American's gloved hand locked on the handlebar and he was dragged forward on his knees some distance before he scrambled up. Behind them a massive block of ice weighing many tons thudded down where Grayson had fallen. Still shaken, still gripping the handlebar, he stumbled forward as the sled kept moving, a little way behind Langer's team. To their rear the pack, caught up in the gigantic collision, was a chaos of movement.

Fissures shivered the weak points. A dark gash knifed past Beaumont's sled and ahead of it. He swerved to avoid it and swerved again to escape a second opening. The noise was tremendous, like a bombardment as the erupting icefield roared and hammered. They kept moving, driving the dogs, running for their lives away from the chopping hell behind them, and when they had covered half a mile, when they were close to the edge of the fog, Beaumont called a halt. Panting for breath like the dogs, the clothes under their parkas clammy with sweat, they looked back. In the distance the icefield was still heaving and writhing. It could be hours before the turmoil ended, before the icefield sealed over once more, locking down the sea while an Arctic silence you could almost hear descended.

'Who the devil were they?'

The flickering image of three fur-clad figures seen from the air hovered in the smoke, then vanished and there was fog and more smoke. The projection screen inside the headquarters hut went blank. Papanin stirred in his seat beside Kramer as the projectionist removed the film reel and someone switched on the light. The smoke came from the little curved pipe he was puffing away at steadily, the smoke which filled the over-heated hut, which obscured the 'No Smoking' sign hanging from a wall. The atmosphere was torrid, glowing with warmth.

'It was interesting,' Kramer ventured.

'That film doesn't tell me a damned thing,' the Siberian replied. 'Just three men and two dog teams at the edge of the fog. Where is the Beaumont force? We're looking for a large body of men—for an expedition. Those thick-skulled pilots aren't looking in the right place.'

Swivelling round in his chair, his little pipe clenched in his teeth, Papanin stared at a map of the lower Arctic spread out on a table. The latest positions of all vessels in the area were marked—the six vessels of trawler fleet k.49, the carrier *Gorki*, the huge research ship *Revolution*, and the American icebreaker *Elroy* which was steaming steadily closer to the icefield.

Alongside the map was a blown-up aerial photograph of Target-5. The picture had been taken four weeks earlier, a routine act to keep up to date their file on all American Arctic bases.

'The ramp at Target-5,' Papanin said, 'that place where they take their Sno-Cats down on to the pack. The sabotage team should be there by now.'

Kramer checked his watch. 10.30 p.m. He didn't know it but the lead was closing on Beaumont at this moment twenty-five miles away to the west. 'Our men arrived there an hour ago,' the Balt replied. 'With their radar they'll have found the American base even in the fog.'

'And the airstrip—that must be sabotaged as well.'

'The same team deals with both—ramp and airstrip. They'll do it the way you suggested. . . .'

'No international incident, remember,' Papanin warned.

'If anything happens it will look like an accident—or a series of accidents. Within thirty minutes Target-5 will be sealed off from the outside world. . . .'

'Not if their wireless hut is still in action!'

'It won't be. The same sabotage team is dealing with that, too.'

But Papanin was hardly listening as he slumped with his arms folded across the back of the chair. 'Beaumont,' he muttered. 'Beaumont,' he repeated. 'That name rings a bell somewhere. Kramer, get me a message pad. I want to send an urgent signal to Petrov at Records in Leningrad.'

'I think you're dead wrong. . . .'

'We go due east,' Beaumont told Grayson for the third time, 'and sooner or later we'll hit Target-5.' He lit a cigarette and it tasted bad because of the fog which had got into everything —including their lungs. The argument had been raging for ten minutes—which was the right way to go?

'We drifted a long way south on that floe,' Grayson insisted. 'Since I'm the navigator I should have some say. . . .'

'You've had your say—and I don't agree with you. Everything is drifting south—and too quickly for my liking. The ice-field, Target-5, the Russian base, the floe we nearly got killed on—it's all drifting south at the same speed, so you discount the floe drift.'

'Up to a point you're right. . . .'

'I'm dead right. And this isn't the House of Commons—where they talk to save themselves doing anything—so we'll get moving.'

'Due east?'

'Where else?'

They started moving through the smothering fog. Over rough ice. So once again they had to keep a tight grip on the handlebar of each sled in an endless struggle to stop them keeling over. And soon after they had moved off they came up against a static pressure ridge they couldn't get round. They had to use ice-axes to chop a gateway in the wall, and it was back-breaking work, work which delayed them and used too much energy. The only bonus on the credit side was that they hadn't recently heard a single helicopter.

'It looks as though the Russians have given up,' Langer said hopefully as they passed through the gap in the ice wall. 'Or else they've run out of fuel.'

'Maybe,' Beaumont replied non-committally. He was wondering whether they ought to pitch camp for the night. It was 11.30 p.m. and everyone was moving lethargically—even the dogs. The tension of the past few hours and the bitter cold was wearing them down—especially the cold. He glanced at the man walking beside him. For a while they had travelled with their snow-goggles over their eyes, but soon the fog had smeared them and they couldn't see where they were going, so now each man wore his goggles pushed back over his hood. The goggles above Grayson's hood were lenses of solid ice. His breath had frozen on the glass.

'We'll stop soon when we find a place to bed down,' Beaumont said.

'Thank God for that!' The American decided he had been a bit too eager to accept the suggestion. 'I could try one more radio-fix,' he suggested.

Among the equipment they were carrying on the sleds was a Redifon GR 345 transceiver and direction-finder, a portable high-frequency set with a peak power of only fifteen watts. But with this set they could communicate with Thule, let alone Curtis Field. They had stopped and listened in on the set three times since the Sikorskys had dropped them on the ice, hoping to hear a transmission from Target-5. They heard nothing—the island seemed to have gone off the air.

Had they heard only one transmission they could have used the direction-finder to locate Target-5's radio hut—to take a rough bearing they could have moved along. The absence of any transmission worried Beaumont, but he kept the worry to himself. 'Probably a lot of static—they know they can't get through so they don't try,' he said airily to Langer when he had queried the air-wave silence.

Ahead of them the fog began to thin out at ground level, but not higher up. They came to a more even area of ice, the best surface for pitching camp on they had come across so far, and Beaumont decided they had better stop. The dogs were slipping on the ice frequently now, a sure sign that they were feeling the strain, and a moment earlier Langer had called out a warning. 'Bismarck's lagging. The whole lot will pack up soon if we try to keep going.'

'I don't think we'll find a motel at this hour,' Beaumont called out, 'so we'll kip down here. . . .'

He broke off, still holding the handlebar, staring straight in front of him. In the thinning fog something flared redly, vanished, flared up more fiercely. He couldn't believe it. He blinked, sure that he was seeing things, stared again. The fog drifted, rolled a curtain across the sight, a transparent curtain. The red flare burst out again, penetrated the curtain, climbed higher and billowed and wavered. There was a faint stench in his nostrils, a stench of smoke, and now the dogs caught the scent and became restless, sensing fire.

'What the hell is it?' Grayson croaked.

Beaumont didn't reply. Taking the compass from the American, he bent over, staring at the luminous dial carefully as he took a bearing. When he looked up the flare had become a dull, dangerous-looking glow, the kind of glow he had once seen from four miles away across the ice when an American research base off Alaska was burning.

'What is it?' Grayson repeated. 'It looks God-awful.'

'Forget about your kip,' Beaumont said grimly. 'We're moving again—as fast as we can drive the dogs. That's Target-5 going up in flames.'

'SOME MANIAC has done this crazy thing deliberately—it's sabotage. . . .'

Matthew Conway, the fifty-year-old station leader, was blazing, blazing almost as furiously as his radio hut had blazed when it became a flaming beacon in the night.

Beside him in the drifting fog, Beaumont studied the wreckage as Dr Conway played a powerful lamp over what had recently been a large hut.

Charred stumps showed where the walls had stood, a twisted hunk of metal lay half-buried under a pile of ash, and an acrid smell of burning was still present in the windless night. The hut had burned down to its foundations and smoke wisps eddied and mingled with the fog.

'Why sabotage?' Beaumont asked as he hitched up the rifle looped over his shoulder.

'When I got here the place was well alight but it wasn't like this,' Conway said savagely. 'Rickard, the wireless operator you met when you arrived, found it on fire. When I got here it was becoming an inferno—but the door hadn't gone. I noticed fresh wood splinters round the lock—it looked as if it had been forced open.'

'Could have been the fire,' Beaumont said casually. He was trying to calm everyone down; since they had arrived ten minutes ago he had detected an air of tension in the three men waiting to be evacuated from the doomed base, a tension which had been there before the hut went up in flames.

'It didn't look like it,' Conway protested. 'Then there was the Coleman space heater—that twisted bit of metal. I could see through the open door and it was lying on its side. It was upright when Rickard left the hut earlier.'

'Maybe the fire caused it to keel over. . . .'

'For God's sake, do you think I'm going out of my mind? I may have been on this island for three years but I've still kept my sanity! Those space heaters are heavy—you'd have to kick one hard to send it on its side.'

'All right, Matt, take it easy.' Beaumont walked round the smouldering ruin. He had known Conway for three years off and on, and twice he had visited Target-5 when it was drifting many hundred miles north of its present dangerous position. But in the fog it had all seemed different. When they saw the fire they had rushed across the ice and made their way up on to the island without trying to find the Sno-Cat ramp. They had dragged the sleds up a gulley in the twenty-foot high cliffs which reared above the pack and headed for the orange glow in the fog.

'That chunk of metal you can hardly see in the corner is our transmitter,' Conway called out. 'Was our transmitter,' he amended. 'Now there's no way of getting through to the mainland—we're cut off until our plane comes in.'

'Which is in ten days' time,' Beaumont said as he stood next to the American. 'Why did they leave it so late?'

'It was my crazy idea.' Conway sounded disgusted. 'We've never had the chance to carry out depth-sounding and salinity tests this far south so I thought it was a heaven-sent opportunity. But I didn't count on the fog coming. And now this. . . .'

'Who could have sabotaged the hut, anyway?' Beaumont asked.

'There are only the three of us here—so no one. I don't know, the strain must be telling on me as well.' He changed the subject. 'What about this Russian that's supposed to be coming here?'

'He's a man called Gorov, Michael Gorov.' Beaumont's tone was off-hand and vague: Conway hadn't got top security clearance for his work. 'I don't know a lot about him, but I gather Washington thinks he could tell them something about the political set-up in Russia. He's supposed to be on his way here from North Pole 17.'

'And that's why you're here?'

106

'I have to pick him up and take him back to Curtis Field. It's as simple as that.'

'Simple—going back across the pack?' Conway stared at the Englishman. 'I wouldn't make that trip for sixty thousand dollars.' Conway grinned as he rubbed globules of ice off his eyebrows. 'And I could do with sixty thousand dollars. Do we get back to the others now?'

'Is there somewhere we can talk first—on our own?'

'The research hut's just across here.' Conway led the way along a beaten snow-track between the surviving huts and Beaumont was pretty sure that the fog was thickening again. He was also sure that Conway was dead right: the radio hut had been sabotaged. But there was no point in increasing the tension on the island and he had a grimmer reason for keeping quiet. If Gorov did get through and they took him out they would be leaving the three men behind on Target-5. Conway he had no doubts about, but Rickard he didn't know and Sondeborg he didn't have to know: one look at the gravity specialist had told him he was on the verge of a crack-up. If the Russians arrived after they had left with Gorov and started putting on the pressure the men staying behind couldn't tell them anything—if they didn't know anything.

'You'll thaw out in here,' Conway said as he unlocked the door of a hut at the end of the line. 'We've left the heater on.'

The hut was about the same size as the headquarters building they had gone inside when Beaumont arrived, one large room measuring about fifteen feet by twenty. Packing crates ready for the evacuation were pushed against the walls, but at one end a huge iron tripod reared up and supported a large winch mechanism.

Conway pointed at the tripod. 'That's where we sling the underwater camera we send down to take a look at the seabed. We've sent the drilling core down through the same hole. Care to take a look?'

Conway bent down and levered up a section of the floorboards under the tripod. It came up as a large trap and Beaumont stared down a square hole about four feet across. Six feet below there were more floorboards. 'That's where we could hide Gorov in an emergency,' Conway suggested. 'He'd be damn cold but it's the best I can do.'

Beaumont stared at Conway across the deep well. 'What are you talking about?'

'Look, Keith, I told you I was still holding on to my sanity. And I can still work things out for myself. You bring two men over the pack from the edge of the fog—and all of you were flown there by chopper, you said. So this Gorov character, who must be pretty important, has taken off from the Russian base to come here—which means the Russian security people will be after him now. Correct?'

'I told you that.'

'Yes, but you didn't tell me that's why my radio hut has been sabotaged! They've done that to cut us off—so we can't signal Curtis Field when your Russian arrives. I worked that out while we were walking here from that mess up the street. Correct?'

'What's under that next lot of floorboards?' Beaumont asked. 'And you're correct—but don't spill any of it to Rickard or Sondeborg.'

'Soul of discretion!' Conway bent down again, took hold of a rope attached to a hook, pulled it. The lower boards opened up as a hinged trap and below there was darkness. Conway switched on his lamp, shone the powerful beam down the hole and the beam lost itself in a blackness which didn't end. A sour tang of salt drifted up into Beaumont's nostrils. At the edges of the beam, walls of ice glistened.

'That's the Arctic down there,' Conway said. 'Two hundred feet down through the ice. Make a good place to hide a body.'

'Let's hope it doesn't come to that,' Beaumont replied tersely.

'It was a joke—helps to release the tension.' Conway lowered the trap on the sinister hole. 'You've probably noticed I'm a bit jumpy—maybe you'll understand why when I tell you I've got Michael Gorov in the next hut.'

The Russian fugitive, the Soviet Union's chief oceanographer, the architect of the Catherine system, lay unconscious in the single bunk which stood against one wall of the hut. Blankets pulled up to his chin showed the hideously scarred face, the thick lips which were half open as Gorov breathed noisily, the mass of straight dark hair pushed back over his forehead. Like Leonid Brezhnev he had thick eyebrows, but his cheeks were pinched and sallow.

'He arrived half an hour before you came in,' Conway explained. 'I was alone by the burning radio hut when he came staggering through the fog. I brought him in here to start with because it was the nearest place.'

It was ironical, Beaumont thought—someone had made a very bad mistake when they set fire to the hut. Because it was the blazing beacon of the burning hut which had shown him how to locate the ice island—and Gorov had undoubtedly used the same flaming landmark to find his way to Target-5. The Russian stirred restlessly in his sleep, murmured something which could have been a girl's name—Rachel—then he subsided again.

'Is he very bad?' Beaumont asked. 'You practised medicine once, so you should know.'

'The frostbite isn't as bad as it looks. Some of it is old scars and the fresh wounds I've treated. He couldn't stop talking and he was a bit hysterical, so I gave him a mild sedative to help him rest. He talked as though I should know he was coming so I let him—I thought that was part of the hysteria.'

'How did he get here?'

'He came over the pack by sled apparently. . . .'

'Don't you know, Matt?' Beaumont demanded.

'There's no need to blow your top. . . .'

'It's important! If that sled is lying out in the open and the Russians find it they'll know he's here.'

'I'm sorry, I see what you mean. He told me he lost his dogs somewhere close to here—he was taking a catnap and he hadn't tethered them properly. He had to manhaul the sled the rest of the way and it nearly killed him. Then he saw the hut blazing in the distance, so he took a quick compass bearing, abandoned the sled and made it here on foot.' Conway took the cigarette Beaumont offered him and the Russian stirred again as a match was struck. 'My guess would be he left the sled maybe half a mile beyond the cliffs. Is that bad?'

'Not too good. How do you know he's Michael Gorov?'

'He said so. . . .'

'Is this his jacket?' Beaumont picked up the jacket off a table and started going through the pockets. 'I don't remember you having a bunk here when I was last on the island.'

'I didn't.' Conway smiled grimly. 'The official reason is I do a lot of calculations in here and when I'm finished I can just tumble into bed. The real reason is it gets me away from the others for a few hours.'

'From Sondeborg in particular?' Beaumont was examining the contents of a wallet carefully, laying out items on the table.

'From Sondeborg especially—he's cracking up fast. And it's going to affect Rickard soon—panic is the most infectious of all human ailments. Is it necessary to go through his personal things?' Conway inquired with an edge in his voice.

'Yes! This card says he's Michael Gorov,' Beaumont replied sceptically. 'The trouble is we've got no picture of him. Did he say the security people were after him?'

'No, he clammed up just before I put him to bed. I think he was suspicious I didn't know anything about him. There was another reason I put him in this hut—kept him here, that is.' Beaumont stared at him without speaking as he picked up the Russian's damp parka. Close to the space heater which Conway had lit, snow had melted on the fur. 'The others don't know he's here,' Conway went on. 'He said enough for me to grasp he was a fugitive and I guessed Russian security might be on his tail—I don't want more panic than I've got on my hands already.' Conway paused. 'And if I had to hide him I didn't trust Sondeborg to keep his mouth shut.'

Beaumont looked at the American with fresh respect. 'That was clever of you, Matt, very clever. And it may be helpful—if the Russians do come. We may have to hide Gorov down that nasty hole of yours yet. . . .'

'I didn't mean a live body,' Conway protested. 'I told you—it was a joke. My God, if you put him down there he'd freeze to death.'

'Not if we wrap him up well—cocoon him—and put a small heater down there with him. It would only be for a short time —while the Russians searched the base.'

'Searched the base!' Conway was outraged. 'They can't run a search here—this place has the American flag flying over it. . . .'

Beaumont fetched up a long tube out of one of the parka's deep pockets, a tube measuring about a foot in length and heavy to hold. 'Matt, you haven't quite grasped it—and this is something else not to tell the other two. We're marooned on this base, cut off. No plane can fly in because of the fog, the radio transmitter has been eliminated. If every man on the island at this moment vanished into thin air no one could ever prove what had happened.'

Conway sank down on a hard wooden chair slowly and stared up at Beaumont. 'Who's panicking now?' he asked with a forced smile. 'You can't really believe that—they wouldn't dare. . . .'

'Get this very clear,' Beaumont said coldly. 'It wouldn't involve much daring, only a touch of ruthlessness. Supposing one of your Sno-Cats was found abandoned on the pack only a few miles away from here—out of fuel. When the fog lifts and someone flies in from Curtis they'd find the base empty, the radio hut burned down, the Sno-Cat out on the ice. What conclusion would they draw? That you'd all panicked when the fog closed the place in, when you lost your only means of communicating with the mainland, that you'd tried to get out on your own. You run out of fuel and start back towards the island—on the way something happens to you. A lead opens up, a moving pressure ridge buries all of you. . . .'

'This is horrible,' Conway protested. 'You're talking about a blueprint for mass murder. . . .'

'I want you to know the score, Matt,' Beaumont said quietly. 'I'm talking about the Russian Special Security Service.'

'When are we moving out?'

Langer asked the question as he settled the dogs inside the hut opposite the headquarters building. The preparations for evacuating the base were well advanced and half the huts on the ice island were now unoccupied. The walls of the hut chosen for the dogs were lined with packing crates filled with equipment and waiting for the plane due in ten days' time.

'As soon as Gorov is fit to travel—sooner if there's an emergency, which there may well be,' Beaumont replied.

Langer adjusted the space heater he had carried to the hut and looked up wryly. 'We're expecting company? The wrong sort of company?'

'They've been here once—when they fired that radio hut. I think they're still very close. Horst, when you've sorted things out here I want you to unpack the transmitter and send a message in clear to Curtis Field. This is the message—Target-5 radio hut out of action. Sabotaged. Go on repeating the word sabotaged a few times, then sign off and pack the set up again.'

Langer patted the sleeping Bismarck who opened one bleary eye and closed it again. 'You mean I don't wait for confirmation on message received?'

'The message isn't for Curtis Field—it's for the Russian monitoring set at North Pole 17.'

'You wouldn't care to explain the mystery, would you?' Langer asked humorously. 'Just so I know what I'm doing, what's going on?'

'Later. And when you've done that I want you to take turns with Sam guarding that hut where Gorov is. If you run into trouble and there's no time left, fire one shot from your rifle into the air. When you're not guarding the hut, try and get some sleep.'

'You could do with some yourself,' Langer observed. 'We had the lion's share when we were drifting on that floe. And I'll forget about sleep if it means moving out of here faster. This place gives me the creeps—you know those three characters waiting for evacuation are on the edge of cracking up?'

'So we tread gently,' Beaumont warned.

He went out of the hut into the icy night and his expression tightened as he shut the door. He could just about see the headquarters hut which was only six feet across the beaten snow-track running between the two rows of buildings. The fog had thickened again, seemed to be intensifying as he stood for a moment and listened. Nearby he heard it, the quiet chugging of the generator which provided Target-5's lighting; and a long way off he heard something else—the muffled creaking and groaning of the polar pack surrounding the island.

When Target-5 cracked under that terrible weight the catastrophe would be very sudden. Fissures would appear out of nowhere, would widen into crevasses, which in turn would open up bottomless chasms as the whole island finally gave up after thirty years' resistance to the ceaseless squeeze of the polar pack.

But it wasn't the island Beaumont was worried about at this moment—it was what might be moving on it out of sight inside the dense rolling fog drifting all around him. He looked towards the hill he couldn't see, that strange forty-foot high eminence with its embedded boulders, floating in the sea a hundred miles from the nearest coast. His eyes prickled with the cold; Horst was right, he was damned tired. He crossed the track, opened the door in the headquarters hut and called out to Grayson to join him. Then he waited outside while the American put on his parka.

Typically, the American asked not a single question while Beaumont explained about Gorov. He only made one comment as he hoisted his rifle over his shoulder before going up the track. 'Trouble in there. I'd like to drop that Sondeborg into the nearest open lead.'

Beaumont stiffened as he went inside and shut the door. He had heard raised voices from the outside but now Sondeborg was shouting as he argued with Conway. 'We can't get through to the mainland with the transmitter busted,' Sondeborg raved. 'Supposing the island starts breaking up before that plane gets here? We're trapped. . . .'

The lean-faced gravity specialist stopped shouting as Beaumont closed the door. Along the facing wall stood a couple of two-tier bunks and Jeff Rickard, the wireless operator, sat on one of the lower bunks, chewing a matchstick as he watched Sondeborg. Conway was leaning against a table in the middle of the room with his arms folded and the flush on his pale face had nothing to do with the heat of the room.

'Get some sleep, Harv, for God's sake,' Rickard snapped. 'We've got company, so stop spilling your guts out.' The wireless operator, a cheerful thirty-two-year-old with curly black hair, reached out a hand to grasp the other man's arm. Sondeborg snatched it out of reach and glared at Beaumont. 'Why have you come here?' he demanded.

'I told you before,' Beaumont explained patiently. 'Our helicopter crashed on the ice and we were very lucky to make it. . . .'

'I don't believe a damn word!'

'Sorry to hear that.' There was an edge in Beaumont's voice as he propped his rifle in a corner. He took off his parka and laid it on the table. 'You've been drinking, haven't you?' It wasn't a brilliant deduction: he could smell the liquor on the gravity specialist's breath six feet away from him.

'He's got a bottle stashed away somewhere,' Conway informed Beaumont. 'I haven't been able to locate it yet. And this is his last Arctic trip.'

'Brother, are you telling me!' Sondeborg sneered. 'When I get on that plane the only ice I'll want to see is in a bar.'

'Which is where you'll take up your living quarters, no doubt,' Beaumont observed nastily.

Something snapped inside Sondeborg. He bent down, grasped an ice pick from under the table, a small-handled pick, stood up again slowly, staring at Beaumont with a blank expression.

'Put that down!' Conway said sharply.

'This big Limey takes up too much room,' Sondeborg said slowly and his right foot moved forward.

'Stay where you are, Rickard,' Beaumont warned. 'It doesn't look as though I'm too popular round here,' he went on as he picked up his parka from the table. 'I don't want to cause trouble, Conway,' he added. 'I'll move to one of the other huts. . . .'

He held the parka as though about to put it on while Sondeborg watched him uncertainly, then with a swift throwing movement like a matador wielding a cape he brought the coat down over Sondeborg's right arm.

Sondeborg flailed with his arm to get the ice pick free and then Beaumont hit him. He hit him very hard with a powerful, short-armed jab which knocked Sondeborg back against the bunks. The gravity specialist sagged, fell half inside a bunk, then collapsed unconscious on the floor.

'Check him,' Beaumont snapped. 'How long before he comes round?'

Conway bent over the man and examined him quickly, then spoke over his shoulder. 'He's out cold. With the drink inside him he could be this way for several hours. . . .'

'Can we get him out of here—into another hut?'

'The one next door has two bunks. . . .'

'I'd like him shifted there,' Beaumont said crisply. 'I'd like him tied up, too.'

'Tied up?' Conway sounded surprised and uneasy.

'Tied up.' Beaumont lifted the ice pick off the floor. 'Any man who would threaten someone with this thing needs restraining. Restrain him—and padlock the door.' Conway opened his mouth to say something as Rickard was lifting Sondeborg over his shoulder. 'I've got a reason,' Beaumont said firmly, 'so padlock the door.' He went over to a tall cupboard standing by the wall, reached up over the top and brought something down in his hand. Conway stared at the object Beaumont put on the table.

'So that's where he kept it.'

'I'm taller than you are,' Beaumont pointed out, 'so I saw it when I came in this time. And there are two more of them up there.'

'Where the hell did he get this?' Conway picked up the bottle from the table and gazed at it as though he could hardly believe his eyes. He was holding a large bottle of Russian vodka. 'He couldn't have got it from Minsky, he's harmless— that's the man in charge at North Pole 17. But he has been here from time to time to see how we're getting on.

'To get information,' Beaumont replied. 'The Russians keep a detailed file on every American base in the Arctic—that's common knowledge. Minsky got his information from Sonde-borg in exchange for the liquor you wouldn't let him have. Now maybe you'll agree to lock him up.'

'That signal worries me,' Dawes said. 'I think a crisis is building up—so I'm sending a plane in to Target-5.'

'But it's still fogged in,' Adams protested. 'How can anyone land?'

'That signal said the radio hut had been burned down—sabotage is the word they used. I'm sending in the transport we have standing by in case the fog clears—I'm sending in Ridgeway.'

'But how can it land?'

'I don't know,' Dawes admitted. 'But if anyone can land it's Ridgeway. He's made five landings on Target-5 in different parts of the Arctic and he's the finest civilian pilot within a thousand miles. Give Fuller the order.'

'I don't like it,' Adams said as he picked up the phone to talk to the airfield controller.

'Ridgeway won't like it either,' Dawes replied.

'I sent the signal,' Langer informed Beaumont as he shut the door. He looked round the hut. 'Where is everyone?'

'Putting Sondeborg to bed—after I'd put him to sleep.' He told Langer what had happened. 'I don't think anyone spotted it, but I tempted Sondeborg into a fight. I'm clearing the decks.'

'You're worried the Russians will come?' Langer dropped his parka on top of Beaumont's on the table. 'God, it's cold out there—I'd better go and relieve Sam in a few minutes.'

'I'm not worried the Russians will come—I'm sure they're coming,' Beaumont replied emphatically. 'The big question is whether they come before or after we've left. If it's before, I don't want a weak sister like Sondeborg available for them to question.' He pointed at the vodka bottle. 'Especially when he's already given them information to get drink. He told them about the radio hut.'

'They needed telling—with the mast sticking up above it?'

Beaumont leaned across the table and poured coffee out of the flask Conway had prepared for them. 'Get some of this inside you. Yes, they needed telling—that no one slept there. In some Arctic huts the operator has a bunk so he can stay on the job. Here it isn't necessary—Rickard only visited the hut when he was using the transmitter.' Beaumont poked at two foot-long metal tubes on the table. 'Recognize them?'

'Twenty-five thousand years of history inside one of these.' Langer picked up a tube and examined it casually. 'Amazing the way they send one of these down at the end of a drill, drive it into the seabed ten thousand feet down, and come up with a core. And the hollow tube they drive in comes back with a sample out of the seabed. Over thousands of years the geological layers at the bottom of the ocean are enormously compressed under the sea's weight, so we end up with this. Twenty-five thousand years and you can carry it about in your coat pocket.'

'Gorov did. See any difference between them?'

Langer examined the two tubes. Both were corroded and abraded by their long vertical journey through the sea, by the frictional drive of the drill forcing them into the far-down seabed, and both were filled with core material. 'They're just cores,' Langer replied, 'like those over there.' He nodded towards a collection of tubes Conway had arranged on top of a crate.

'This one is Gorov's.' Beaumont took the core and levered at its extremity with the tip of his penknife.

A solid piece of core about three inches long dropped into his hand when he upended the tube. The piece of core at the other end remained in place as he shook the tube, and then something shiny and tightly rolled fell into his palm.

He winked at Langer as he held a section of the 35-mm. film up to the light. 'And this, unless I'm very much mistaken, is a microfilm of the Catherine charts.'

'My God. . . .'

'Exactly. I'm holding in my hand a record of Russia's entire underwater system in the Arctic.' Beaumont re-rolled the film, slipped it back inside the tube, replaced the piece of core. 'So if we do lose Gorov we've still got this.'

'When he wakes up he'll notice it's gone,' Langer warned. 'In his place it would be the first thing I'd check the moment I did wake up.'

'So we'll keep him happy—by putting this one back in his parka.' Beaumont held up the second core tube, then checked his watch. 1 a.m., local time. 'You might do that for me when you relieve Sam. And now I'm going to get some kip before I fall asleep in this chair.'

He had just taken his boots off and climbed into one of the lower bunks when the door was thrown open and Langer came back.

'I think the Russians are here—Sam heard their engines. . . .'

The Siberian came across the ice from North Pole 17 by helicopter which landed at the eastern edge of the fog bank. Here he transferred to a waiting Sno-Cat, the curious tracked vehicle used for short-distance journeys in the Arctic. It has four caterpillar tracks—two at the front which support the driver's cab, and two more at the rear which carry the truck-like part of the vehicle.

'We should reach the American base at about one o'clock,' Kramer said as he settled himself beside Papanin who had elected to drive the Sno-Cat.

'Which is the approximate time we estimated Gorov might arrive—if he was very lucky.'

Despite the fog they had no trouble locating the ice island. The security detachment which had made its way to Target-5 earlier had planted an electronic device at the summit of the hill behind Conway's encampment, a device which the box Kramer was holding locked on to, guiding them straight to their objective. But it was a hideously cold journey and Kramer was shivering when they arrived—as were the ten armed men huddled close together in the compartment behind the cab.

They avoided the snow ramp which would have allowed them to drive up on to the island; instead they left the Sno-Cat on the pack and went the rest of the way on foot. As in a chess game played by a grandmaster, everything was foreseen. When they came to the cliffs they used climbing equipment to haul themselves up the twenty-foot-high obstacle. When they had scaled the cliffs Kramer used his little box to guide them through the fog to the top of the boulder-strewn hill. And from the summit an erratic compass bearing showed them which was north—the side where the group of huts lay.

'Something's gone wrong,' Papanin whispered when they had gone down the slope and found nothing.

Something had gone wrong; since the last aerial shot of Target-5 had been taken, since the fog had descended, the island had turned a few degrees, so it was only by good luck that the Siberian crashed into one of the empty huts before he knew it was there.

A few minutes later, stumbling round like a blind man, he found the headquarters hut which now had a light burning outside it. He hammered on the door with his gloved fist, shouted in English, then opened the door and walked inside.

The Siberian's command of English was fluent; trained in a language laboratory at Kharkov in the Ukraine; perfected during long conversations with Guy Burgess in Moscow—when the English defector was sober enough to enunciate clearly— the Siberian had spent most of 1967 attached to one of the Soviet consulates in the south-western United States, consulates which have only one purpose to justify their expense: espionage.

Coming out of the fog the light dazzled Papanin. He lifted his hand to cut down the glare and saw three men inside the hut—the number Minsky had reported as still on Target-5 waiting to be evacuated. A very large man in his thirties was sitting on a bunk while he cleaned a rifle—and the muzzle was aimed at the doorway. A shorter man, fair-haired and also in his thirties, stood nearer the door with a rifle crooked in his arm while he held an oily rag in the other hand. The oldest man, in his fifties, was leaning against a table with his arms folded and a tense look.

'Come inside and shut the damned door,' the big man snapped. The rifle elevated. 'No! Just you—the others can stay outside.'

Behind Papanin more fur-clad figures, all of them at least a foot shorter than the huge Siberian, stirred in the fog as he stepped inside the hut and stared at the man on the bunk. 'I am from North Pole 17. . . .'

'I said shut the door,' the big man said very quietly.

'Dr Kramer should be present,' Papanin insisted stiffly, 'he has something important to warn you about.'

'All right, Kramer comes in, too—the rest stay outside. . . .'

'It is very cold. . . .'

'No one invited you here.'

Papanin's expression was grim and he felt his temper rising as Kramer pushed in behind him. The fair-haired man with the rifle slammed the door in the faces of the men outside, bolted it with a savage, grating sound.

Papanin glanced quickly round the hut for any sign of Gorov's presence on the base. He saw drilling cores laid out on a crate, an ice pick beside them, more packed crates, a flask and cups on the table the oldest man was still leaning against. Papanin was tall enough to have seen the two remaining bottles of vodka on top of the cupboard—except that they had been removed. The Siberian took off his damp parka and dropped it over the back of a chair.

'My name is Vassily,' he explained, his eyes still wandering round the hut. 'I am the administrative officer for various Soviet research bases, including your neighbour, North Pole 17. Dr Kramer is the medical officer there. Is everything all right here?' he inquired.

'Shouldn't it be?' Beaumont asked.

'I smelled something when we came through the fog, something burning. . . .'

'Our wireless hut burned down,' Conway burst out. 'It was burned down deliberately. Is that the sort of trouble you had in mind?'

Beaumont inwardly congratulated Conway; the American had reacted exactly as he had suggested, which gave him his opening to throw the Siberian off-balance. 'It's a pretty serious business this, Vassily—we've sent a signal to Greenland reporting the sabotage and someone's going to have to answer a lot of awkward questions.'

'You sent a signal about the fire?' There was a mocking tone of disbelief in Papanin's voice. These people must be wood from the neck upwards. 'Can you tell me how it is possible to use a transmitter when it was destroyed in the fire?'

'Spare transmitter,' Beaumont informed him laconically. 'We always keep a spare—do they only let you have one on Russian bases? I suppose we'll have to put it down to the extravagances of the capitalist system. Incidentally,' he went on, 'your monitoring unit at North Pole 17 will tell you about the signal when you get back.'

Beaumont waited, wondering whether his insurance policy was going to pay a dividend. The Siberian clearly hadn't yet been told about the signal, but it was vital: so long as he grasped the fact that a signal had been sent, that it had already been reported to Greenland that something very strange was going on at Target-5, he would hesitate to take extreme action. And this was all that Beaumont hoped for—hesitation, delay to give them time to get Gorov away from the ice island.

'Monitoring unit?' Papanin asked blankly.

'Oh, come off it!' Beaumont stood up and the two men seemed to fill the hut as they faced each other. 'Monitoring unit! Everyone knows you've got monitoring units all over the Arctic checking up on our signals. It's normal procedure, Vassily, so why make a big secret of it?'

Conway quietly put both hands inside his trouser pockets to hide the fact that he was sweating profusely. Beaumont was walking a high wire he could so easily fall off; there were armed men, a lot of them, just outside the hut, and no one might ever know what had really happened on Target-5 inside the fog. He was still doubtful whether the Englishman could out-manœuvre the Russian, still horribly conscious of the fact that Gorov was hidden only yards away from where he stood.

'This is not what I came here to talk about,' Papanin snapped. 'I am afraid that one of our people may be responsible for burning down your hut,' he went on.

'So there'll be a big inquiry,' Beaumont said bluntly. 'By now Washington will have heard about it—you can imagine how they're going to react to the word sabotage!'

'If you will let me continue . . .'

'It could be hitting the world's headlines tomorrow—Russians attack U.S. base. . . .'

'That's ridiculous. . . .'

'Buy tomorrow's paper and see.'

For the first time in many years Papanin was rattled. In case a signal had been sent he was going to have to tread carefully here. 'No international incident. . . .' He could hear Comrade Brezhnev's instructions repeating in his brain as he tried to regain command of the situation.

'I am talking about Nikolai Marov, a junior oceanographer,' he explained. 'He has gone mad and murdered another man called Gorov. Then he escaped in this direction with a sled team. Marov has taken his victim's papers and may try to pass himself off as Michael Gorov. . . .'

'Why should he do that?' Beaumont demanded.

'Because he left his own papers in his hut,' Papanin said smoothly. 'He would know that you might ask to see proof of his identity. . . .'

'What makes you think he's mad?' Beaumont interjected.

Papanin glared at him, his patience wearing thin with the constant interruptions. He tried a new tactic, raising his voice. 'For God's sake, he burned down your hut! He committed a brutal crime! It was not a pleasant murder. . . .' He took a step closer to Beaumont, trying to break him down by the force of his personality. 'He killed poor Gorov with an ice pick and then hacked him about the face! Don't you understand? He has spent three years in the Arctic and his mind has gone —he is like a wild animal roaming round somewhere out there on the ice. . . .'

'Then you'd better stop wasting time and get out there and find him.'

Papanin calmed down suddenly, gestured towards Kramer. 'This thing is a great worry to us. When you have heard what it is all about you may wish us to stay. I think Dr Kramer had better explain—then you will understand how serious it is. I may sit down?' He pulled out a chair and sat down, smiling amiable round the hut. 'Get on with it, Kramer.'

'Marov is a psychopath . . .' Kramer began in careful English.

'We don't want his medical history,' Beaumont said unpleasantly, determined to get the Siberian on his feet again. 'We've got quite enough on our plate without you people settling in for the night.'

Papanin stood up slowly, flexing his fingers to release some of the tension building up inside him. He had to be very careful; somehow the whole thing had been turned round—instead of frightening these Americans Papanin himself felt dangerously off balance.

'We came here to warn you,' he began as he collected his parka off the table, 'to ask for your co-operation . . .'

'We've been warned, we co-operated, we listened. Thank you. And now we've work to do,' Beaumont broke in crisply.

'I was going to suggest we searched your huts—one of you could accompany us—in case Marov is hiding here.'

'Not necessary—we searched them ourselves when we saw that someone had fired the hut. . . .'

Conway intervened, made a magnificent job of his intervention as his voice shook with genuine fury. 'This is an outrage! You come here and suggest searching the place? This is United States territory, Mr Vassily.' He stood away from the table as he faced Papanin. 'I hope I don't have to remind you that the American flag flies over this ice island?'

Papanin paused, stooped over, half inside his parka as he looked at Conway. He was going to shake these people before he left. 'I saw the flag when we came in—hanging limp like a piece of frozen cod.' He stood upright, fastening his coat. 'It might be safer if none of you leave this ice island until your plane arrives.'

'Safer from what?' Beaumont asked.

'If we see something moving on the pack my men may assume it is Marov and shoot,' Papanin said grimly. 'I have told them he must be taken unharmed—if possible. But Gorov had many friends and some of them are outside this hut—and all of them are armed.' He pulled the fur hood over his shaven head. 'Kramer, we did ask for these people's co-operation.

Since we are no longer welcome we will go.' He glanced round the hut. 'A pleasant trip back to the United States, gentlemen. Here you are living on borrowed time.'

When they had gone, Beaumont sent Grayson out to make sure they had really gone, then he looked at Conway who was drying his moist palms with a handkerchief. 'It's going to be extremely tricky from now on,' he warned. 'The man who called himself Vassily is Colonel Igor Papanin, head of Special Security in Leningrad—I was shown his photograph before I left Washington.' Beaumont checked his watch. 1.45 a.m. 'I'm going to take Gorov out by sled at eight o'clock this morning—in six hours' time. That will give us the best chance of avoiding the Russians.'

'Why eight o'clock?'

'Because by then they'll have been up all night somewhere out on the pack—waiting to see what happens. They'll have had six hours of it—listening hard, shivering, straining to see any sign of movement. By eight o'clock they'll be bad-tempered, bone-tired and not very alert. But it would help if I had a diversion when we move off.'

'I'll drive the Sno-Cat around,' Conway suggested quickly. 'I can take it across the island, down the ramp and move round on the pack a bit.'

'Which was what I was going to suggest—up to a point anyway.' Beaumont stood up, his eyes heavy, his limbs sluggish. He started walking around to keep himself awake. 'They found their way here in Sno-Cats—God knows how—and they may be carrying some kind of mobile radar. If you take the Sno-Cat out they'll concentrate on it—while we slip off the western end of the island.'

'It should fox them. . . .'

'Listen, Matt.' Beaumont spoke with deliberation to stress the risk Conway would be running. 'There's a bunch of armed Russians within a mile of this hut, so you're not to take any unnecessary chances. I think I knocked Papanin off his perch when I said a signal had been sent. . . .'

'He'll find out when he checks with his monitoring unit.'

For a moment Beaumont wondered whether to tell Conway

about his own transmitter, then he decided against it. It was an even chance that Papanin would be back again, and next time he might ask questions rather more forcefully. 'That won't be until he gets back to North Pole 17,' he said. 'You can drive your Sno-Cat safely round the eastern part of the island—in this fog?'

'I've lived on this island for three years—in all weathers,' Conway assured him. 'I can put on the airstrip landing lights to guide me, I've got an angled beam on the Cat which shows me the way down the ramp. . . .'

'Not down the ramp!' Beaumont said sharply. 'The island has your flag flying over it—once you go down on to the pack it's no-man's land. If you're going to help at all you just drive around slowly on the island for an hour or so. On the island,' he repeated.

They had a great deal to do during the next half-hour. They called Langer out of the hut where he had stayed with the dogs to keep them quiet during Papanin's visit. They released Rickard from the hut next door where he had been locked in with the unconscious Sondeborg—ostensibly to keep an eye on the unstable gravity specialist, but also to prevent his hearing about the presence of Gorov on the island. Beaumont was determined that Conway would be the only man left behind on Target-5 who would know about Michael Gorov.

They left Conway and Rickard in the headquarters hut, and then Beaumont took the others with him to 'get Gorov out of the refrigerator,' as he put it.

Mercifully the Russian oceanographer was still asleep, still under the influence of the sedative when they lifted the trap-door in the research hut and hauled up his cocooned body. Had he woken up inside the deep tomb alone his reaction was something the imagination preferred not to dwell on—until he discovered the scribbled note Beaumont had left beside the lamp they had lowered with the heater.

Wrapped in many blankets, Gorov was surprisingly warm when they lifted him into the single bunk Conway had installed inside the research hut. He woke up as Conway slipped inside and closed the door. 'I wanted to see if he was O.K.' the

American explained. 'It gave me the horrors to think of him lying down there.'

'This place is different,' Gorov said as he eased himself up on one elbow. 'You have moved me to a new hut. Why?'

Surprisingly alert, Beaumont noted, but a man who had made his way alone across the pack from North Pole 17 had to be unusually tough. He asked Conway to examine him again and lit a cigarette while he waited impatiently for the verdict. He was convinced they only had a few hours to get away from the ice island. Papanin would soon recover from the shock of his initial reception and then he would be back—and the second visitation would be much more dangerous than the first.

'He seems in good condition,' Conway said as he stood up from his patient. 'I can't understand it—after that ordeal.'

Beaumont started his interrogation at once, firing questions at the Russian who spoke good English. Like Papanin, Gorov had learned his English at the Kharkov language laboratory, a knowledge essential to his work. Once French had been the international language of the scientific fraternity, but for a quarter of a century it had been replaced by English—and Gorov liked to read scientific works in the original language. He was obviously taken aback by Beaumont's verbal onslaught.

'When were you last in Kiev?'

'Last week.'

'Meet any relatives there?'

'My brother, Peter. . . .'

'He's in the Navy?'

'No, he's on a trawler. . . .'

'What was the name of your girl friend who died?'

Gorov's thick lips tightened. He stared bleakly at Beaumont. 'She was my fiancée. We were going to be married. . . .'

'I asked for her name.'

'Rachel Levitzer. Is all this really necessary?'

'Yes! Is it by God?' Conway burst out, appalled by Beaumont's brutality.

'Yes, it is by God,' Beaumont replied tersely. He watched

126

Gorov very carefully. 'Colonel Igor Papanin was standing in this very room half an hour ago.'

Fear flashed into the Russian's eyes. He stared round the hut like a trapped man, tried to say something, swallowed uncomfortably. It was the instantaneous reaction Beaumont had been hoping for; if this man had been a stooge—sent to the island by Papanin as a spy—he couldn't have pretended naked fear so spontaneously.

Beaumont explained what he had been doing and the reasons for it. No photograph was available in Washington of Michael Gorov and this was the only way to check his identity. At least now when they started out across the ice on their terrible journey they would know they were taking the right man.

Conway gave Gorov a drink from the bottle of brandy he had brought with him, a bottle he kept securely locked away in a cupboard so that Sondeborg wouldn't guzzle the lot. At Beaumont's suggestion he prepared food for the Russian on a primus in the research hut, and all the time the fugitive sat at the edge of the bunk, lacing and unlacing his strong fingers, running them nervously through his lank black hair.

Earlier, soon after the interrogation had ended, he had got up to stretch his legs and had wandered over to the chair where his parka lay draped. Casually, he had lifted the parka to sit for a moment; even more casually he had run his hand over the pocket which contained the core tube, had felt its cylindrical shape under the fur. Langer, standing near the door, smiled to himself as Gorov sat down, visibly relaxed that his precious possession was still safe.

That night it was fatal for Beaumont to think of sleep. He had just said that he was going back to the headquarters hut to lie down for a while when they all heard it. The distant drone of an aircraft coming in. The Hercules C.130 transport which Dawes, worried stiff by the 'sabotage' signal, had sent, was circling overhead, waiting to land.

Colonel Igor Papanin was also listening to the drone of the American transport plane. A few hundred metres away from the snow ramp leading down from Target-5 he sat in the cab of his Sno-Cat alongside Kramer, calmly puffing at his little curved pipe. The atmosphere inside the sealed cab was thick with smoke, so thick that Kramer thought he would soon expire. But he dare not open a window because that would let the Arctic flood in.

'They've switched the landing lights on,' he said nervously. The blurred glow of a single landing light wobbled beyond the top of the cliffs, then the fog masked it.

'Naturally,' Papanin said, 'they have to show their plane where to land.'

'And you still think Gorov isn't there?'

'I said I wasn't convinced that he had yet arrived—a different thing, Kramer. I was looking for fear and anxiety when we arrived but all I detected was indignation. That big man was very aggressively indignant,' he said thoughtfully.

'But if he has arrived—and the plane lands?'

'You worry too much. It's going to be all right—you'll see.'

Seven hundred feet above Target-5 the plane's pilot, Alfred Ridgeway, sat in front of his controls as he circled over what another pilot, Arnold Schumacher, had called the oatmeal, the thick bank of dirt-grey fog below him. In the cargo compartment behind him two rows of bucket seats lined the fuselage and the rear seats were occupied by twelve men in Arctic clothing who carried concealed weapons.

The twelve men belonged to the U.S. Coastguard Service and they had been specially chosen for this job. In Leningrad the Russians had sent a Special Security detachment to the Arctic because this gave the expedition a non-military character—which neutralized the danger of an international incident building up only a few months before the Summit meeting in Moscow. Washington was taking the same precaution for the same reason: there must be no danger of an international incident.

The two seats nearest the pilot's cabin were occupied by a different type of passenger, by a doctor and a nurse. Dr Maxwell Hergsheimer, forty-eight years old and grey-haired, who was equipped with a medical kit and oxygen cylinders for his Russian patient, stared out of the window as the fog rolled in great banks below. Behind him sat Nurse Anne Clyde from Brooklyn, the thirty-year-old girl who had volunteered to come with him. Hergsheimer was worried about her; not every girl would have so calmly contemplated a trip out over the polar wastes. And to emphasize the civilian character of their mission she wore her uniform. She leaned forward over his shoulder. 'Do you think Captain Ridgeway will get us down?' she inquired.

'I think so, yes. He comes from my home state, Illinois, and I've known him for years. He'll go on circling until he does see his way in.'

In the pilot's cabin Ridgeway's sentiments were rather less optimistic. In fact, Ridgeway was very worried indeed. There was no sign of a gap in the fog anywhere; if anything it was getting worse as it floated like a dark, poison-gas cloud under the pallid light of the moon. He glanced at the fuel gauge. Plenty left: he'd damned well go on circling until there was only enough gas to get them back to Curtis.

'I'm beginning to wonder whether I saw those landing lights at all,' van Beeck, his co-pilot, commented.

'Want to go home, Jim? You said you saw them—did you?'

'I saw them, Captain.'

'O.K. So we keep circling.'

Beaumont was sweating with anxiety as he stood close to one of the landing lights Conway had switched on. In the fog it glowed like a small greenish fire. He was standing with Conway at the edge of the airstrip, a quarter of a mile away from the cluster of huts where five more men waited in equal anxiety. Then he heard the faint drone of the plane coming back, a drone growing steadily louder.

'Thank God,' Conway muttered. 'I thought he'd given up.'

Thank God, Beaumont agreed to himself. And the fog was thinning a little. The plane only had to land to secure their salvation; at Curtis Field Dawes had told him about the coast-guard detachment standing by and Beaumont was confident it would be on board. With a detachment of a dozen armed men on the island Papanin would be checkmated.

'Do you think he can land in this stuff?' Conway whispered.

In the fog, whispering came naturally. It shifted all around them, assuming strange, menacing shapes, and the cold was intense. They shifted their boots frequently, stretched their toes inside them, anything to keep a fraction of circulation moving while they waited and the invisible plane's engines built up into a muffled roar.

Soon it was dead overhead, and the fog thinned a little more. But not enough, Beaumont was thinking. 'He can't be thinking of landing yet,' he murmured. 'I wonder what visibility is like up there. . . .'

Visibility from five hundred feet up had improved: instead of being impossible it was bad to awful. Ridgeway banked the plane more steeply to get a better look down and grunted. It was a habit of which he was unaware—grunting—but the noise was significant for van Beeck. It told the co-pilot that his captain had just taken a tricky decision. He waited while Ridgeway stared hard into the fog.

The pilot had seen the landing lights, he had guessed that this improved situation would be short-lived, that soon the fog would roll over again. It would have been a considerable over-statement to say that the parallel lines of lights were visible—they showed to Ridgeway in the banked plane as two vague strings of pale glows: no more, but they showed him where the airstrip was. It was between those two faint lines and that was enough for him.

'We're going in,' he said. 'Tell them.'

The co-pilot left his seat, went back into the cargo compartment and called out to his fourteen passengers. 'Time to strap yourselves in—we're going down. . . .'

'You see,' Dr Hergsheimer told Nurse Clyde, 'I was right—he's from Illinois.'

In the control cabin Ridgeway was banking his machine away from the island, turning in a wide sweep to give himself a good run-in.

The lights had vanished now and he was praying he would see them again when he had completed his turn. The sweep continued, swinging out over the desolate polar pack which was invisible, then he was on course, screwing up his eyes as he stared ahead.

The damned lights seemed fainter now, hardly more than a blurred phosphorescence beneath the fog. The machine went into a shallow glide, the blur came up to meet it. Gear and flaps down. The four propellers whipped through wisps of fog, the motors beat steadily, the ice island came up to meet them. It was an exercise Ridgeway had repeated many times before. He had landed five times on Target-5 in various parts of the Arctic—all of them hundreds of miles north of this latitude.

Don't overshoot! The warning flashed through his brain. There was just sufficient length of airstrip to land on—provided he touched down in time. The lights merged into glow-lines, the skids touched down, the machine wobbled as though starting to skid, so they were tearing over the ice blind except for the glow rushing past them on either side. So long as there was no obstruction in the way. . . .

The propellers beating the air thrashed up a storm of snow, obliterating the glow on either side, and then Ridgeway completed the landing, reversing propeller pitch and braking to bring the machine to a halt.

Beaumont and Conway were at the edge of the airstrip when they heard the increase in engine sound and realized the transport was coming in to land. 'Get well back!' Beaumont shouted. They moved away from the airstrip, went back a short distance, and when they turned round the lights of the plane were visible, dropping towards them at what seemed slow-motion speed.

'God! He's going to overshoot. . . .' Conway stood quite still, frozen with fear as well as with cold.

'He'll make it!' Beaumont shouted the words above the roar of the engines. The fog made distance impossible to judge, visibility from above must be better than it seemed at ground level—otherwise the pilot would never have attempted the landing.

Beaumont saw the wings which carried the lights, a dark silhouette plunging through fog swirls as it thundered along the airstrip. In the Arctic night the engines were deafening, a thudding roar, then the machine touched down, sent up spurts of snow as the skis sped along the ice, sent up cloudbursts of snow as the propellers churned. The plane seemed enormous bursting through the fog. Then it was past them and Beaumont thought he heard the hiss of skis above the roar. Their aerial taxi had arrived.

The plane went on through the fog. They heard the engine sound change as the pilot reversed propeller pitch. In a moment the machine would be stationary, its propellers ticking over as the pilot cut his motors. They could still see it as a blurred, retreating shape when the silhouette altered. One moment it was horizontal, the next moment it was swinging up vertically, the tail high in the air, then the tail smashed down, vanished. The vibration of the impact travelled through the ice, echoed up their legs. The petrol tanks detonated, deafened Beaumont. The flare of flame, the flash which seared right through the fog, blinded him for a moment. Then there was crackling fire, black smoke.

As the echo of the detonation died away Papanin opened the window and knocked out his pipe. 'You see, Kramer, I said it would be all right.'

There were no survivors. The heat was so intense that for a brief time it burned a hole in the fog, exposing moonlit sky before the smoke masked it again. The plane was burning itself to cinders on a carpet of ice and the inferno faded suddenly, leaving only creeping smoke and a nauseous stench which turned Beaumont's stomach, a stench compounded of petrol, plane—and people.

He had completed a careful circuit of the disaster when Conway, breathing heavily, caught up with him. 'There must be someone alive. . . .'

'It's hopeless, Conway. No one could survive that—they might just as well have been shoved into an incinerator.'

'Beaumont—look at this. . . .' The American's voice trembled and he was holding something in his hand, something crumpled and smeared with oil. He opened it out, reassembled it into a caricature of its original shape. 'Beaumont, it's a nurse's cap.'

'They must have brought her to attend to Gorov. . . .'

'Why the hell had that plane to crash? It was down—it was safe, it was stopping when . . .'

'Come over here.' Beaumont walked a few paces on to the airstrip, bent down and heaved at a large object close to a skidmark which scarred the snow. 'This is why, Conway. The plane caught this rock and somersaulted. One of the machine's skids is over there—it must have ripped away when it struck the boulder.'

'I swept the airstrip with the snow-plough—swept it two days ago.' Conway sounded bewildered, in a state of shock. 'I just couldn't have missed a thing that size. . . .'

'You missed this one, too.' Beaumont moved a few feet further across the airstrip and hammered his boot against a second snow-covered boulder. 'And that one. . . .' He had only just seen the third obstruction and he bent down to examine it, telling the American to focus his lamp on it. Conway stared down at the rock in silence as Beaumont heaved it over and scraped at the underside with his gloved fingers.

'You missed all three of them,' Beaumont continued, 'for the very simple reason they weren't here when you swept the airstrip. There's very little snow underneath this rock and not much more on top—what there is came from the whirling propellers.'

'You mean . . .'

'Yes! These boulders are from the hill behind the camp—and boulders don't walk a quarter of a mile. They were carried here in case a plane did try to land. It's sabotage again, Conway—sabotage of the most brutal kind. God knows how many poor devils were on that plane besides the nurse.'

'The bastards!'

'Take it easy. We've got to get back to the camp.'

'I'll see this gets into every newspaper in America. . . .'

'You won't, you know.' Beaumont took a grip on Conway's arm and started him moving. 'You haven't got a shred of evidence to back up that statement. . . .'

'The boulders, for God's sake!'

'The Russians would say the rocks must have been there all the time, that the wind blew snow away and exposed them—maybe even that it was your fault for not sweeping the strip properly. Someone has organized a very nasty and very effective accident. I just hope it's not setting a pattern for the future.'

The Sno-Cat ground its way through the fog, the two pairs of heavy tracks kicking up the devil of a row as they revolved over the ice. One headlight beam poked at the fog beyond the cab, the second light mounted outside the cab window was angled downwards. Inside the cab Conway leaned well over to check the angled light: he was going to depend on that lamp soon, depend on it to stop him plunging twenty feet over a sheer drop down on to the polar pack.

Muffled inside his fur parka and fur hood, he checked his watch. 8 a.m. exactly. So he had got the timing right; in a few minutes he should see one of the airstrip landing lights he had switched on. He moved the gear lever, moved the big lever which turned the tracks, checked the milometer as he changed direction. Conway, a peaceable man, had a loaded rifle on the seat beside him as he drove on into nothing with the memory of the nurse's cap vivid in his mind. Screwing up his eyes, he frowned: the windscreen was messed up and the wipers were spreading dirt over the glass. He stopped the Cat, left the engine ticking over and climbed out with a cleaning rag.

Fog rolled over the Sno-Cat, blotted out the rear of the vehicle, and Conway looked round nervously as he rubbed at the glass. Fog everywhere, fog which could conceal an army of Russians. He cleaned the glass quickly, got back up into the cab, and the closing of the door was a relief, made him feel safer because he was high up and enclosed. He checked the milometer, moved the big lever and the cumbersome machine ground slowly forward. The dangerous part was coming.

Crouched over his levers, the American leaned close to the windscreen where the wipers kept a fan-shaped segment clear of moisture. He must be close to the cliff now—if he had any idea of where he was going—and now he was staring at the ground below the angled headlight. Entirely on his own, Conway was extending Beaumont's deception plan—he was going to drive the Sno-Cat to the ramp, take it down on to the pack and drive it a quarter of the way round the island. With the aid of the angled headlight he could keep the cliff in view and avoid any risk of losing himself out on the pack.

Then he was going to abandon the Sno-Cat, walk back to the ramp and return to camp. He would leave the Sno-Cat with its nose pointed north, its steering mechanism jammed. When the Russians found it they would assume that someone had escaped from the island—panicked by the plane crash— and that they were heading north instead of west.

With one hand he lit a cigarette, and that made him feel a little better. Then he changed course suddenly. The angled light had projected its beam into a vacuum, into nothing. He was moving along the edge of the cliff-top. For safety's sake he took the vehicle back a dozen yards, then he watched for the lamp on top of the wooden post which would tell him he had made it. In a few minutes he would be going down the ramp.

'East . . . east . . . east. The ramp.'

Kramer switched off the microphone which linked him with the men on the pack surrounding the island, the men equipped with the Soviet version of the American walkie-talkie transmitter. They would all now be converging, hurrying towards the Sno-Cat—and the ramp.

The Balt was sitting next to Papanin inside the Sno-Cat which was stationary in the fog. In the compartment behind them the radar operator gazed at his scanner, tracking the slow approach of Conway's vehicle across the island. Above him on the roof the radar wing revolved, turning through the fog. It was very quiet out on the pack as Papanin clenched his pipe and stared towards Target-5.

'Do you think Gorov will be with them?' Kramer asked.

'How the hell do I know? There are two possibilities—he is with them, or he isn't. If he is, the problem will be solved. If he isn't, we can go and take possession of an empty camp and wait for him. Can't you work out anything for yourself?'

The Siberian looked through the window to his left. When the fog drifted he could just see the outline of a second Sno-Cat, also stationary and with its engine silent. It carried eight more men, four of them armed with automatic weapons. He looked at his watch. 8.5 a.m. By 8.15 another piece would have been removed from the board.

Conway was on top of the ramp. He manœuvred the Cat with great care as he felt the front tracks dropping. Three years ago they had built up the ramp with supporting rocks taken from the hill, they had curved it to follow the cliff wall with a drop to the right so he had to turn the vehicle to the left slowly, keeping very close to the cliff wall.

He braked, kept the engine running, peered out of the window. The angled light shone on no firm surface: it dropped into the fog, gave you the feeling you were looking down a mountainside. Conway's hands were sticky inside his gloves as he went on peering down. Normally he would never have attempted the descent in conditions like these—he was wondering whether to reverse, to go back on to the island.

'To hell with that!'

He spoke the words aloud, a habit he had developed because he was so often alone, carrying out experiments on the pack. The fog obscured everything on the dangerous side; on the other side the light showed a blur of cliff wall. He'd have to concentrate on keeping close to the blur, resisting the temptation to look towards the drop.

Releasing the brake, he started the vehicle turning down the curve, a tricky operation because the huge rear tracks had to haul themselves round after the front caterpillars. He stared at the blurred wall barely a foot away and his seat tilted him forward as the Sno-Cat slanted downwards, its right-hand tracks less than a foot from the brink where the fog hid the pack below. The tracks crawled down the ramp, Conway's hand gripped the lever tightly, sweat dripped off his forehead. Thank God the Cat was responding, was going down nicely. Without warning the vehicle keeled and Conway felt it turning, dropping.

The outer edge of the ramp, where supporting rocks had been levered out of the ice, collapsed. The huge weight of the vehicle completed the disaster. While Conway was still fighting with the controls the Sno-Cat went over sideways, then went straight down twenty feet on to the hard pack. Conway had switched off the engine, an instinctive reflex when he was going over, and then he was upside down. The roof struck the ice and the terrible weight of the tracks came down on the up-ended floor of the cab, concertina-ing the tiny compartment, crushing the man inside into an unrecognizable shape of smashed bone, tissue, metal and glass.

A mile away on the far side of the island, unaware of the tragedy, Beaumont led his small party down to the pack the Russian security guards had just left, and headed westward.

Tuesday, 22 February: 10 a.m.—Noon

THIS WAS HOW the whole world—Europe, the Americas, Australasia, Asia, Africa—might look one day; a lifeless, sterile, frozen desert when the earth moved away from the sun and became an extinct satellite. It was like a preview of the death of the human race.

Wafted by the merest of breezes, a chilling stream of ice-cold air which came direct from the North Pole, the fog had shifted south, exposing the moonlit frozen desert Beaumont and the two sled teams were moving over. They had an endless view to the west and the north, the same God-awful expanse of ice, ice and more ice. Even in the land deserts of the world something grows somewhere; there are isolated oases, pockets of green trees and burning blue water. Here there was nothing but hideous ice—going on for ever.

Pressure ridges loomed in the moonlight ahead of them, a chaos of static ridges ten to twenty feet high. Guided by Grayson's erratic compass they were heading due west, sledding towards distant Greenland over a hundred miles away, and Beaumont was still wondering whether to take out his insurance policy—to head due south instead of west, south to the most dangerous place on earth, Iceberg Alley.

Since the fog had withdrawn its concealing curtain over an hour ago they had seen no sign of the Russians. It was possible that Papanin's men were still patrolling the fringes of Target-5, waiting for Gorov to come in.

Beaumont glanced over his shoulder as he drove his sled and Grayson hurried up to him. 'How is our first-class passenger getting on, Sam?'

'Gorov is a pain in the ass,' Grayson said inelegantly. 'He's still sulking over that cross-examination you put him through, and he sits on Horst's sled as though he's some kind of emperor. I'd make the bastard hoof it.'

'Later. He'd just hold us back at the moment. . . .' Beaumont broke off, looked quickly into the sky. A small dark blip was coming in from the north-east, heading directly towards them. Like an ugly bird it cruised across the night sky, too far off yet for the blur of its rotor disc to be seen, for the sound of its engine to be heard.

'Chopper! Get under cover. . . .'

Beaumont cracked his whip as he shouted the warning, driving the dogs faster towards the shelter of the pressure ridges while behind him Langer shouted at Gorov to get off the bloody sled, to run. The Russian tumbled off the moving sled, fell over on the ice, swore in his own language and then stumbled after them in desperate haste. The sound of the engine beat of the oncoming machine could be heard now, a faint sound growing louder by the second. Beaumont's team plunged through a gap in the first ice wall and then they were inside a corridor, halting as Beaumont pulled at the sled. Langer followed them through the gap as Gorov tried to catch up, still out in the open as the Soviet machine drummed closer. With a curse Grayson grabbed at the Russian and threw him under the lee of the ice wall.

They waited, staring up while the dogs, huddled together, also gazed at the sky.

The machine they could no longer see was flying low, no more than two hundred feet above the ice, and if it passed over them they were bound to be spotted. Crouched against the pressure wall which climbed fifteen feet above them, its crest curling over them like a breaking wave, they listened and watched for the helicopter to appear overhead. The throb-echo grew louder, vibrated down the ravine where they pressed themselves against the ice. And then Langer was in trouble with the dogs as two of them started to jump about, hating the helicopter's noise, equating it with the machine which had brought them to the edge of the fog bank. He slapped one hard and the animal turned on him, showed its teeth, let out a menacing growl. If the dogs careered out into the ravine it was certain they would be seen. Nothing shows from the air like movement.

Beaumont glanced over his shoulder anxiously, unable to leave his own team which was becoming infected by the commotion. He was astounded to see Gorov crawling along the ground on his knees, stretching out a hand and squeezing the rebellious animal's neck as he called to it in Russian. The animal relaxed, permitted itself to be stroked, and the second dog stopped struggling, staring as though it resented the special treatment its colleague was enjoying. Then something flashed over the ravine, the shadow of the machine.

Before there had been tension, anticipation, now they froze with fear, holding their breath without realizing it. And the dogs froze, too, remained absolutely still. They didn't see the helicopter—only its shadow—then it was flying westward, away from them. 'Stay here till I get back,' Beaumont ordered. Shielded by the pressure wall, he stood up and walked along it until he found a high point on its crest. He clambered up the wall carefully, jabbing his boots into crevices until he could peer over the crest.

It was a good lookout point. Beyond him more jagged ridges spread away, lower ridges he could see over, and about half a mile away the ridges ended and the ice flattened out. The belt of flat ice stretched into the distance like a sheet of plate glass, ideal terrain for them to sled across except for one thing— the Russians were in the way.

Small groups—he counted a dozen—were spaced out over the belt with long distances between them. And they were all sled-teams, moving slowly away from him, heading west towards far-away Greenland. Several miles across the ice two helicopters flew above the pack as though patrolling. The machine which had passed near them landed while he was watching, came down on the level ice close to one of the sled-teams. The rotors had hardly stopped whirling when the door opened and a stream of dogs poured out on to the ice. Men followed the animals, sleds were unloaded, and within minutes the men were harnessing the dogs. The speed of the operation impressed Beaumont. Ten minutes after he had first looked over the crest the helicopter took off, climbed to about five hundred feet and flew off to the north-east. Beaumont slithered back into the ravine, hurried back to where the others were waiting. The argument flared up almost at once.

'Well it missed us, thank Christ,' Grayson said.

'It wasn't looking too hard—it's just unloaded more sled-teams.'

'More?'

'Sam, not more than half a mile away to the west the ice is lousy with Russian search teams. Some of them are a long way west—and they've got choppers above them.'

'They're coming this way?'

'At the moment they're heading away from us. . . .'

'O.K. So we creep along behind them.'

'It won't work. Remember that wide belt of smooth ice we saw when we flew in over the pack? They're spread out across that. If we try to cross that belt they'll spot us. Papanin just slammed the door in our faces.'

Short of sleep, the memory of the air crash horror still fresh in his mind, Grayson faced Beaumont and his temper was going fast. 'You're dead wrong, Keith,' he said quietly. 'The only safe way out is westward. We have to hit the Greenland coast. Once we get there we're O.K.—the Russians can't invade Greenland.'

'A perfect plan,' Beaumont said sardonically, 'except the bit about hitting the Greenland coast. I keep telling you—the Russians are in the way. . . .'

'We can slip through those search teams. The ice is big—too big for them to cover it all.'

'You're not getting the message. It's not only the men on the ice—they're patrolling that belt from the air. . . .'

'So which way do we go?' Grayson flared. 'North towards the bloody Pole? East back to Target-5 where Papanin's waiting for us? South . . .'

'South,' Beaumont interjected. 'That's where we're going.'

Gorov, who had been listening intently, added his own contribution to the growing tension. 'South? That is madness. . . .'

'You're not invited into this debate,' Grayson told him

roughly. He turned back to Beaumont. 'We'd be heading straight for the edge of the icefield, straight for Iceberg Alley. I suppose when we get there we make the sleds seaworthy and float 'em all the way down to Cape Farewell?'

'Stop busting a gut,' Beaumont rapped back. 'We'll be going aboard the icebreaker *Elroy*. She's already coming hell for leather up Iceberg Alley—I fixed that with Dawes in Washington in case something like this happened.'

Grayson was astounded. 'And you really think we have a snowflake's chance in hell of rendezvousing with her?'

'We will rendezvous with her. She's coming up the tenth meridian and we go down it to meet her. You'll have to take frequent star-fixes to check our position.' The decision taken, Beaumont started forming up his own dog team, but Grayson hadn't finished yet.

'You make it sound like we'll be going down the New Jersey Turnpike. The star-fixes may not be accurate—you know that. It would be one pinpoint trying to find another pinpoint. . . .'

'With the aid of a little science.' Beaumont pointed to his sled. 'Don't forget we have the Elliott homing beacon. When we get within range of where the *Elroy* should be we'll send them a signal on the Redifon set. They'll send up the helicopter they have on board and it will home in on our beacon.'

'I don't like it.' Grayson looked at Langer who had listened to the argument in silence. 'Do you like it?'

'Look, Sam. . . .' Beaumont's voice hardened. 'That's the way it's going to be. We did the same thing once before when we made rendezvous with the *Edisto* near Spitsbergen.'

Grayson exploded. 'We were heading for land then! This time we'll be heading for the edge of the icefield—beyond that there's nothing but Iceberg Alley, the ocean . . .'

'Sam,' Langer intervened, 'before Keith started talking what was the last thing you'd have expected him to do?'

'Head south. . . .'

'So that's the last thing Papanin will expect us to do.'

Gorov, who had been clasping and unclasping his gloved hands, burst out suddenly. 'I do not think we should do this very crazy thing.'

Grayson turned round and spoke very deliberately to the Russian. 'If it wasn't for you, we wouldn't be in this mess. If you don't like it, you'd better start hiking your way back to Leningrad—because we're going south!'

He formed up his dogs and they moved off with Beaumont in the lead. Within five minutes they were turning through an angle of ninety degrees, heading south away from the great belt of ice where the going would have been so much easier. For over two hours they travelled across ice littered with ravines and pressure walls they had to thread their way through, then Beaumont called a brief halt. It was Grayson who sent the signal on the prearranged wavelength, the signal Dawes was waiting for at Curtis Field.

'Oxygen . . . Strongbow . . . Oxygen . . . Strongbow . . .'

He repeated the signal for five minutes before Curtis acknowledged, which was too long because it might be long enough for the Soviet monitors at North Pole 17 to take a radio-direction fix. But the signal had to get through. 'Strongbow' informed Dawes that Michael Gorov had been picked up; 'Oxygen' told him that Beaumont was heading south. Grayson telescoped the Redifon aerial back inside the set and looked up at the sky.

'No Russian planes for two hours,' he said. 'And no American planes either,' he added. 'Those pilots at Curtis must have gone home for the winter. I hope to God the icebreaker *Elroy* hasn't gone home too. . . .'

'. . . *urgent you penetrate icefield for possible rendezvous. Maximum risk must be accepted. Repeat. Must be accepted.*

Commander Alfred Schmidt, U.S.N., captain of the 6,515-ton icebreaker *Elroy*, still didn't like the signal he had received from Washington three days earlier, and the more he thought about it the less he liked the last part of the signal. 'Maximum risk. . . .' What the hell was a maximum risk in these waters? Did you decide that maybe you'd had enough when the ship was going down because it was overladen with ice, because it had just struck an iceberg? Schmidt, forty-three years old, five feet eight tall and very wide-shouldered, had thick dark hair and thick dark brows. His expression was invariably bleak, not to say grim. And he only smiled in moments of extreme danger, which was the origin of the toast seamen drank to when they had their last beers in a bar in Milwaukee, the *Elroy's* home port.

'Here's hopin'—no smilin' from the cap'n till we hit port again.'

'Care to take a look, sir?' Vance Carlson, the mate, stood back from the radarscope and pulled up the collar of his coat. The high bridge of the *Elroy* was heated but something seemed to have gone wrong with the system. Perhaps the something was the Arctic conditions outside which were keeping a team of men permanently at work shovelling ice over the side, ice which seemed to form as rapidly as they cast it into the floe-littered sea.

Commander Schmidt didn't care to take a look, but he looked all the same. Three hours earlier when he had looked down inside the rubber hood he had seen isolated blips showing on the scope, blips which were not ships, blips to the north-west and north-east. He stared down as he watched the sweep turning remorselessly round the greenish glow inside the hood. No more isolated blips now; instead a solid unbroken pattern of echoes filled the screen, congealing into a wall-to-wall band.

'The barrier,' Carlson commented unnecessarily. 'Dead ahead.'

Schmidt remembered the end of the signal again as he continued staring down into the hood. The barrier. A solid wall of icefield was stretched across his path and the *Elroy*, its engines beating heavily, its reinforced bow brushing aside great floes of ice like matchsticks, was heading straight for the dreaded wall which stretched from the coast of Spitsbergen to Greenland. The trouble was that Schmidt had to find a way in, a place where the icefield was barely above sea level, a point where he could use the massive bows of the ship to smash his way inside the ice. At least they had the radar to show them what lay ahead. He prayed to God there wouldn't be fog.

Two hours later the menace drifted off the icefield. Fog trails like wisps of steam floated off the ice across the *Elroy's* path. Schmidt was standing close to the clear-vision panel at the front of the bridge, looking down at the deck and ahead alternatively. Neither view enchanted him. The ice on the fore-peak was piling up faster, the new team of men was fighting a losing battle as they heaved it over the ice-coated rails where it toppled down on to more ice drifting on the sea. The temperature was fifty below.

'Polar bears. . . .'

At the starboard side of the bridge Carlson was looking at the top of the ice wall that was as high as the bridge itself and no further away than a few cable-lengths. On the foredeck below men glanced up at the wall above them; it was like looking up the side of a building. In the moonlight three yellowish blurs stared down at them, three polar bears at the brink of the ice-field attracted by the smell of the garbage the cook had just emptied overboard.

The engines were dead slow, a regular, powerful throb which reassured Schmidt: earlier they had been badly delayed in their dash back to the north because of engine trouble. The view ahead did not reassure him at all. 'Vance, I think you'd better take a spell in the cage. We don't want to miss our way in. . . .'

There was reluctance in the voice which gave the order, a reluctance certainly shared by the mate a few minutes later as he mounted the ice-sheathed ladder up the hundred-foot mast leading to the observation cage. It wasn't the most comfortable post on the *Elroy*—not in a temperature of fifty below and not with fog coming up. The observation cage at the *Elroy's* mast-head wasn't larger than two telephone kiosks and Carlson experienced his usual sense of claustrophobia as he settled on the leather-topped stool. Thirty-two years old, the same age as Beaumont, Vance Carson had got married only one day before his ship left Milwaukee. He had been counting the days of the voyage home when the ship had turned round and headed back to the icefield. Like the Captain, the mate did not love Beaumont.

After a quick glance through his clear-vision panel Carlson hitched the harness over his head, adjusted the mike under his chin and checked with the bridge. 'In position, sir. There's a big berg dead ahead.'

'We've seen it. . . .' Schmidt's voice came up the wire. 'Any sign of an entry point?'

'None at all, sir. It's as solid as a mountain.'

'Keep looking.'

Carlson experienced a sense of claustrophobia inside the cage; perversely he also experienced a sense of being horribly exposed. The walls which surrounded him, which he could reach out and touch with his extended elbows, were armour-glass, and their transparency made him feel, if this were possible, even colder. On the bridge below the heating wasn't totally effective; inside the observation cage it seemed totally ineffective, as though it had lost itself on its way up the mast.

One hundred feet above the deck, Carlson had an all-round view. To port, to starboard, below. The vessel seemed to be hardly moving, the bow slamming into huge floes as big as houses, cube-shaped floes which looked like sugar lumps seen from the cage. The flock of cubes divided, slid past either side of the ship, and beyond them the minor monster loomed, its peak high above Carlson's head, apparently motionless as though anchored to the seabed. But the berg wasn't anchored, it was drifting south, south towards the *Elroy* while the ship steamed north.

Carlson clubbed his gloved hands together, leaned sideways off his stool as he stared one way, then another. Above where he sat the large radar wing revolved steadily, transmitting its warning echoes to the hooded scope on the bridge. To starboard the ice wall slid past, the polar bears long since vanished. Below, the lozenge-shaped deck was so laden with ice that from the cage it appeared to be a fragment broken away from the main icefield. Carlson pressed the send-switch. 'Heavy fog coming up, sir. About a quarter-mile away—dead ahead. . . .'

Thirty minutes later Carlson was isolated. He couldn't see a thing. He was also very cold. The numbness which had begun in his feet and hands was spreading. To keep himself alert he was standing up and the four walls of glass were frosted over, coated with a deadly white rime which was growing thicker by the minute. His only view was through the clear-vision panel, and when he peered through this he saw only fog, creeping, ice-laden fog which had blotted out the icefield. Even the deck was invisible and he might have been inside the cabin of a plane in the night.

'You'd better come down, Carlson,' Schmidt ordered.

'I'll stay up a bit longer. It may clear.'

'Fifteen minutes. Then come down. . . .'

Carlson pressed his face against the clear-vision panel and the glass was freezing, like pressing into ice itself. He saw nothing. A dense mass of moisture. Nothing more. The vessel was almost stationary, moving at slow-slow speed with the aid of the radar wing above Carlson's head, the metal eye which would throw back a warning echo when an iceberg loomed dead ahead. But the mechanism wasn't foolproof under these conditions and on the bridge below, DaSilva, deputy mate and an experienced radar man, was staring anxiously down at the scope, waiting for it to go wild, to ping-ping-ping—warning that something big was close to the bows. The engines beat with a slow monotony while Carlson, the loneliest man aboard, went on staring hypnotically at the fog rolling inches from his face.

'Anything yet, Vance?'

'Nothing yet.'

In the cage Carlson had checked every window when he saw a change in the fog ahead. He couldn't see anything specific, but there was a change, a faint motion as though the vapour was affected by the merest of air currents. He stopped banging his gloves together, stood quite still with his face again pressed into the panel. Yes, there was something, something which was disturbing the fog like a giant spoon stirring it gently.

The warning ping on the scope came too late, too suddenly, and afterwards Schmidt had to speak forcefully to convince DaSilva that there was nothing he could have done. Nothing. It was too quick. On the scope the sweep went round and abruptly there was a new image. DaSilva raised his head, started shouting. . . .

Carlson probably never saw it coming. If he did it could

only have been for a fraction of a second. The ice claw, the huge rampart projecting across the *Elroy*'s path was eighty feet above the deck surface. It stretched out like a gigantic arm, thrust out across the path of the *Elroy* as though trying to hold it back. The ship steamed on, slowly. The claw came over the bows, over the deck. The masthead struck it. One shattering, shearing blow. They heard the crack on the bridge as DaSilva had his mouth open to shout a warning, a crack which sent terror into their brains. The masthead was sliced off, eighty feet above the deck. The cage, eighty-five feet up, toppled with the severed mast. Sealed inside the cage, Carlson went down with it. It hit the deck-rail, eighty-five feet below, on the starboard side, smashed away a section, went on down into the sea with Carlson inside it. The severed head weighed five tons and went straight down, taking Carlson and the radar wing with it, down into the Arctic where the depth varies between nine and ten thousand feet. It can only be hoped that the mate was dead before the sea burst in.

The roll of the dead was beginning to mount. Vance Carlson was the twentieth casualty so far—including Nikolai Marov, Gorov's security guard, Tillotson, the sixteen who died aboard the plane on Target-5, and Matthew Conway.

And the radar was gone. The *Elroy* was blind, engulfed in fog, surrounded by ice, on the verge of the icefield itself, an icefield no one could see. This was beyond maximum risk, far beyond it; if any situation justified Alfred Schmidt in turning round and making slowly for home, this was it.

At Curtis Field the code-signal, 'Oxygen-Strongbow', had been received and understood. 'We have Gorov, we are moving south to rendezvous with the *Elroy*.'

It was not the only information Dawes had received as he paced round the small office which had been made over to him, an office which glowed with warmth from the three heaters under the windows. The atmosphere was seventy degrees and the warmth caressed his red face as Adams perched on a chair tilted against a wall and watched him.

'The ice west of Target-5 is crawling with Russians,' he

growled as he chewed at his unlit cigar. 'They've got choppers over the ice and sled-teams down on the pack—and the Cats are beginning to appear.'

'It looks tricky,' Adams said.

'In Washington you said it would be simple,' Dawes reminded him. He looked up as Fuller, the airfield controller, hurried into the room. 'Time you got here. I want intensive air surveillance over the entire area between the coast and Target-5. I want one-third of the machines you send up concentrated on the ice north of Target-5. . . .' He went over to the map he had brought with him which was pinned to the wall. 'Here—and here.'

'Nothing to the south?' Fuller queried.

'Nothing! And I want non-stop surveillance. They go out, they come back, they refuel, they go out again. . . .'

'There's a limit to how much the pilots can take,' Fuller pointed out.

'Find that limit—then push them beyond it.'

'I don't get it,' Adams said when Fuller had gone. 'Beaumont's heading south, so why send the aircraft west and north?'

'If you don't get it, maybe Papanin won't. Our chances of spotting Beaumont from the air in the polar waste are nil—unless we got lucky. I'm not counting on that. So I'm launching a deception operation.' Dawes paused as the blast of a helicopter's rotor went past beyond the window. 'Papanin has a whole fleet of choppers scouring the ice. In a couple of hours he'll hear of my air surveillance, so what will he assume? That I'm looking for Gorov—that I know where to look. He'll withdraw his machines from the south and that may give Beaumont a chance to get out of range.'

'It could work, I suppose. . . .'

'It will work!' Dawes grinned crookedly. 'I'm sending that bastard Siberian a signal—Beaumont is coming out north or west.'

'North or west?'

Papanin muttered the words to himself as he gazed down at his pocket chess board in the North Pole 17 headquarters hut.

On the table beside the board was a book open at the page recording the moves in the Fischer-Spassky game at Santa Monica in 1966. The Siberian prided himself on being able to do three things at once: play his own game, study another mans' game, and take a decision on the current operation.

'All the machines are in the air,' Kramer reported from behind his chair. 'They are concentrating on the northern and western approaches to Target-5—all except the six helicopters you told me to hold back.'

After the American Sno-Cat had crashed over the ramp they had paid a second visit to Target-5 and they had found the island deserted. No one was there—although Papanin did not realize that two men, Rickard and Sondeborg, should have still been at the camp. The Siberian had left a small detachment to wait in case Gorov arrived, and had then gone straight back to his own base. Until he received the signal from Petrov at Leningrad Records he had been puzzled.

'The Beaumont force we kept talking about doesn't exist,' he commented as he fingered a pawn.

We? The Balt said nothing. When things went right Papanin invariably referred to events in the first person singular. When trouble loomed there were references to 'we' as the Siberian included him in the mess.

Papanin pushed back his chair, placed one booted leg carefully on the table beside the little chess board, and explained. The signal had come back from Leningrad in reply to his query. The diligent Petrov had burrowed deep into the massive archives and the mystery was solved.

In 1971 the Americans had sent a three-man team clear across the pack from Greenland to Spitsbergen. The achievement was never reported in the press, but a Soviet agent in Spitsbergen had sent a vague report. The expedition had obvious military implications: in case of real trouble Soviet forces might attempt to occupy Norwegian Spitsbergen—as the Americans had occupied Iceland in the last war. The Americans had foreseen this; if they could send men in over the pack they had a chance of occupying Spitsbergen first. So they had quietly sent a small team to see if it could be managed.

'It doesn't seem relevant,' Kramer protested.

'Doesn't it?' Papanin grinned unpleasantly as he filled his pipe. 'Beaumont is the name of the British Arctic expert who led the team to Spitsbergen. He had two men with him—an American, Samuel Grayson, and a German, Horst Langer. I think that big swine who had so much to say for himself at Target-5 was Beaumont.'

'They wouldn't send in only three men to take out Gorov. . . .'

'Wouldn't they? It could be clever, it could be enough. How easy is it to spot four men from the air in the polar wastes, Kramer?'

'So there's no large expedition?' Kramer said dubiously.

'Just Beaumont and his friends. Remember those three men we filmed slipping into the fog two days ago?' Papanin's tone changed. 'Send a coded signal to all planes in the air—they are looking for a very small group. Probably two sled-teams and four men only.'

'And the six machines still waiting?'

'They are to fly south—due south of Target-5.'

'But the Americans are looking north and west. . . .'

'Carry out my orders immediately,' Papanin said quietly.

Alone in the hut, the Siberian dropped his leg to the floor and frowned as he studied the chess board. Some of his more bizarre decisions he never explained: it was part of his technique for keeping his subordinates in permanent awe of their huge chief.

Like De Gaulle, Colonel Papanin believed in surrounding himself with a certain mystic aura—it also helped when some of the decisions turned out to be wrong. No one knew what you had been trying to do in the first place.

But Papanin had a definite suspicion in his head, a growing suspicion. During the flight of the Bison bomber from Murmansk he had studied a dossier on Lemuel Quincey Dawes, whose speciality was deception operations. He couldn't ignore the obvious—that the concentration of American machines north and west of Target-5 was indeed searching for the Beaumont group; if it all went wrong he would be severely criticized for not checking those areas. But the southern sector was beginning to interest him.

Kramer came back into the hut a few minutes later. 'They will be airborne within five minutes,' he informed the Siberian.

'Excellent. Now send a signal to the carrier *Gorki* that I need an immediate check on the position of the American icebreaker *Elroy*.'

Mystified again, Kramer hurried away to the wireless hut. And again Papanin carefully did not give reasons. When the Beaumont team was approaching Spitsbergen in 1971 it had made a prearranged rendezvous with the icebreaker *Edisto*; now another icebreaker was involved, the *Elroy*. Papanin had an idea he was getting close to Beaumont as he made up his mind and moved the pawn.

Tuesday, 22 February: Noon—7 p.m.

BEAUMONT wouldn't listen to reason; perhaps it would be more accurate to say Beaumont wouldn't listen to anyone as he kept men and dogs moving remorselessly, driving them on, refusing to stop for food or drink, refusing to stop for anything or anyone as they moved further and further south down the tenth meridian and closer and closer to the edge of the ice-field, to Iceberg Alley.

Hemmed in by pressure ridges, huge walls of jagged ice which loomed all around them, they sledded south down the ravines in the moonlight. And Beaumont had now taken over Langer's team, had the powerful Bismarck as his lead dog as he gripped the handlebar and cracked his whip over the dogs' heads.

Which was an unmistakable sign that they were all going to be driven to their limits as Langer observed to Grayson—to their limits and beyond them.

This was what had happened during the last stages of their drive over the pack to Spitsbergen and their rendezvous with another icebreaker, the *Edisto*. Beaumont had taken over the Bismarck dog team and they had never let up for twelve hours —not until the *Edisto* was in sight, the Elliott homing beacon had been switched on, the radio signal had been sent and the chopper from the icebreaker had come winging towards them. This time it was Langer who started the argument, who thought that Beaumont had over-reached himself. He handed over his sled-team to Grayson, ran ahead down the ravine and caught up with Beaumont.

'I don't think we can keep this up much longer . . .' he panted.

'Keep moving!'

Beaumont, his face set inside the narrow aperture of fur hood, cracked the whip, coaxed a little more speed out of Bismarck and the other animals increased pace. They came to a bend in the ravine but Beaumont didn't slacken pace; he took the sled round on one runner and it scudded over the hard ice.

'This is crazy,' Langer blazed. 'We need some rest—the dogs need some rest. The *Elroy* is miles and miles away. We can't possibly make it tonight. . . .'

'We have to keep moving, for Christ's sake! Every half-mile is a half-mile closer to the *Elroy*. It's better than that—the bloody ship is moving towards us!'

'Gorov is feeling the strain.'

Beaumont glanced quickly over his shoulder. Behind him Grayson was driving the second team, forcing them to keep up with Bismarck—and Beaumont. Behind them the Russian followed on foot, his teeth gritted as he fought to keep up with them. It was a deliberate, brutal act of policy on Beaumont's part to put him at the rear; travelling on a sled he slowed everything down, but following them on foot Gorov was constantly afraid that he would be left behind, lost in the polar waste, and his fear of being left was keeping him moving, was forcing him to summon up reserves of energy he didn't even know he had. 'He'll move if he's scared,' Beaumont had said three hours earlier, 'so keep him scared.'

'He knew it wouldn't be any picnic when he left North Pole 17,' Beaumont snapped. 'Don't talk to him—I want him running scared. And don't talk to me—I have to watch this sled.'

Langer dropped back: Beaumont was in one of his foulest moods, you couldn't reason with him any more. They'd just have to keep moving. But Beaumont's temper was under perfect control: he had simply chosen the simplest method of shutting Langer up. And his grim rush across the ice was based on cold calculation. For three hours they had seen no sign of a Russian helicopter. Why, he had no idea, nor did he care, but now the moonlit sky above the pack was clear of the enemy he was determined to make the most of it, to get as far south as possible while they didn't have to worry about hiding from Papanin's eyes in the sky.

Nor had he thought it wise to reveal to the others that if humanly possible they were going to keep moving until they sighted the *Elroy*. For some unknown reason they had been given a golden opportunity to get clear, an opportunity which might never recur. Privately he doubted whether they would sight the *Elroy* that night, but it wasn't an impossible hope and he was going to drive them until they dropped. An hour later the American plane appeared to the south-east.

'Halt!'

Beaumont jerked up his arm to warn those behind him and it felt like jerking up a heavy weight. He pulled at the sled to stop the dogs, handed the whip to Grayson, then forced himself to start climbing the pressure wall to his left. His fatigue was so enormous it felt like climbing a mountain and as he clawed his way up the ice wall the distant murmur of the machine's engine urged him to hurry, hurry. It was a different sound, not the deadly beat-beat of a Soviet helicopter. Once he slipped but his clawing gloves saved him as he grabbed at the crest of the ridge and hauled himself over it. The night-glasses slung round his neck struck his jaw but he was hardly aware of the pain as he sat astride the crest and raised the glasses.

They were almost out of the pressure ridge maze: just ahead of them the frozen sea stretched away like a level plain; very much like a frozen sea with ripples congealed on its surface. The plane, two thousand feet up, was flying south-west and would soon pass them at a distance of about half a mile. He fumbled with the focusing mechanism. Russian or American? The silhouette came up as a blur, so he thought he had the focus wrong, then he realized it was his tired eyes. His eyes cleared, the machine crisped in the lenses, a white star painted on its fuselage. American!

'Sam! Get a smoke flare off my sled. It's American. . . .'

The exhausted men down in the ravine were galvanized. Grayson tore open the fastenings, Langer grabbed a flare while Gorov watched the dogs, climbed half-way up the ice wall with the flare which Beaumont took from his extended hand. His fingers were so frozen he had trouble dealing with the flare. He tried to set it off, tried again. Nothing happened. 'Give me another,' Beaumont shouted. 'This one's a dud. . . .'

There was a frantic scramble as Grayson and Langer struggled to locate a second flare, and while they searched, the plane with red and green lights at its wingtips began to turn, moving in an arc which would take it on a fresh course due south. 'Hurry up, for God's sake!' Beaumont roared. He saw that Grayson had found a flare, was going to bring it up to him. 'Set it off down there in the ravine!'

The flare ignited, gushed dark smoke, climbed in the still air like an Indian signal, billowed, went higher and higher. And the plane went away, continued south, growing smaller and smaller by the second. Grayson and Langer scrambled up on to the crest beside him.

'It hasn't gone. . . .'

There was anguish in Grayson's voice, crushing anguish, and his shoulders sagged. 'Look back, you bloody fool,' Beaumont said quietly. They watched the plane to vanishing point. A silver pinhead in the moonlight, it disappeared suddenly, leaving behind only the fading sound of its engine. 'It was a routine weather flight,' Beaumont observed, 'they weren't looking for us.'

'I would like to shoot the Goddamned so-called observer in that machine,' Langer said with quiet venom. 'Maybe we should have used the radio.'

'No!' Beaumont's tone was sharp. 'We're not using that till we're within range of the *Elroy*. At this very moment there will be a Soviet monitor crouched over his set waiting for us to do just that—so he can take a radio-direction fix. We'll get moving.'

The smoke flare climbed above them as they moved off in silence. Even the dogs seemed subdued, felt to be pulling the sleds with less vigour as they emerged from the pressure ridges and went out on to the plain of ice. Afterwards Beaumont blamed himself for not thinking of the danger, for taking them out on to the exposed ice too soon, but the disappointment and the fatigue had dulled his brain. His arms and wrists were aching with the strain, felt as though they were on fire, half-pulled out of their sockets after hours of wrestling with the bucking sled. The numbing cold was weakening his grip on the handlebar, he had to make an enormous effort to keep tramping forward with an appearance of vigour, to keep the others moving.

'Look out!'

It was Langer who shouted the warning. 'Keep still!' Beaumont shouted his own warning as he brought the dogs to a sudden halt. Behind them the night was shattered with a beating roar. Rat-tat-tat throbs echoed across the ice. The nose of the shadow was bulbous with a second, smaller bulb below it. Twin rotors whipped the air, one above the other. A double-finned tail. Like an evil metal bird it swept over their heads at fifty feet, the ground shadow slicing over the ice. A twin-jet submarine killer. The latest Soviet helicopter.

'Don't move!'

Beaumont reinforced his warning as the machine flew away from them, climbing now and beginning to turn. There was a chance that the men inside the Russian machine hadn't seen them. Moving at fifty miles an hour—Beaumont's estimate of the helicopter's speed—flashing over the ice where it had suddenly burst upon them from behind the pressure ridges, a Soviet observer would need sharp eyes to spot them. Seconds later he knew that sharp eyes had looked down on them from the machine. It was coming back. It was the smoke flare which had caused the disaster: the flare the American plane had never seen had guided a nearby Russian machine to them.

'What the hell is he going to do?' Langer asked.

'Depends how many men he has aboard,' Beaumont replied tersely.

It was travelling slower—and higher—coming in at least two hundred feet above them. So they had not only spotted the sled teams, they had also seen the rifles looped over the men's shoulders. Beaumont handed over his restless team to Grayson and stood a few yards away, his rifle in his hands. The oncoming submarine killer was a menacing shape, all bulges and rotors, and when it was almost above them it began hovering while its drumbeat hammered the ice. Beaumont hoisted his rifle.

The helicopter ceased hovering, banked and began swinging in a wide circle, trailing a gauze of vapour in the cold atmosphere. They had to swing on their heels to follow the helicopter as it went round them, its engines drumming away. Then Langer grunted, hoisted his weapon. 'They've got a telescopic sight on us. . . .' Looping his rifle over his shoulder, Beaumont snatched up his night-glasses.

'Drop that rifle!' Beaumont spoke quickly as he continued watching the machine through his glasses, pivoting on his boots. A window had been lowered in the dome and the moonlight reflected off something with a cylindrical muzzle. 'It's a cine-camera,' Beaumont warned. 'They're taking pictures of us—a nice peaceful occupation. With a telephoto lens,' he added.

As he spoke the helicopter turned away, presented its double tail-fins towards them and flew off to the north-east. The beat of its twin rotors was fading rapidly as Beaumont ran back to his sled and took over from Grayson. 'I can't figure why it didn't land,' the American said.

'My guess would be they hadn't enough men aboard.' Beaumont stared across the belt of level ice into the distance where more ridges reared up like hill ranges. 'And now we really have to get moving before they catch us in the open again. Because when the Russians do come back they'll have more than enough men.'

'Hold that frame!'

The Siberian's voice roared in the silence of the smoke-filled hut, a silence broken only by the whirring of the film projector. The operator stopped the machine, the image on the screen froze, the image of four men staring up at the camera, one man with a rifle, another man aiming a pair of glasses. A bloated shadow crossed the screen as Papanin stood up and pointed, his shadow fingertip touching a man holding the handlebar of a sled.

'That's him,' Papanin rumbled. 'That's Gorov. I'll bet my pension on it.'

'You can't see his face,' Kramer objected from the darkness. 'You can't see any of the faces. . . .'

'Bugger the faces! I watched the way this man moved, the way he cocks his head to one side. That's Gorov, that's our target.' The enormous fingertip shadow moved, touched the fur-clad figure with glasses. 'And I think that's Beaumont. The other two must be Samuel Grayson and Horst Langer.'

'We recall all the planes from the north and west?' the Balt asked, anxious to anticipate the next order.

'You switch on the damned lights in this hut first,' Papanin said softly. He looked round at one of the men sitting behind him. 'Vronsky, you can find them again?'

The twenty-eight-year-old Russian who had led the security detachment brought from Murmansk stood up and went over to a wall map. Small, lean and mournful-faced, Andrei Vronsky had lost both his parents a month earlier when they had tried to drive over the frozen Volga near Stalingrad: the river had cracked and swallowed them up. 'Here, Colonel,' he pointed to the cross he had drawn. 'We took a star-fix. . . .'

'So you are confident?'

'We did find them. . . .' Vronsky stopped speaking when he noticed the Siberian's expression.

'You found their bloody smoke flare!' Papanin roared. 'You saw it from five miles away and changed course—you said so when I questioned you. God knows why they let off that flare—maybe it went off by accident.'

'I suppose we were lucky. . . .'

'So I'll show you how to be lucky again!' Papanin took the pencil off Vronsky and stared at the map. 'They are heading for a rendezvous with the American icebreaker *Elroy* which is here. Draw a line down from Target-5 and you see they are moving down the tenth meridian.'

'So we fly down that. . . .'

'You shut up and listen! They will change direction for awhile to throw us off the scent—they'll go either south-south-east or south-south-west.' Papanin drew two slanting lines from the south to the point where Beaumont had been seen. 'Later they will resume their course due south. Allowing for star-fix error, for ice-drift, you will find them inside this triangle. Understand?'

'It makes sense, Colonel. . . .'

'Everything I say makes sense.' He looked over his shoulder at Kramer. 'This time every machine must carry a section of armed men.'

'We haven't enough for all the machines.'

'Who the hell said we were going to withdraw all of them— and immediately warn Dawes that his deception operation has failed? I'm leaving half the pieces on the board to the north and west of Target-5. The other half come back here, refuel, and then scour my triangle.'

They left the hut quickly before the Siberian could comment on their slowness while Papanin remained staring up at the wall map and sucking at his little pipe. 'I think I've got you this time, Mr Beaumont,' he said to himself.

Tuesday, 22 February: 7 p.m.—11.30 p.m.

IT HAD BECOME a nightmare: Russian machines were within hearing all the time. Sometimes the deadly rat-tat-tat beat was a long way off, little more than a murmur in the bitterly cold night as they dragged their weary limbs down more ravines, under the lee of more pressure ridge walls, but even when it was only a murmur you had to listen hard, to concentrate—so that you detected the moment when it started becoming louder, when it was coming in your direction.

At other times it was close, far too close for comfort, the wicked beat rising to a loud cacophony which echoed along the ravines and reverberated over the icy crests. It was, Beaumont admitted to himself, only a matter of time before they were seen—unless they were incredibly lucky. It was only a matter of time because, despite the frequent requests of Grayson and Langer, he obstinately kept them moving—and movement can be seen from the air.

The constant need to listen, to stay on the alert, was now wearing them down as much as driving the sleds, driving their own legs to keep on the move. By ten in the evening the four exhausted men were moving like automatons, their limbs sluggish, their eyes half-closed with the fatigue and the cold, and Gorov had twice said he couldn't go any further, that he must travel on one of the sleds. Beaumont's reaction had been quick and to the point. 'You'll either keep up or die on the ice.'

'But this is why you are here!' Gorov had protested as he stumbled alongside Beaumont's sled. 'You came to collect me!'

'It's got beyond that now,' the Englishman had told him grimly. 'It's a question of our survival—so keep up or drop, I don't care which any more.'

When Gorov had dropped back, Beaumont sneaked a look

over his shoulder, and the Russian was plodding on beside Langer's sled while in the distance Grayson was completing another star-fix. Beaumont had no intention of leaving the Russian behind; if he collapsed he would have to be carried on a sled. Oddly enough, faced with the prospect of a lonely death on the ice, Gorov was able to keep going.

But the real havoc was played with their nerves and tempers, and now it was becoming dangerous for one man to speak to another because whatever was said it was always the wrong thing. It was just after ten o'clock when Grayson decided that he had had enough, that they had run out of luck, that this time they had to stop before Beaumont's madness destroyed them all. He finished packing the sextant back inside Langer's moving sled and hurried to catch up with Beaumont.

'Another plane coming up—from the east. I'm getting on top of a ridge to check. . . .'

'Conserve your energy,' Beaumont snapped. 'It's a long way off. . . .'

'It's coming this way! It's louder already. Do we wait till the bloody thing is on top of us?'

'Yes!'

'Why, for God's sake?'

Beaumont took a tighter grip on the handlebar, and there was barely suppressed fury in his voice as he replied. 'Because we are not playing their game—Papanin's game. Haven't you grasped what's happening? These are random flights—criss-crossing the ice.'

'One of them will spot us. . . .'

'If he's lucky, yes. But he'll have to be damned lucky to spot us down inside these ravines. To do that he'll have to fly direct overhead. When that's going to happen we freeze against the wall—I've already hammered that into you.'

'It may be too late then.'

Beaumont took a deep breath, stared at Grayson, then grabbed at the sled with both hands as it nearly toppled sideways. He spoke in a cold, deliberate monotone. 'We have to get further south than Papanin thinks is possible before we rest. These planes are looking for us, yes. But they're also trying to wear us down, to make us stop every time we hear one, so that we never get a chance to reach the *Elroy*. . . .' He stiffened as the rat-tat-tat he had been listening to while he talked loudened to a roar. 'Get under cover!'

They stopped the dogs, sprawled beside them to calm the animals, crashed down full length on the ice and seconds later the helicopter boomed over them, the hellish clatter of its engines deafening them. It swept over them from east to west, flashed across the ravine two hundred feet up, then it was gone. They remained perfectly still because they didn't know yet— whether they had been seen. If they had, it would come back. Dropping prone on to the ice shook each man badly, muffled as they were in their layers of clothing, because prone they didn't feel like getting up again. They lay in the ravine along-side their twitching animals, calming them, their bodies frozen, their resistance very low indeed. When the machine didn't come back they clambered slowly to their feet and Grayson tried once more, croaking the words.

'Keith, we ought to stop . . . to eat. . . .'

Beaumont shook his head slowly, listened, and couldn't hear the sound of any machine. Painfully, he began to climb up the nearest ice wall, slithering back several times before he got anywhere near the crest. It was time to check the view ahead. Once more. Reaching the top, he nearly fell backwards, but regained his balance. He rubbed at the lenses of his night-glasses to clear them, perched his elbows on the crest, raised them to his weary eyes. He could see a long distance, a very long distance indeed. He scanned the blurred horizon, dropped the glasses a fraction, stared through them steadily, then lowered them as he looked down into the ravine. 'I think you'd better come up here,' he said quietly.

'Well?' Papanin demanded.

'Nothing yet.' Vronsky closed the door of the hut. 'I've just come back—it looks pretty hopeless.'

'Hopeless, did you say?' Papanin stood up slowly from his chair and Kramer, who knew him, took an involuntary step away from the Siberian. 'You're gutless, Vronsky. You're not fit to lead a detachment. In this game it's the man who goes on longest who wins. I'll have to consider your position when this is over. You were going to eat? Skip the meal, Vronsky— you're aboard the next helicopter that takes off.' He waited until the Russian had left. 'It's going to be difficult if they reach the *Elroy*, Kramer,' he remarked.

The Balt was startled. It was the first time Papanin had even suggested that Beaumont might reach the ship. 'Difficult?' he queried. 'Impossible once Gorov is aboard an American ship. . . .'

'Not impossible, but difficult, yes.' The Siberian's tone was deceptively quiet. 'The thing would begin to assume huge dimensions. Our people back home would start fretting— because of the American president's visit to Moscow in May.'

'We may be lucky. . . .'

'I make my own luck!' Papanin's fist crashed down on the table which was now bare: the little chess set was inside his pocket. 'We are changing our tactics,' he rumbled. 'From now on we sweep north from the *Elroy*—we'll meet them coming in over the ice. When a machine finds our target it lands as close to them as possible—I don't care how bad the ice is under them.'

'And if the men with Gorov resist?'

'This is the second order you will issue at once. Give it personally to each leader of the armed parties—the pilot must not hear you. We don't want the men with Gorov—they are an embarrassment, so lose them. Bury the bodies under the ice— If an open lead is available drop them into it. The dogs must be killed as well—poisoned meat would be best. And lose the sleds. By midnight, Kramer! Earlier if possible. . . .'

It had to be a mirage, Beaumont thought when he first saw it in his night-glasses. The image blurred, went away, then came back again as he readjusted the lenses to their original fix. He called down to the men inside the ravine. Langer reached him first; caught by something in Beaumont's voice he mounted the ice wall quickly, then flopped beside the Englishman on the crest. His face was whiskered as he pulled open his hood to use the glasses, whiskered and still smeared with fog-streaks many hours old.

'Over there. The thing sticking up.'

Beaumont pointed and Langer, his fingers trembling with anxiety, tried to get a fix. For another three miles ahead the terrible jumble of pressure ridges continued, like a stormy sea with massive waves coming towards them, a stormy sea frozen suddenly in mid-fury. Beyond this was level ice, very level ice indeed, a vast sheet gleaming in the moonlight. In the middle of it was the mirage, something which, if photographed, would look totally unreal. 'Good God!' Langer muttered the exclamation and fell silent.

The mirage was a high-masted ship with a high bridge, a ship made of ice and snow, almost like an unsuccessful wedding cake. In the night-glasses Langer saw that its bows pointed towards him, that it was crusted and coated and mired with ice so that in the moonlight it glittered like a ship made of glass. Icicles hung from the crosstree, from the jagged tip of the mast. Its rails dripped a curtain of ice like the edge of a counterpane flung casually over the foredeck. The bows were very high, as though mounting a huge wave, but the vessel was absolutely stationary, embedded in the pack, and the only clue that it might not have been abandoned was the lights at the tips of the crosstree. It was not a mirage. It was the American icebreaker *Elroy*, ten miles from the nearest ocean, hemmed in by the pack.

'Good God!' Langer muttered again.

'You said that before,' Beaumont reminded him. 'You must be getting old—you're repeating yourself.'

'I feel old.' Langer corrected himself. 'I felt old! Hey, Sam, it's the *Elroy*!'

Leaving Gorov to watch over the dogs, Grayson had hauled himself up on to the crest. 'Don't kid me,' he croaked. Langer handed him the glasses. 'See for yourself.' The American opened his hood, exposed an equally haggard, grizzled face, and focused the glasses.

'How the hell did it ever get in so far?' Langer wondered.

'Guts,' Beaumont said. 'I've never met Schmidt, the captain, but he's smashed his way through that stuff inch by inch to get in close to us. The funny thing is I can't see his radar.'

'I do know him,' Grayson said quietly. 'He's a number one bastard—and that's why he's here. How close do you reckon he is?'

'Seven miles away at a guess,' Beaumont replied. 'Any objections to us pushing on?'

They pushed on for two miles at a speed they hadn't achieved for hours, threading their way through the maze of ravines until they were within one mile of the open ice. And because there were still no Russian choppers in the sky Beaumont decided that now they could send the signal and activate the Elliott homing beacon which should bring the *Elroy*'s helicopter over their heads.

It was very cold, colder than ever it seemed, but this could be their overwhelming fatigue. And it was still clear, clear except for the plume of steam-like vapour which hung over the sled-teams as they moved forward, the vapour which was breath of dogs and men condensing in the bitter atmosphere. Unlike the popular conception of the Arctic, screaming blizzards were rare in this latitude; it was simply one of the coldest places on earth.

They halted inside a ravine. Grayson had pointed out that no helicopter could land in this mess but Beaumont had told Langer to unload the transmitter. 'They can winch us up, Sam, one by one,' he explained, 'then I'll take the dogs out on to the open ice.' Langer was unfastening the canvas flaps round the transmitter when Gorov came down the ravine, moving so quickly that Beaumont watched him in surprise. The Russian was breathing heavily as he stopped and spoke almost hysterically. 'Now we are safe I demand you return my property immediately!'

'What the hell are you talking about?' Beaumont was looking down as he spoke, gently heeling his right boot into the ice. It didn't feel too hard and he suspected that the pressure ridges on either side had only recently been formed by the closing of a lead.

'My core! You stole my core! One of you stole it!' Gorov

was getting excited as he pulled out the heavy tube from his parka and waved it in Beaumont's face.

'You're holding it,' Beaumont said. He frowned again as the heel of his boot suddenly sank a few inches. When he pulled it came up with an oozing plop. Soft ice. Gorov was too absorbed to notice anything wrong.

'This is not the same core. . . .'

'You mean the other one had the Catherine charts inside it?' Beaumont was staring directly at Gorov. 'As you said, we may be almost safe. Not a good time to start shouting the odds, is it?'

'The odds?'

'Go back and give Horst a hand with that set.'

Langer had hoisted the man-pack transceiver over his shoulder and was now a long way back down the ravine, carrying it to a more level section before he set it up. It was almost too much for him in his weakened state but he plodded on and then found a level gap in the wall. He put it down carefully as Gorov raved on in the distance.

'I must have my core! It is that core which makes me valuable to Washington. . . .'

Gorov was still waving the metal tube about like a blunt instrument when Grayson took it off him. 'Valuable?' the American said. 'Until we reach that ship not one of us is worth a bent nickel. We may not have heard one of your choppers for over an hour, but we're not on board that ship yet. Now, give Horst a hand with that transmitter when he's finished.'

'Ground's sticky underfoot, Sam,' Beaumont murmured as Gorov went back up the ravine. 'We'll have to watch it.'

'I suppose it figures,' Grayson replied as he fondled Bismarck to keep him quiet, 'we're getting close to the sea. . . .'

They heard the Russian shout, looked along the ravine, saw him falling. He crashed full length along the ravine, tried to get up, fell down again. 'Christ!' Beaumont snapped. 'He's twisted his ankle.' Langer was ready to transmit, had the telescopic aerial extended, and he was just moving the set to a more level patch of ice when he heard the shout. Swearing, he left the set and went down the ravine to help the Russian.

167

Gorov had twisted his ankle. He tried to stand up a second time and collapsed as Langer reached him. The German grabbed him under the armpits, lowered him to a sitting position with his back to the ice wall, then noticed the boot of his right leg, the one which had brought him down. Black ooze clung to the boot, ooze which was already freezing. 'Keith! Soft ice here—and Gorov can't walk. . . .' With Grayson to help him, he formed an arm cradle and they carried Gorov back to the sled where he settled himself, looking anywhere except in Beaumont's direction.

'Better hurry up with that signal,' Beaumont said.

Langer and Grayson went back up the ravine slowly, careful of where they placed their boots, and when Langer reached the gap in the ice wall he stared, wondering if he was going mad. Then he let out a shout which brought Grayson running. The Redifon set had sunk. The main part of the transmitter had vanished and only the disappearing aerial still showed above the surface as a froth of bubbling ooze closed over the box. Langer dropped to his knees, scrabbled desperately in the icy mess, but the box had gone below the level his gloved fingers could reach. In despair he grabbed at the aerial. A piece snapped off and he was left holding it as the rest of it went down. It was gone. They had lost their only means of communicating with the *Elroy*.

'You have dealt with the caviar?' Papanin demanded.

The Siberian had a new temporary headquarters, a mobile headquarters a thousand feet above the pack as the submarine killer flew steadily south. And he was talking to Vronsky in another machine much further south, using the code-word caviar for *Elroy* because he was talking direct on the radio-telephone.

'The caviar is sandwiched,' Vronsky replied.

Papanin grunted as he switched off and stared down at the icefield below. It was getting close to some kind of climax in the game and he wanted to be there to direct the moves himself.

'By midnight we'll have them,' he said.

'They haven't been seen yet,' Kramer pointed out, ever pessimistic.

Papanin frowned ferociously to shut him up as static crackled in his ear. He listened with an expressionless face, acknowledged the new message, then glared at the pilot. 'Get this thing moving,' he said coldly, 'or are you anchored to the ice?' He turned round and stared at Kramer who was perched on a flap seat at the back of the cabin. 'By midnight, I said. They have just located the target.'

'Keith, the bastard's coming in to land!'

'I expected that.' Beaumont stared up from the top of the ice wall while he watched the submarine killer dropping, both rotors moving more slowly as the machine came down vertically to a point on the level ice a quarter of a mile from where he crouched.

They had been spotted. The helicopter now landing had flown over them twice, and it was landing between them and the icebound ship. He lowered his glasses. Papanin never missed a trick: a second helicopter was hovering over the ice-encrusted silhouette of the ship, poised over the launch pad so Schmidt couldn't send up his own machine.

'We were nearly there,' Grayson said bitterly as he crouched beside Beaumont. 'Another couple of hours and we'd have made it. . . .'

'Might as well be a couple of hundred,' Langer said from the other side of Beaumont. He slithered back inside the ravine quickly as the dogs started jumping about. The beating roar of the descending machine echoed along the pressure ridges which criss-crossed the ice in all directions. It touched down, its rotors still whirling. A door opened and men began dropping to the ice, men with rifles. Furry and hooded in the moonlight, they spread out in a broad crescent and began advancing towards the pressure ridges. Again the speed of the operation impressed Beaumont.

'I didn't know that machine could hold so many,' Grayson said grimly.

'You know what you have to do,' Beaumont reminded him.

'Keep a close eye on Gorov—I don't want him panicking at the psychological moment.'

'You're committing suicide. . . .'

'We'll die if we just wait for them. They want Gorov and we're expendable witnesses.'

Beaumont slipped down the side of the ice wall, trailed his rifle and began running down the ravine. Behind him the others watched him go until Grayson gave them a sharp order. Despite the fact that the ice walls on either side towered above him Beaumont ran in a stoop, ignoring the fact that there could be soft ice ahead, praying that the ground would stay firm. In the emergency the fatigue had temporarily left him; he was clear-headed and he had complete control over his limbs. It was hardly surprising that Grayson had called what he was trying to do suicide—Beaumont was running straight towards the Russians.

It was not quite as foolhardy an action as it seemed. He had waited to see what came out of the machine, now they were advancing towards the pressure zone, and now he was running towards the approximate centre of the crescent of men he couldn't see. They would come inside the ravines trying to keep their crescent-shaped formation—so when the right moment came the security detachment could close their crescent, encircling their target. It was the element of surprise Beaumont was counting on: the last thing the section leader would expect would be for one of the hunted men to run towards him.

He ran light-footed, making as little noise as possible as he followed the snaking ravine which twisted and turned; from his high point on the crest Beaumont had noted the course of this ravine, and so far as he could tell it eventually led out on to the open ice at a certain point. In places the ice corridor was in shadow, in other places as he went round a corner he ran into moonlight. Soon he would have to slow down because soon he would be close to the incoming Russians. As he ran he heard in the distance the faint humming beat of the helicopter muffled by the ice walls. The pilot wasn't taking any chances; he was keeping his engines going for fear they might never start again in this temperature. He stopped running, began moving very cautiously. He would meet the Russians soon.

Crouched close to the lee of the right-hand wall, he crept forward, noting alcoves he could dodge back into when he heard them coming—if he heard them coming in time. Beaumont was under no illusion that he faced amateurs: the Soviet Special Security detachments which operated in the Arctic were trained men accustomed to operating in sub-zero temperatures. But they weren't too accustomed to moving on foot over the pack. He was holding his rifle in both hands when the fur-clad Russian came round a corner very quietly.

Both men were startled, but the Russian hadn't been expecting to meet anyone so close to the helicopter. He was carrying an automatic weapon over his shoulder and he made a mistake: he tried to unsling it. Beaumont reacted without thinking, swinging the rifle round in his hands so that the heavy metal butt-plate faced the Russian. He slammed it forward at head height. At the last moment the Russian jerked his head sideways and the butt-plate only grazed his jaw, but it was enough to unbalance him, to send his boots slithering over the ice as he fell backwards and Beaumont moved forward.

The Russian hit the ice with the back of his head. The blow was cushioned by the fur hood he wore. Still sprawled on his back, his own weapon dropped and out of reach, he grasped the Englishman's right boot and the hand was large enough to encircle the ankle. The fingers locked and prepared to heave sideways. Beaumont ignored the danger, concentrating on what he had to do. The rifle came down from high up, hammered down on the Russian's forehead, and the force of the down-stroke was so great that the butt rebounded. The hand locked round his ankle relaxed, the head flopped sideways and the man lay still as Beaumont bent down and heaved him over on to his stomach. The impact points—jaw and forehead—were now in contact with the ice, so when they found him—if they ever found him—it would look like an accident, an accident caused by the Russian tripping and smashing his face down on the iron-hard ground.

He took an even bigger risk now: he started running again. He had counted about twenty men coming out of the machine and they had to be spread over a rabbit warren of ravines, so probably the arrangement was that when one of them located the fugitives they would open fire to bring the others running. He was still running when he turned a corner and a sheet of light came into view. He had reached the exit—the open ice was ahead.

The roar of the waiting machine's rotors blasted his eardrums coming inside the ravine and he saw it barely a hundred yards away, its double fin facing him, the pilot's cabin looking the other way. It was a point he had noted from the ridge crest and he had been praying the pilot hadn't swung his machine round. He hadn't. And there was no guard waiting at the edge of the ice. It didn't surprise Beaumont; when you have twenty men at your disposal and you go in to capture a group of four men you'd hardly anticipate that one of them would be mad enough to head straight for the machine. Beaumont headed straight for the machine.

He looped his rifle over his shoulder and began walking at a moderate pace towards the rear of the helicopter. It seemed a crazy thing to do, to walk slowly, but Beaumont was gambling on elementary psychology in case the pilot inside the cabin did look behind him. Reflexes moved fast when jerked into action —the sight of an armed man running across the ice towards the machine would provoke one reaction in the pilot. He would pull the lever, take the machine vertically off the ice. A five-second job.

Beaumont kept walking slowly, coming closer to the submarine killer.

Beaumont was fairly confident now that he was going to make it; although his fur hood and parka hardly matched the security men's outfit it was similar—similar enough when seen by moonlight through the ice-rimed dome of a helicopter. As he neared the machine, as the deafening drumbeat increased in decibels, every nerve in his body was screaming at him to run, to cover the last fifty yards before the pilot turned his head. Beaumont kept walking at the same even pace, coming up directly behind the old-fashioned-looking tail, the kind of tail biplanes had once sported. Unlooping his rifle, he walked past the tail, climbed up and hammered with his gloved fist on the misted dome.

The vibration shuddered him and nothing happened. He beat with his fist a second time and then the window slid open. The rifle went inside at the same moment as warm air wafted in his face, the muzzle pointed at a helmeted figure who had jumped back into his seat behind the controls. 'Get out! Come on! Get out—quick!' Beaumont shouted in Russian and jerked his head to show the pilot what he wanted—with the drumbeat going full blast the pilot probably couldn't hear a word. Beaumont leaned in through the window, jabbed the rifle muzzle hard into the pilot's side. The Russian had goggles down over his eyes but Beaumont had the impression he was young, maybe in his late twenties. Young enough to be a hero. The pilot's right hand moved towards a lever.

The lever, Beaumont guessed instantly, would elevate the helicopter. Suddenly the machine would be climbing and he would be suspended in mid-air, maybe jerked off to smash on the ice below. 'Don't try it . . . !' To drive the message home he rammed the muzzle harder into the pilot. The Russian stared sideways and Beaumont read the man's mind. He had guts: he was checking the weapon, wondering whether he could survive the bullet. The calibre must have scared him: his hand moved away from the lever. 'Get up! Up! Up!' Beaumont jerked his head and the pilot disconnected his headset and slid carefully out of his seat.

Something in the pilot's stance warned Beaumont. The Russian paused half-way out of his seat, crouched like a cat, the lenses of his goggles catching the light from the instrument panel so his eyes were invisible. 'Come on,' Beaumont snapped, 'hurry it up.' The Russian came closer as Beaumont withdrew the rifle, cuddling it under his arm, his finger still inside the trigger guard as he used his other hand to press down the door handle, to slide it open. The pilot spread his hands in a slow gesture of surrender.

But the heroics weren't over yet. The pilot came slowly

173

through the doorway and then he was very close to Beaumont. He turned, as though obeying Beaumont's gesture for him to drop to the ice; then, still crouched under the whirling rotors, he grabbed for the rifle, a reaction the Englishman had anticipated. Beaumont slammed down the butt, struck the Russian on the shin, and the pilot grabbed for the door frame to regain his balance. Holding on to the frame he straightened up on one leg. He came within range of the steel blades of the lower rotor.

They beheaded him.

Still crouched and clinging to the window frame, Beaumont was stunned with horror. He swallowed bile. The corpse was below him on the ice. Dark spots flecked the ice around the huddled heap. The head had been hurled God knew where by the whipping blades. It was incredible—a helicopter pilot decapitated by his own rotor—but the majority of accidents happen in the home, and for the pilot the machine had been home. Shaking—and not only from the vibration—Beaumont went inside the cabin and closed the door on what lay below it. Then he eased himself into the pilot's seat and stared at the control panel.

It was not entirely unlike the Sikorsky's control panel. And a year earlier Beaumont had visited the Soviet base, North Pole 15, now orbiting the Pole somewhere off the Siberian coast, where a vodka-filled pilot had shown him his submarine killer before the security man had arrived to drag them both out of the machine. Beaumont had sent a report to Washington and London about that machine and now he desperately tried to recall its details.

The altitude readings were in metres, of course. Most of the dials and levers he understood, but there was one dial and two switches he couldn't fathom. Cautiously he touched the lever the pilot had reached for. Nothing happened. He pushed it a shade further and the machine left the ice. He pulled it towards him and felt the bump as the skids touched down again. The spare helmet he had taken from a hook and put over his head as soon as he sat down was loose-fitting. He fastened it more tightly, clamping the ear muffs closer to cut out the hellish row. The instrument panel was juddering badly but he suspected some of this was his own fatigue. Fiddling with several other controls, he sorted out the set-up calmly, knowing that at any moment the Russians on the ice might reach the sled-teams. But he had to grasp the mechanism of this thing. He opened the throttles and the twin jets boomed. He took a deep breath, operated the ascent lever.

Tuesday, 22 February: 11.30 p.m.—Midnight

THE MACHINE CLIMBED faster than he'd expected, shot up vertically with a drumming roar. When the altimeter registered one hundred metres he hovered, then flew forward. He changed direction, flew through the arc of a circle. Beyond a clear patch in the perspex dome the *Elroy* appeared like a stranded toy, then vanished. The small lever which had puzzled him banked the helicopter. It was responding to his touch now. Reluctantly. He had a feeling of enormous power locked in behind the panel, power itching to break loose, and in flight the cabin vibrated more than a Sikorsky's, vibrated like an old washing machine.

From above, the ridges looked weird in the moonlight, levelled down to ribs of ice like the burial ground of prehistoric monsters, their long-dead bones bleached a pale colour. He saw two men moving along an ice corridor. He ignored them, searching for the assembly point, the strangely-shaped area they had crossed shortly before they heard the Russian machine coming. He sent the sled teams back there to wait for him because it was the only place inside the ridges where a helicopter could land—a tiny amphitheatre of ice, a bowl surrounded with pressure ridge walls.

He flew over more Russians who stopped and stared upwards, flew on some distance, then realized he had overshot the amphitheatre and turned.

Beaumont was becoming worried now. If he couldn't find the amphitheatre first the Russians would reach the sled teams, might even have reached them already. He saw other fur-clad figures moving along the ravines, some of them running, and all of them stopped to stare up at him, wondering why the hell their machine had taken off from the ice. And conditions inside the large cabin could have been better: the heaven-sent warmth was counteracted by a smell which kept intruding on his stomach, a stench of petrol fumes which was nauseating. Either there was something wrong with the machine or Russian engine technology lagged sadly behind British and American. Then he saw it—a white circle among the shadows.

He operated the lever and started going down. Three men, two sleds, the dogs were in the middle of the bowl, and one of the men was waving frantically. Then five Russians came over a nearby ridge crest and looked down into the bowl with rifles in their hands.

Under the helmet Beaumont's expression was grim: he had arrived too late.

Pressing himself hard against the seat back, he banked the machine, lost altitude, increased the revs, flew straight for the Russians. Beyond the perspex dome he saw them standing on the crest, frozen with astonishment. The helmet and goggles he had put on helped the illusion, heightened the tension—because from the crest the five men saw their own machine, piloted by their own comrade, come screaming down towards them.

The row inside the cabin was deafening. The frame was vibrating as though soon it would shake every rivet free from the fuselage. Beaumont increased the revs again and beyond the dome the five men flew towards him. He moved the stick and the machine thundered over the crest, rotors whipping, the skids just clearing the ridge—and the men were gone, tumbling down the far side of the ridge as they took desperate evading action. Beaumont climbed again, turned, saw the Russians on their feet inside a wide ice corridor. He dived, aimed the machine point-blank along the corridor, and the security men, seeing what was coming, fled. Beaumont continued his power-dive, took the machine down dangerously low, levelled out just above the crests, continued on course along the corridor.

The skids missed the men's heads by feet—down inside the corridor it must have seemed like inches as they flung themselves to the ground and the reverberations of the engines pounded their eardrums.

When Beaumont looked back they had started to run again —away from the amphitheatre, demoralized. His terror campaign was beginning to work. And it must seem terrifying to the security detachment who were bound to assume their own pilot was behind the controls, a pilot who had gone berserk. The irony was that no one would fire a single shot at him—the machine he was flying was their only transport out of the terrible polar wasteland.

He made three more circuits of the amphitheatre and then went down.

His eyes were watering from the petrol fumes which had seeped under his loose-fitting goggles as he descended into the bowl. In his anxiety to get down fast he landed heavily on the ice: it was only a matter of time before the Russians pulled themselves together and then they would be swarming towards the place where they had seen the helicopter landing. Leaving the rotors running, he unfastened his seat-strap, went to the door, opened it. He was rather careful of the whirling blades above his head as he jumped down on to the ice.

'Watch those damned rotors,' were his first words. 'Get the dogs aboard first—if trouble comes we leave the sleds.'

The dogs had already been released from the traces and they scrambled them inside the machine, lifting each kicking animal and shoving it unceremoniously aboard. Beaumont waited a short distance from the machine, leaving it to Grayson and Langer to hoist dogs and Gorov inside while he stared round the circle of crests with his rifle ready.

The sleds went on board last, and when Beaumont followed them there was no trace left on the ice that the Beaumont party had ever existed.

Beaumont went straight up to a thousand feet, taking them out of range of rifle fire before he set course for the *Elroy*.

Langer stood close to the transparent dome as they climbed, hemmed in by whimpering dogs. He pointed downwards. 'We were only just in time.'

Beaumont nodded. A group of six Russians was moving close to the amphitheatre as they ascended.

From their altitude of one thousand feet the *Elroy* looked like a ghost ship, one of the legendary vessels which drift round the oceans of the world without a crew, a ghost ship set in solid ice. As they came closer Beaumont saw a channel beyond its stern, a dark slash of sea where the icebreaker had battered its way through the polar pack, but beyond the slash there was continuous ice. As the ship hammered its way north the ice-field had closed behind it, locking it in.

'That other sub-killer is still hanging over the ship,' Langer said suddenly.

'I know,' Beaumont replied. 'We're going to have to shift it.'

He moved the stick and they started losing height, close enough to the ship to see men running to the rails and staring up as a second Russian machine homed in on them. And some of the seamen carried rifles. Aft of the high bridge, close to the stern, they could see now far below another helicopter, a Sikorsky, resting on its launching pad while the Soviet machine clung to the air above it. So long as the hovering machine held its present position it was impossible for the American plane to leave its pad—it would have ascended directly into the other machine.

'I suppose that other sub-killer thinks we're his pal,' Grayson remarked as he patted one of the dogs.

'He's in for a shock,' Beaumont said tersely.

'They may try to crash us. . . .' Gorov who had sat in silence on a folding seat at the back of the cabin was now alarmed enough to speak. He stood up to get a better view, holding on to a rail to take the weight of his injured ankle.

'Sit down, Gorov!' Beaumont shouted. 'Didn't you hear what Grayson said? The pilot will think we're Russian, which gives us the edge.'

'Two pairs of rotors whirling close together, Keith,' Grayson warned. 'We could end up with both of us taking diving lessons. . . .'

'I want that machine out of the way,' Beaumont insisted. 'I

want it out of the way before we land. . . .' He was almost over the ship now, flying slowly at an altitude of five hundred feet while four hundred feet down the other submarine killer maintained its hover, hanging over the Sikorsky like a threat. The ice-coated rails of the ship were lined with seamen now, all of them staring up at the new arrival, wondering what was going to happen.

Standing close to the dome, Langer stared straight down on the machine below, saw the dizzy circle of its rotors whipping through the night, the gauze of vapour spiralling up towards him.

'Keith!' he shouted above the throbbing din. 'Could you take us down slowly alongside that bastard?'

'Yes. Why?'

Langer took down a folded toolkit bag hooked to the side of the dome, opened it, extracted a large steel monkey wrench. 'With our window open I might get his dome. Then he would . . .'

'Got it—we'll try it,' Beaumont shouted. 'You know I can't get too close to his rotors?'

'I'm ready.' Langer pushed two of the dogs away, took a firm grip on the monkey wrench and opened the window. A blast of icy air streamed inside the heated cabin as Beaumont started to go down.

Langer's dark hair flew out behind him as he pushed back his hood to see clearly and leaned out of the window. No one spoke again inside the cabin; Gorov hunched nervously on his flap seat; and Beaumont was acutely conscious that he was handling a strange machine, that he was attempting a dangerous manœuvre which could easily end in total disaster.

The drop went on as Beaumont took the helicopter down slowly. From the window Langer watched the deck of the *Elroy* coming up, the line of heads staring towards him, a peaked cap which poked out of the bridge window to look up, but above all he watched the giddy ellipse of the lethal rotors below him, slicing the air, rising up to meet him. So far as he could tell, Beaumont was gauging his descent with murderous accuracy—accurate because when he came alongside the second machine his own racing blades should clear the rotors below, murderous because the margin of safety was so small.

Exposed to the bitter night air after the brief spell of warmth, Langer's face was already numb and frozen; his eyelids felt like leaden weights, desperately wanted to close, but he forced himself to keep them open, to stay hanging out of the window. Then he saw the vague shape of the top of a helmet under the dome; as he watched it the helmet tilted and something pale came into view, a pale blur seen under a clear patch in the ice-rimmed dome—the pilot's face watching Beaumont coming down almost on top of him. He had had no signal to leave his post. Now it was too late.

For the Russian the position was reversed. He had successfully immobilized the American helicopter, holding it down on its pad, but now he was sandwiched, unable to go down, unable to climb, caught in a press between the other two machines, and the press was closing, coming down on top of him. Beaumont had hoped that the pilot's nerve would crack, that the slow descent would make him run, and while they had been at five hundred feet the Russian could have escaped. Now it was too late. Caught in an emergency the Russian pilot's nerve hadn't broken, it had frozen. Unsure of what to do, he did nothing. Beaumont's descent continued, the gap closed, the skids of his machine hovered close to the Russian's transparent dome.

They were so close now that the air disturbance was exerting full power, sucking air down, and Langer had the sensation that it was about to tear him out of the window down into the mincing machine of the whirling rotors. He pulled his head in, slammed the window shut, continued watching from inside. The air disturbance was now causing another dangerous reaction—the machine was rocking from side to side. It wasn't impossible that a whirlpool reaction would start—drawing both helicopters towards each other until their rotor tips met in one brief grinding clash.

Then they were alongside each other and Langer opened the window again.

There was an observer as well as a pilot in the Soviet

machine and Beaumont could see him operating his headset, talking non-stop as he kept glancing across at them. A signal was being sent to someone.

Then Gorov did a stupid thing. Restless with anxiety, he stood up and peered towards the dome of the other helicopter. 'Sit down!' Beaumont roared. He didn't think Soviet pilots were insane enough to use suicide tactics but he didn't know what instructions they had received regarding Gorov. Beaumont held his own helicopter in a hover, ready to fly forward, much of his attention focused on the thick silhouette of the mast which had to be avoided whatever happened.

'O.K., Horst,' he shouted. 'Get on with it!'

Below them the deck of the *Elroy* had cleared suddenly; either by order of the ship's commander or through instinctive self-preservation, the American seamen had disappeared, taken cover. Beaumont watched Horst, his hand on the lever which would take them forward, away from machine, ship and mast in a burst of speed. The noise inside the cabin was terrible now, shattering as the engines of the other machine added their blasting roar to the din. And the Soviet helicopter was rocking badly too, quaking as though about to split open.

Langer screwed up his eyes to see more clearly, saw the curve of the Russian's dome only yards away. For seconds they wobbled close to each other. Langer leaned well out of the window and was deafened, paralysed with the cold. He raised his right arm, paused, hurled the monkey wrench in a careful arc, slammed the window shut.

The missile struck the shatter-proof dome, a dome shuddering with vibration, hurtled away at an angle into the night. Langer stared through his own dome. It had worked. Shatter-proof, the Russian's dome hadn't shattered—it had crazed. No longer transparent, its curved surface was milky—the pilot inside was blind, couldn't see a damned thing. Beaumont shot away from the blinded Russian, banked away from the ship's mast which loomed like a gigantic flagpole, flew on out over the ice.

Every helicopter has a smaller rotor at the tail. Without a tail rotor mounted at right-angles to the pitch of the main rotor no helicopter would fly. The enormous power of the overhead rotor has a natural torque reaction—whirling through the air it would sweep the fuselage it supports round and round at ever-increasing speed—but for the counter-force of the tail rotor. This was something the Soviet pilot and his observer were about to experience for brief killing seconds.

As Beaumont had anticipated, the Soviet pilot did the wrong thing. It was understandable; it was also fatal. At one moment, sitting behind his controls, the pilot still had a clear view of his surroundings. Then Horst's wrench struck and he was surrounded by opaqueness, by crazed windows he couldn't see through at all. The world went milky on him. He was confined to a view of his cabin. He panicked.

He had to get away from the mast, to fly clear of the ship and out above the open ice where Beaumont had gone. He moved a lever, misjudged it, went forward in a shallow curve, banking to escape the menace of the huge mast. He was only half successful, his main rotors swung clear, but he forgot his tail and curved too sharply. The tail rotor kissed the mast and the whole mechanism left the machine. The balance-force which countered the torque tendency was gone. Basic aerodynamics came into play.

Once in Sydney, Australia, Beaumont had seen a film taken from an automatic camera mounted in a helicopter which flew too close to a building in Sydney Harbour. The tail rotor kissed the building, dropped into the water, and the camera recorded what happened. Later it was dredged up from the wreckage containing two bodies and the film was re-run. It was terrifying. He recalled the film as he saw what happened to the Soviet helicopter, knew with a horrible clarity what was happening inside the doomed machine.

The cabin began to rotate, to whirl like a top, and the two men inside rotated with it. . . . Faster and faster they revolved on their own axis with the machine still in mid-air, spinning round and round and round at ever-increasing speed in endless gyrations. In seconds both men were disorientated, powerless, spinning, spinning, spinning. Strapped into their seats, they experienced the full force of the terror, whirling like a round-about gone mad, at a speed no roundabout out of control would ever attain.

They would have gone mad had it lasted long enough, but it didn't last long enough. The machine lost its equilibrium, banked over sideways, fell towards the ice. The whirling rotors were still hurtling the fuselage round when the smash came. The fuselage broke in two pieces, flew across the ice three hundred yards away from the *Elroy* as the rotors disintegrated. The fuel tanks detonated, sent out a sheet of flame which melted the ice on the port rails. Black smoke rose and wavered in the breeze which came from the north.

There was another watcher who saw the Soviet helicopter's destruction. Two miles away, flying at three thousand feet, Col. Igor Papanin lowered his night-glasses and sat in silence while the pilot beside him waited for instructions.

'What happened?' Kramer asked from the seat behind. 'What was that flame?'

'Shut up! Let me think.'

Papanin was in a state of shock. Only an hour earlier he had flown to where the *Elroy* was hemmed in by ice to see what was happening. On the way he had received the signal from one of his helicopters: the Beaumont party had been found, men were being landed on the ice to cut them off from the American ship.

It had sounded like a triumph.

He had arrived in time to see the Soviet helicopter still hovering over the *Elroy*. He had sent a signal over the radio-telephone himself, ordering it to keep its position. Then the second machine had appeared. For a few minutes Papanin had no idea what was happening, then the helicopter over the ship had started reporting. For once the Siberian had listened without interrupting, without saying a single word as the com-munications became more and more tense, climaxing in a report which had chilled him as he listened to the taut words coming through the earphones.

'Machine coming down on us . . . several men inside . . .

window opening . . . Gorov! Gorov! In the machine! . . . many dogs . . . three other men. . . .'

Then the message ceased. Papanin saw why when he raised his night-glasses and aimed them with difficulty, focusing just in time to see the obscene spectacle of his own helicopter whirling crazily in mid-air before it crashed.

Sitting behind him, Kramer saw the sagging shoulders stiffen. Papanin swung round in his seat and his expression frightened the Balt. 'Send a signal to the *Revolution*! Tell them I am on my way. Tell them to start radio-jamming at full power immediately! All vessels! We will establish our head-quarters on board the *Revolution* and wait for the *Elroy* to come to us.'

'Hydrogen-Strongbow . . . Hydrogen-Strongbow . . .'

The two-word signal which Beaumont asked the *Elroy*'s captain to radio immediately to Curtis Field the moment he arrived on board reached Dawes close on midnight. 'Hydrogen-Strongbow . . .' The signal told Dawes everything—or almost everything. 'We have Gorov, we are aboard the *Elroy*.' He asked for a call to be put through to Washington immediately on the hot line.

The hot line went through Curtis Field on its way to Iceland and Europe; the other way it went back through Dye Two, a remote Distant Early Warning Station perched on the icecap, before it continued its long journey to Washington. When the call came through Dawes spoke to a man in the Defence Department and Adams listened, hearing only one end of the conversation.

'Sure we've got Gorov aboard an American ship,' Dawes said at a later stage in his call, 'but for the third time I'd feel a lot happier if we could send an escort ship to take the *Elroy* home. . . .'

'No, I'm not suggesting they'd board an American vessel . . .' he growled at an even later stage.

Two minutes later he slammed down the phone and absent-mindedly lit his cigar, the first live smoke he'd enjoyed in seventeen days. 'They won't give her an escort,' he said. 'They say it's all over.' He began pacing the overheated office and staring at the wall map which showed the position of all ships in the area south of Target-5. 'All they can think of is that the president is at this moment in Peking clinking glasses with the Chinese.'

'You lit your cigar,' Adams pointed out. 'You're celebrating?'

'Not yet.'

When Adams had gone to bed Dawes was still pacing slowly, still gazing at the wall map, so uneasy that he knew he wouldn't sleep even if he did go to bed. And in this foreboding Dawes showed more insight than the man in Washington who had said it was all over.

It was, in fact, just beginning.

Checkmate

THE KILLING GROUND

Wednesday, 23 February: 1 a.m.—5 a.m.

'TAKE HER DOWN! You have to land on that blasted thing one day!'

Papanin shouted the command to make himself heard above the drumming of the rotors as the helicopter hovered uncertainly, hovered over the 16,000-ton research ship *Revolution*. The aircraft canted sideways, caught by a gust of wind, and Papanin, standing up, grabbed at his seat to save himself. Bloody amateur! The so-called pilots the flying schools turned out these days were a disgrace. Behind the pilot Kramer clung nervously to the flap seat he was perched on: he hated flying and this had been a very rough ride. The pilot regained control of his machine and spoke to the Siberian without looking at him.

'It would be safer if you sat down, Colonel!'

'It would be safer if we were already aboard that ship! Take her down, I said!'

'Landing conditions are very dangerous. I have enough fuel left to stay up. . . .'

Papanin sat down next to the pilot in the observer's seat, put his face close to the pilot's, enunciated the words carefully. 'I am ordering you to land on that ship. I have not got the time to hang about in mid-air because you require the sea to be as smooth as a baby's bottom! Take her down!'

He turned away from the pilot and looked down at the ocean. The view was scarcely encouraging. The huge research ship, the showpiece of the Soviet merchant marine, her vast radar dome aft of the bridge gleaming in the moonlight like some strange seaborne mosque, was heaving slowly in a considerable swell. Three hundred feet below them, she rode great sea crests trundling south, her whole structure tilting and then falling, the spike at the top of the radar dome tipping sideways, pausing, climbing again as the seas lifted the vessel. Close to the icefield, ice floes drifted in the surging waves, climbed a crest, slammed down against the bows. The helicopter began to descend.

The pilot, his facial muscles tight, leaned well forward for his first sight of the radar dome. Under these dangerous conditions the dome was his only guide to the whereabouts of the landing pad, immediately aft of the dome. He had to touch the pad at just the right moment—when it was level—otherwise they would tip over sideways. Spume, caught by the wind, came up and splashed over the perspex, obscuring his view. Feeling the Siberian's stare, he continued the descent. Something like a huge pendulum swivelled beyond the perspex. The masthead, topped by a radar wing. The mast was laden with electronic gear. The *Revolution*, launched officially as the world's greatest research vessel, was really the Soviet Union's largest spy-ship.

The machine went lower. The dome filled the view now, sliding with the massive sea swell, but the pilot hardly saw it: he was watching the masthead beyond, swinging towards the vertical. When it reached the vertical, paused there for brief seconds, the invisible landing pad would be level. The skids below the undercarriage hit the pad, slammed into it. Waiting technicians rushed forward, clamped the anchor rings tight. The Siberian opened the door while the rotors were still whirling, looked back at the pilot.

'You see! You never know what you can do until you try!'

He jumped to the deck as the pilot glared at him, crouched to avoid the rotors, splayed his huge legs to hold his balance, then he was clawing his way along the rail when the sea sent an avalanche inboard. He clung to the rail, holding his breath until the water receded, and there were frozen spits of ice on his sleeves as he hauled himself up the tilting ladder leading to the great bridge. Captain Anatoli Tuchevsky, the ship's commander, opened the door to let him in.

'Colonel Papanin!' The Siberian, dripping water, took off his sodden parka and dropped it on the floor. 'You are Tuchevsky?

Good. A change of clothing, please! Something belonging to the largest rating aboard! Why are you heading north at this turtle pace?'

Tuchevsky, a lean, self-contained man with a beard, grim-faced and thoroughly alarmed about what was happening to his ship, gave an order for fresh clothing to be brought and then led Papanin to the chart-room behind the bridge. He sent away an officer working over a chart with a pair of dividers, shut the door and faced the Siberian.

'I have to protest most strongly . . .'

'Protest noted!'

'I haven't told you what I'm protesting about yet. . . .'

'I'm not interested!'

'These are dangerous waters for a vessel of this size. . . .'

'Now tell me something new!' Papanin stripped off his outer gloves, peeled off his mittens underneath, dropped the sodden articles on a side-table. Taking out a pair of steel-rimmed spectacles, he stared at the chart on the table, picked up a pencil, made a cross. 'The American icebreaker *Elroy* was about there when I last saw her. She will now be smashing her way out of the ice. She will sail due south. . . .' He scrawled a brutal line down the chart. 'We continue sailing due north.' His pencil went straight back up the line. 'So get on this course. And make this old tub of yours move!'

Tuchevsky took off his cap, dropped it on the chart so the Siberian could make no more markings, folded his arms and stared straight at Papanin. 'I command this vessel. I have an order to receive you, to carry out your instructions—but I am still in command. . . .'

'Of course!' Papanin towered over the five-foot six Tuchevsky as he beamed down at him. 'I fashion the bullets, you fire them!' Sitting down on the floor, he tugged off one boot and then the other, still grinning at the captain.

'I wish to protest formally about this order to proceed due north,' Tuchevsky continued with an edge in his voice. 'The *Revolution* is our latest and most modern research vessel. It cost millions of roubles. And yet I am ordered to take this vessel into a sea littered with icebergs. . . .'

'The *Elroy* made it—and part of the way without radar. I saw she had lost her masthead equipment. You have that damned big ear twitching at the top of your mast—use it!' Papanin stood up in his stockinged feet and began padding about the chartroom, looking at things. 'I want to speak to the radio-jamming officer,' he went on. 'There will be a short pause to send a signal to the *Gorki*—all helicopters are to search for the present position of the *Elroy*. The first one to find it flies here immediately to report. . . .'

'Why?' flared Tuchevsky. 'Why are we doing this insane thing? I shall radio an immediate protest to Moscow.'

'No you won't!' Papanin looked at him over his shoulder. 'The pause in the jamming will be very brief—only sufficient to send off my signal to the *Gorki*. The *Elroy* is sailing south into a sea crammed with icebergs. She will be sailing blind—her radar is gone. She will be lost to the outside world—the radio-jamming has isolated her. Get me some tea, please, Tuchevsky, and I will tell you what it is all about.' The Siberian paused. 'You see, we are going to intercept the *Elroy*.'

The murderous, shuddering impacts of steel smashing into solid ice woke Beaumont after three hours' sleep at four in the morning. Had an earthquake been erupting outside the effect would have been mild compared with the quivering, grinding sensation he woke to as the bows smashed and drove into the polar pack. And of all men aboard Beaumont was receiving the full treatment—his cabin, the only other quarters available apart from the one amidships he had given to Grayson and Langer, was under the bows.

Befuddled with sleep, he blinked, wondering why the cabin walls seemed to be oscillating, as though some tremendous force just beyond was about to burst through the plates and crash down on him. He checked his watch. 4 a.m. He'd had three hours' sleep since coming aboard. The oscillation of the cabin walls was quietening down but the reverberating crash was still in his ears when the door opened and Pat DaSilva, acting mate, peered in cautiously with a mug of steaming coffee.

'I wondered if you were awake,' he said solemnly. 'And you'd better swallow this fast before the next ram.'

'Thanks.' Beaumont took the mug and sipped cautiously while he studied DaSilva. The acting mate was a short, stocky man of about forty with curly black hair and a squarish head. At first glance he looked tough and uncompromising, but there was a glint of humour in the steady grey eyes if you studied him carefully. Beaumont swallowed a lot of the scalding liquid. American coffee. Very strong.

'Here it comes again,' DaSilva warned as he grabbed hold of the door frame. The vessel was moving forward, its engines throbbing with power. Just beyond the wall of the cabin was the bow. Somewhere just beyond that was the ice as the steel bow cut through black water. Beaumont put out a hand and waited, his coffee mug three-parts empty, his hand pressed against the end of the bunk. The ship struck.

The cabin vibrated with the massive collision. DaSilva almost lost his grip and was hurled across the cabin, but he saved himself. Beaumont had the feeling that the bows were breaking, the plates buckling, that within seconds the cabin wall would crumble while an avalanche of smashed ice deluged in over them. But at the back of his mind he knew this wouldn't happen: this was an icebreaker. The ship stopped, the engines still throbbing. Beaumont looked at the coffee splashed over the opposite bulkhead. 'Are we getting anywhere?' he asked.

'No place fast. It's been going on for over an hour—God knows how you slept through it—and we're stuck solid. The trouble is we've lost not only the radar—the observation cage went down as well. With the mate inside it,' DaSilva added soberly. 'Which promoted me to acting mate. I could have done without it—Carlson was a good guy. We need someone up top,' he explained, 'to see what angle to hit the ice at. The trouble is there's no top to send anyone up to.'

Beaumont was getting dressed, putting on his boots and his parka as the vessel withdrew from the ice. The cabin shuddered again; the grinding, grating sound of steel withdrawing itself from the vice of the pack was appalling. 'I'm going up to the bridge to see what's happening,' Beaumont said as he fastened the parka. He looked directly at the mate. 'Could I have imagined it,' he inquired, 'or was there a certain lack of enthusiasm as we came aboard?'

DaSilva looked uncomfortable. 'You don't want to take any notice of it.' He hesitated. 'The fact is, Schmidt wasn't too happy about bringing the ship as far north as this in February. The rumour is he received some gut order from Washington—get the hell north and damn the consequences. He kind of blames you for being alive, for bringing him up here.'

'Some of the crew too?'

'Maybe a guy here and there. We were going home to Milwaukee when the order came through. They'll get over it. . . .'

But they hadn't got over it yet. Beaumont sensed the hostility around him as he made his way up to the bridge. He'd have had to be blind not to have sensed it. Seamen he passed didn't seem to see him coming. One burly character on his hands and knees in a companionway who was cleaning the floor moved his bucket in front of Beaumont.

'Shift that bucket fast, Borzoli,' the acting mate snapped.

The burly man looked up. 'I didn't see you, Pat. . . .' He moved the bucket quickly. It wasn't just that they had been sent up Iceberg Alley, Beaumont reflected as he mounted a staircase; DaSilva hadn't told him the whole story. He was being blamed for the death of the mate, Carlson. It looked as though the voyage could be marred by the odd incident; the men who crewed an icebreaker weren't the gentlest characters who went to sea. Commander Schmidt's opening remark wasn't exactly encouraging either.

'I'd keep to your quarters if I were you, Beaumont. You need the rest.'

The high bridge gave a good view out over the ice ahead and the vessel was driving along the channel for another ram. At least the surviving channel had been wide enough for Schmidt to turn his ship round before he attacked the pack, searching for a way out south. At the end of the channel the ice was battered but still intact, and when the bows struck, no crack appeared. Beaumont released his gloved hands from the rail he had gripped and looked at Schmidt. 'We're in trouble. At this time of the year the icing up will go on—if we don't get out soon we'll be stuck here till spring. . . .'

'You think you're telling me something?' The dark-browed commander stared bleakly at Beaumont from under his peaked cap. 'Against my better judgement I came up here on account of you people. What I can do without is your comments.'

'You need a man high up,' Beaumont insisted, 'a man eighty feet up so he can guide the angle of the ramming, so he can detect the slightest trace of a fissure which will tell him where to ram next time. . . .'

'Come with me!'

Schmidt's expression was even bleaker as he gave an order for the ship to be stopped and then left the bridge quickly. They went backwards down a slippery ladder which had recently been cleared of ice, and on deck teams of men were shovelling ice over the sides, great slabs of ice which other men were levering off the deck with crowbars. The *Elroy*'s Sikorsky was just coming in to land, hovering over the pad aft of the bridge and then dropping. 'Checking up on those Russians out on the ice,' Schmidt snapped. 'Like you suggested,' he added grudgingly. 'A Soviet chopper airlifted them out half an hour ago.' They arrived at the base of the huge mast. 'Take a good look,' Schmidt growled.

The huge structure speared up into the moonlight. Eighty feet above them, the tip of the spear was jagged and torn, looked as though it had run into the wall of a building. The crosstree below was intact, and even from their great distance below it Beaumont could see that the crosstree was sheathed in ice. A seaman levering up an enormous slab of ice tipped it over. It smashed down inches from Beaumont's right foot— because Beaumont had moved the foot just in time. 'Do that again,' Schmidt roared, 'and I'll have you in the brig. Get over to the port side!' He waited until the seaman had gone before he spoke again. 'They all liked Carlson,' he said.

'And they hold me responsible for his death?'

'I didn't say that. Now, for God's sake, look at it! And you say I ought to send a man up there!'

A metal ladder ran up the side of the ice-coated mast, its rungs encased in gleaming ice; the rigging was festooned with ice; ten-foot long icicles hung from the tips of the crosstrees. Seen from the deck as Beaumont stared up, the mast was like some weird glass pylon. It looked totally unassailable.

'I didn't say you ought to send a man up,' Beaumont replied. 'I can get up there myself. I'll need a leather strap to hold me, canvas padding round the mast, and a telephone set to communicate with the bridge. . . .'

'And a coffin to bury you in,' a voice behind him added.

'This is Quinn, the chopper pilot,' Schmidt said gruffly, so Beaumont shook hands with Quinn, the first man who had extended him this courtesy since he had come aboard. Lean and lanky, in his early thirties, Quinn reinforced his warning.

'You should have died on the ice. You didn't—so stick to your cabin till we hit Quebec. We'll get there one day.'

Schmidt was staring resignedly up at the mast. 'It's what we need—someone high up. But what damned use would you be up there?'

'I did the same job for your sister ship *Exodus*,' Beaumont replied quietly. 'Three years ago north of Baffin Bay. She was trying to head up Smith Sound and she had the same sort of problem—solid ice ahead. I knew the area so I went aloft and guided them through.'

'That's MacDonald's ship.' Schmidt stared at Beaumont and then up at the mast again. 'We have a telephone box up there already and the mast is padded—DaSilva went up to locate a way into the icefield, but I brought him down before we started hammering the pack.'

'Mac was the captain when I was on the *Exodus*.' Beaumont smiled dryly. 'He wrote out a dummy certificate for me afterwards—to show I could act as pilot in Smith Sound. And I think we ought to get out of here—that radio-jamming bothers me.'

'Standard procedure when Ivan is in a bad temper. You know what's going to happen if you're up there when I slam into the pack? It's suicide.'

Beaumont looked round the deck where seamen were continuing to heave ice overboard. Heads turned away when he caught their gaze, one man spat on the deck and then hurriedly resumed work as Schmidt glared at him. 'Suicide?' Beaumont repeated. 'Then everyone here will be happy.'

Three hours' sleep had revived Beaumont, but he was hardly his normal energetic self as he mounted the ice-coated ladder, swaddled in clothing, the leather chest-strap clamped round his body, the second snap-clip strap for fastening round the mast dangling, the telephone headset in position under his fur hood. Below him on the deck a subtle change had come over the seamen who ten minutes earlier had been so hostile. They paused in their work, staring up with some awe at the huge Englishman climbing the deadly ladder. Beaumont had noted the change when he came on deck the second time, had ignored it. To hell with them.

Twenty feet above the deck he stopped to smash his boot down hard to break the ice. His boot slipped, his gloved hand tightened on a rung, and the ice he had hammered was intact. He was mounting a ladder of pure ice. As he went on up he felt the sub-zero temperature penetrating his gloves, seeping through the mittens inside them, rasping at the raw skin of his fingers. He felt the bitter night air freezing his face, prickling his eyelids, catching his throat. His eyes watered, his vision blurred. He went higher and the sensation of relentless cold began to blot out everything else—the throb of the waiting engines, the searchlight Schmidt had projected over the bows, the endless icefield planing away to the south.

He was forty feet up when the snap-clip dangling from his chest-strap hooked on to one of the rungs; he went on up, not realizing what had happened. He had one foot on a lower rung, the other reaching for a higher perch, when his body jerked taut in mid-air. It caught him off-balance and he lost his equilibrium. The foot in mid-air thrashed about in space and the boot lower down, poised on a rung of ice, had to take all his weight, the shock of the sudden halt. Then the lower boot slipped off the rung. He dropped.

Suspended forty feet above the ice-coated deck by only his

hand-holds, gloves clawing at slippery ice, he fought to regain control, his boots swinging in air as he tried to find rungs he couldn't see. He felt his hand-holds losing their grip, slithering round the icy rungs, then one foot found a rung, took some of the weight, and within seconds he had his other foot back on the ladder. As he paused for breath he had a glimpse downwards of the deck, of tiny faces staring up at him. He waited for his heart-beats to slow down to something nearer normal, then he resumed his ascent.

The crosstree was a right royal bastard. The steel ladder ended just below it, so he presumed it must have led straight up through a trap into the observation cabin where Carlson had died. He now had to climb beyond that, climb up over the crosstree before he could straddle on it and attach the chest-strap to the mast above it. And he was now eighty feet above the deck. Before he attempted this tricky manœuvre he reached up with one hand to test the canvas padding wrapped round the crosstree. He found that it revolved, gave no safe purchase at all.

It took him ten agonizing minutes to get up over the cross-tree, to get seated on the unstable canvas sleeve with the mast between his groin, to get the second strap looped and fastened round the mast, to attach the telephone terminals into the box already fixed to the mast. Only then did it occur to him that under his clothes his body was covered with sweat, that sweat was running down his face. He fumbled a handkerchief out of his coat pocket and used it to wipe his face. Beads of ice came away from his forehead.

Before communicating with the bridge he looked around and the view was spectacular.

He pulled back the side of his hood to listen. No, he hadn't imagined it: weird gibbering and squeaking echoes were coming across the ice, then a low rumble like a volcanic upheaval. Half a mile away he saw the turbulence starting—half a mile ahead of the *Elroy*. Walls which seemed no larger than ripples from that height and distance began to heave up, to creep over the plain of ice, moving away from the *Elroy*, moving south. As he watched a ribbon of dark water appeared, spreading away from the icebreaker. The night was full of the sound of ice cracking, ice shattering against itself. And the lead went on expanding, creeping towards a distant belt of darkness which was the ocean. The *Elroy* had to break through to that lead.

Twisting round, held to the mast by the chest-strap, he looked beyond the stern. A half-mile of open channel lay behind the vessel, and at the end of that channel, a long way down, lay the ruins of the Soviet helicopter Beaumont had flown to the ship. He had deliberately landed the machine under the bows of the *Elroy* and later Schmidt had completed the job, reversing his vessel a short distance and then ramming into the ice, into the machine perched at the brink. When he withdrew, the steel bows dragged the remnant with it, dropped it into the sea. But it wasn't the end of the channel Beaumont was staring at now; appalled, he was looking at something well beyond it.

Carried forward by a rising breeze from the north, a black pall was creeping towards the ship, a pall quite different from the fog which had blanketed Target-5, a black curtain hundreds of feet high, a curtain which glittered ominously in the moonlight. A bank of black frost was drifting towards the ship, the most dreaded phenomenon in the Arctic. What Beaumont was staring at was a bank of frozen fog, a rare weather condition so insidious that it can cause frostbite requiring instant amputation if it settles on a man. If it caught him at the masthead he could be dead within seconds. And it was already invading the pressure ridge zone. He spoke quickly into the mike dangling from his chin.

'Schmidt! Reverse her!'

He clung to the canvas-padded mast as the engine throbs increased in power, then the vessel was moving back, sliding through the dark water behind its stern. The immediate effect at the masthead was more gentle than Beaumont had feared; no more than a slight sway as the icefield drifted past below and dark water appeared on both sides, a dark stain against the pallor of the pack. Then the vessel slowed, stopped. Knowing what was coming Beaumont felt his stomach muscles tighten. It took a conscious effort of will to start the process, to give the order into the mike.

'Half speed! Forward!'

'O.K., Beaumont, here we go! Hold on tight.'

Beaumont hugged the mast, his head to one side, prepared to take the impact. The power increased, quivered up the mast, the vessel moved forward. The icefield slid past in the opposite direction far below, the water stain narrowed, and Beaumont watched the narrowing stain—because when the stain vanished the icebreaker would hit, ship against ice, steel against the barrier, a moving force against an immovable force. The stain narrowed, faded to a ruler-line, vanished. The ship went on, moving faster. . . . Grkkk! The steel bows struck. The impact shuddered the entire vessel, raced up the mast, and the mast shuddered, whipped, vibrated to a maximum at its tip. It hit Beaumont like a hammerblow as he clung desperately to the mast, his body pressed into the canvas. Then the vibration slowed, stopped. The icebreaker was stationary, locked into the ice.

Beaumont relaxed his grip, stared ahead. A dark crack extended beyond the bows, but no more than a few feet. He looked either side of the crack, searching for a more promising fissure, found nothing. The ice was intact. His concentration was so great that it took him a few moments to realize that Schmidt was talking to him. He took a firmer grip on the masthead, saw half a mile away that the lead was still growing wider, then he heard Schmidt again and there was a hint of anxiety in the firm voice.

'Beaumont, are you receiving me? Beaumont. . . .'

'I'm O.K. We didn't do much this time. Same again is the answer—and hit the ice in exactly the same place if you can.'

'Reverse?'

'Take her back, Schmidt.'

The engine power built up, the screw thrashed the dark water at the stern, and from his great height Beaumont could sense the icebreaker fighting to tear herself free. Hurling her great bulk against the ice the *Elroy* had trapped herself; the ice had parted, let the bows bite into it, then closed round them like a massive vice. The throbbing built up a second time, built up greater power, and when Beaumont was certain Schmidt had failed again the ship suddenly wrenched herself loose. The sound of rending ice came up to him above the engine throbs, then the *Elroy* slid backwards, leaving a dark smear on the port side where the remnants of her paint stained the damaged ice. As the vessel went back Beaumont looked back. The black frost curtain was advancing over the belt of smooth ice, coming closer to the ship. He waited until the ship stopped again.

'Half speed! Forward!'

Schmidt had taken the ship further back down the channel this time, so when the bows met the ice they would be moving faster. Beaumont braced himself. Eyes half-shut, staring down, he watched the narrowing stain of water, not knowing that Grayson and Langer were on deck, gripping a rail, staring up in horror. The gap closed, the ice was under the bows, the impact was far greater. The tremor shot up the mast and Beaumont was in trouble, shaking like a leaf with the mast's brutal vibration. He had his eyes still half-open and the vast icescape shuddered horribly, shuddered as though in the grip of an earthquake. Then the ship was still.

Thirty minutes it went on at half speed, thirty bruising, battering minutes. Beaumont changed the angle of attack, used the *Elroy* as his own personal battering ram, hammering into the icefield, and slowly something began to happen. The ice began to fracture, to show a pattern of dark zigzags. And something else was happening, not so slowly. Beaumont was methodically being reduced to a state where he hardly realized what he was doing. His face was horribly sore and bruised, sore with the aching cold, bruised with pressing it into the canvas at the moment of impact. And now the black frost had almost reached him—they had to break out quickly before it killed him.

'Reverse, Schmidt,' he croaked. 'Take her back to the end of the channel this time.'

They went back. They went too far back. A finger of black frost was creeping out over the point where the submarine killer had gone down. The finger curled out to the masthead and Grayson, seeing what was happening, bellowed up to the bridge in a way passengers don't normally address ships' captains. 'You stupid idiot—get her moving! Beaumont's in the frost!'

Beaumont felt the deathly freeze as darkness blotted out everything. The icefield went, the water below disappeared, the damned deck vanished. He had been looking ahead, gauging the next ram, when the black frost closed over him. Panting with exhaustion he took a deep breath and a grisly sensation passed through him. His lungs felt as though they were congealing, filling up with liquid ice. He was gasping for breath, felt a great weight descending on him, trying to drag him off the crosstree. The vessel started moving forward, took him clear of the freezing menace. He opened the eyes he had instinctively closed and saw with a shock of horror that his parka was coated with ice crystals, layered with them. He had been freezing solid.

'Are you O.K., Beaumont? Beaumont, Beaumont. . . .' Schmidt's voice had lost its normal detached control, was filled with urgency and anxiety.

'I'm O.K. This time we do it.' Beaumont paused for breath. 'We hit the port side of the ice fifty yards before the crack. Got it?'

'Fifty yards before the crack?' Schmidt sounded incredulous.

'Yes. Port side! Fifty yards! I'm going to bounce her—into a starboard crack. Full power!'

'Full power! It'll kill you . . .'

'Get this fucking ship moving, Schmidt!' Beaumont was shouting down the mike. 'When I say full power I mean full power!'

'O.K. It's your decision.' Schmidt just stopped himself in time: he had been on the verge of saying it's your funeral.

The *Elroy* sheered forward, throbbing in a way it hadn't throbbed before, pushing aside the dark water, sending a bow wave coursing against the ice on both quarters, building up maximum power for its next run against the barrier. Beaumont's tactic was unusual: he was directing Schmidt to hurl the massive weight of the moving vessel against one point of the ice so that its rebound would strike a segment of ice it couldn't otherwise have reached, a segment where a wide zig-zag extended a long way towards the ever-widening lead in the distance. It was a tactic he had experimented with—which had succeeded—when he had led the *Exodus* into Smith Sound three years before. But not at full power.

He talked Schmidt in this time, guided the ship's onrush, taking it towards a precise point on the port side of the ice. Below him there was a significant development: Schmidt had ordered the deck cleared of men prior to the coming impact. Grayson had gone up to the bridge, was leaning out of a window, staring up at the tiny figure he could hardly see poised on the crosstree. Full power. . . . If it had been possible he would have countermanded Schmidt's order.

At the masthead Beaumont was staring to port, laden down by his outer clothes which were like a steel canopy, solid with the crystals. He issued one last instruction. 'If you feel her going through, Schmidt, keep her going. . . .' The vessel surged forward, the engine throbs echoed in Beaumont's brain, he clasped his arms tightly round the canvas-wrapped mast, he took a deep breath, the vessel hit.

The *Elroy*'s bows slammed into the ice on the port side, hitting the barrier at an angle, a glancing blow. They bounded off the barrier, swung at an angle, rammed forward with terrible momentum into the starboard ice. Beaumont had used the icebreaker like a gigantic billiard ball, cannoning the bows off one side so they would strike the opposite side close to the zigzag. Above the throb of the beating engines came a different sound, a grinding smash which travelled through the ship, which stunned the crew below.

But the effect at sea-level was nothing compared to what happened at the masthead.

The mast began to vibrate like a tuning fork, whipping back and forth as though about to rip itself out of the ship, whipping Beaumont back and forth, whipping like a flexible cane instead of an eighty-foot-high mast. The ordeal was appalling, well-nigh unendurable, and Beaumont became disorientated as the whipping went on—back and forth at incredible speed. He felt his strength, his mind, going. He felt as though his teeth were being shaken out of his head, his head loosened from his body, his whole body structure coming apart.

He opened his eyes, his hands still locked round the mast, and everything was blurred. He couldn't make out whether they were stopped or still moving forward. He looked down, saw a huge crack, a crack which was almost a lead, and flopped against the mast he felt the cold mike against his chin. He spoke without realizing it, spoke like a man repeating a rote. 'Keep her moving, Schmidt . . . keep her moving. . . .' There was a salty taste in his mouth, blood, an agonizing pain across his shoulder blades. He wondered whether his back was broken. 'Keep her moving, Schmidt. . . .'

Schmidt kept her moving. From the moment they struck the starboard ice, from the second he felt the penetration, Schmidt kept her moving. The scarred bows battered, heaved, forced their way forward, thrust aside huge slabs of ice, upended them, bulldozed them, bit deeper and deeper, went on and on and on, smashing through the barrier which was at last giving way. Below decks the chief engineer stared at his gauges, unable to drag his gaze away from the needles quivering well above danger point. If Schmidt wasn't careful the boilers would blow.

Schmidt wasn't careful, he maintained full power. And the vessel responded, wouldn't stop, was mounting its bows on top of the ice, riding up on it, breaking it down with sheer weight and power. From the masthead, barely conscious, Beaumont began to grasp what was happening, saw the ice parting, the crack widening to a lead, the lead spreading back and back, and he knew they were going through all the way. Then he lost consciousness, relaxed his hand-grip, slipped from the crosstree, and like a man hanging he hung there, suspended by the chest-strap, his body swaying like a pendulum.

It was Borzoli, the burly seaman who had shoved a bucket in Beaumont's way, who went up to get him. Grayson had one foot on the icy ladder when Borzoli pushed him aside with an oath, 'You're too small for this job, friend. . . .' And probably the seaman was the only man aboard who could have attempted it; a couple of inches shorter than Beaumont, he was built like a wine cask. He clawed his way up the swaying mast, went up and up while the icebreaker continued driving through the ice.

'Christ, he must be dead. . . .' Langer stood beside Grayson, holding on to the ladder to keep himself upright as they stared up in horror at the body swinging eighty feet above them in the night. Like a man hung from a yardarm two hundred years ago, Beaumont swung backwards and forwards, swung free of the mast as he pivoted in space. 'That strap won't hold his weight much longer,' Grayson murmured. Borzoli was smaller now, was moving up at an incredible pace, and Grayson had his heart in his mouth for both men—for Beaumont whom he expected to see spin off the crosstree at any second, for Borzoli who had only to make one mistake to bring himself crashing down sixty feet—or was it seventy?—he was close to the crosstree now.

Hardly daring to believe the evidence of his own eyes he saw the tiny climbing figure stop. Grayson looked away, not able to watch any more, and then the vessel lurched with a terrible violence and he lost his grip on the ladder, went hurtling across the icy deck to crash against a bulkhead. He lay there for some time, the wind knocked out of him, trying to get his breath back as Langer bent over to make sure he was all right. That terrible impact had, of course, knocked both men above them off the ship; they were now lying somewhere on the pack, dead.

'Get me up, Horst. . . .'

Langer helped him to his feet and he stood there, holding on to a rail, not daring to look up. Both men stared upwards at the same moment and then went on looking, hardly breathing, scared out of their wits. Borzoli was on his way down, was on his way down with Beaumont suspended from his back by the chest-strap he had released from the mast. How the hell could the seaman stand it, Grayson wondered? He was descending a ladder of sheer ice, a ladder rocked by the continuous collisions of the bows with the pack, descending with another man's weight trying to tear him backwards off the ladder with every downward step he took.

Borzoli grew larger, Beaumont grew larger as the descending

men came nearer the deck, and now, feeling his strength ebbing, the seaman was coming down as fast as he dared, his great boots hammering at the ice-coated rungs, smashing off the ice because it was the combined weight of two outsized men battering at the rungs. Splintered ice showered over Grayson and Langer. They ducked their heads to save their eyes, and when they looked up again Beaumont's swaying body was only just above them. They grabbed at it, took the weight off the exhausted Borzoli, and then both men were at deck level as the *Elroy* surged forward into the open lead, towards the ocean beyond.

Thursday, 24 February: 6 a.m.—Midnight

'WHAT WOULD HAPPEN if there was a collision?'

Papanin stood on the bridge of the *Revolution* close to Tuchevsky who was watching the radar. The bridge was very large, had a great sweep of armoured glass beyond the helmsman, was fitted with every scientific device available that might help navigation. Compared to the Russian ship, the 6,500-ton *Elroy*, her radar gone, was back in the nineteenth century.

The vibration of the powerful diesel motors was gentle, barely more than a persistent humming, and a battery of searchlights poised at different angles beyond the bridge shone out into the dense mist. The helmsman was several yards away as Papanin spoke in a low tone, too low also for the officer of the watch to hear as he stood in front of an outsize clear-vision panel. 'What would happen,' Papanin continued, 'if we came out of the fog and struck the *Elroy* amidships with our bows?'

The *Elroy* was at sea, a weird and terrible sight, and she was sinking. It was dark, total darkness, although somewhere above the screen of black frost the moon still shone down. Her lights —the searchlights projected over the heaving ocean—showed glimpses of the horror.

The bridge, the mast, the rails, the deck were mantled with the deadly crystals where the atmosphere itself had frozen over the ship, coating her, polluting her, tarring her with the evil black sheen which glistened when light caught it. The temperature was —39°F—seventy-one degrees below freezing point. The air was colder than the ice-cold sea, was liquid ice which hung over the ship like a black cloud, a cloud of death. And there were over five hundred tons of ice on the deck which listed dangerously to port. It was only a matter of time before the *Elroy* capsized, went down.

It was horrible on deck—horrible and dangerous where groups of men, all the crew which could be spared, fought to heave the ice overboard in time, and as they fought the black frost hovering all round them added more layers to overwhelm them. They couldn't see—except by the glimmers of light from bulkhead lamps smeared and half-obscured by the molasses-like frost encrusted on the glass. They couldn't stand upright—because the deck was permanently canted over to port by the great weight of ice they desperately tried to shift. They could hardly breathe—because when they took in breath they took in air which had crystallized to liquid ice, air which it was no cliché to say was as heavy as lead.

Frozen with the terrible cold, their clothes weighted down by ice crystals, they used picks and axes and hammers and shovels to smash at, break up, lever up and heave overboard the tonnage which was killing them. The sound of the slow-beating engines was almost muffled by the hacking, smashing, cracking noises. And the unquiet sea heaved the vessel up and down, made their impossible task infinitely more dangerous as, caught off balance, they grabbed for lifelines sheathed in ice. It had been going on for twenty-four hours.

Beyond the plunging bows the sea hissed and rolled in the searchlight, and in the beam, looking down from the high bridge, Schmidt saw ice descending in mid-air, black ice. 'It's beating us, DaSilva,' he said grimly. 'More ice is forming than we're getting rid of.'

At the port window DaSilva peered down and he wasn't prepared to give the captain an argument: the ice on deck was nearly rail-high. He pressed his face close to the armour glass, withdrew it quickly as his nose felt the temperature. A seaman, Borzoli he thought, had pulled his hand up quickly and the glove he should have worn was gone, trapped under a slab of ice. Even though he wore mittens under it frostbite would attack him within seconds, Borzoli was running, his hand tucked under his armpit, running for the nearest stairwell, and DaSilva prayed it wouldn't mean amputation. Then he could not see anything as spume from a wave hurtled through the air and hit the glass with a crack, freezing as it landed.

'I hear Beaumont is O.K.,' Schmidt said.

'Beaumont is recovering,' DaSilva agreed. 'He must be like this glass—armoured.'

Inside Langer's cabin Beaumont was sitting up alone, listening to the thump of ice floes against the hull beyond the cabin wall. He could tell that something was wrong from the tilt of the cabin: it was almost permanently canted to port. But he was thinking about Papanin, about things Schmidt had told him three hours earlier soon after he had woken.

'They're about forty miles south of us—the six Soviet trawlers,' Schmidt had said, pointing to his chart. 'Spread out across our path like a screen. Quinn found them—before the black frost caught us he took his machine south to the limit of his fuel—and he thought he had a glimpse of a much bigger ship just about here.'

'Less than thirty miles away. The *Revolution*?'

'Could be. The fog down there closed in just as he spotted her. He thought he saw a big radar dome—the equipment she uses for tracking our satellites. We'll just have to make sure there's no collision when we're passing them. . . .'

Beaumont eased himself to a more comfortable position in the bunk. McNeill, the ship's doctor, had told him in a voice of some wonderment that he was still in one piece. 'Your clothes and that canvas buffered you. The fact that you swung free from the mast without striking it helped—but you'll be here till we hit Quebec. . . .'

Beaumont didn't think so: he'd be up soon now. His torso was badly bruised, felt twice its normal size, which meant it felt very large indeed, but soon now . . . as he settled himself he winced. Well, maybe in a few hours. As he stared at the opposite wall without seeing it he thought about the short time he had spent with Papanin in the hut on Target-5. He was remembering the Siberian's huge, shaven head, the very wide mouth, the almost Mongolian bone structure. A ruthless man.

And now there were at least seven Soviet vessels in front of the *Elroy* which was carrying Gorov—and the Catherine charts.

Reaching behind him, he fumbled in the pocket of his parka and took out the core tube. He weighed it in his hand—the entire Soviet underwater system, and Papanin knew where it was. 'We'll just have to make sure there's no collision . . .' Schmidt had said, and Schmidt had been thinking of an accident. Beaumont was thinking of something quite different as he returned the core to his parka pocket, pulled the blankets up under his chin, and stared into the distance, trying to see the future. Then, without realizing it, he fell asleep.

The *Elroy* had increased speed dangerously, was ploughing forward at half speed, her bows plunging deep inside a trough as a wave crashed over the port rail and submerged it. When the bows lifted again half the wave crest was attached to them, frozen solid to the rail which was now six inches thick with ice.

'We'll have to take a chance,' Schmidt had decided ten minutes earlier. 'We'll have to increase speed in the hope that we take her out of the black frost.'

'She'll go over . . .' DaSilva had stopped speaking when Schmidt looked at him, understanding the glance: they were going over anyway, so what was the difference? And every possible factor was deteriorating.

The wind had increased to thirty-five knot strength, was howling like a banshee among the ice-clogged rigging, hurling spume inboard, spume which froze in mid-air so it landed on the backs of the stooped men on deck like lead shot. They were losing the whole battle for survival on every front—and they knew it. The ice still piled up faster than they could get rid of it, was now solid to rail height on the port side. The rising wind was turning the sea they had to plough through into a churning cauldron of forty-foot waves, great green combers which came rolling above them, half as high as the remnant of the mast which was also canted to port.

The giant combers inundated the deck frequently, swirled waist-high round men clinging to the icy lifelines, submerging the ice they were struggling to shift overboard. And frequently it brought with it floating spars of ice which crashed into the bulkheads with lethal force, such force that one spar shattered into pieces before the sea retreated. They lost one man in this way—hanging on to a lifeline he was pinned to the bulkhead, the whole of his middle crushed in by a heavy spar which came at him like a torpedo. It worried the men that they hadn't saved the body, but privately DaSilva thought it a blessing—the mangled corpse would later have had to be buried ceremonially. As Schmidt had said, they had to take a chance. So they went up to half power.

'I think we ought to clear the decks,' DaSilva said fifteen minutes later.

'Why?'

Schmidt joined him at the port window and saw why. The port rail was submerged again and looking down from the bridge it was an extraordinary, terrifying spectacle. Only the top half of men waist-deep in water showed. The rail was gone, the mountain of ice had vanished, it was as though the bridge was floating by itself. Frozen spume bombarded the window and Schmidt had to move to find a still-uncovered patch he could peer down through. Schmidt went back to keep watch on the bows.

'Keep them at work,' he ordered.

'They can't work, for God's sake! How can they—waist-deep in sea?'

'Are they waist-deep now?'

'No, not at the moment, but they will be when the next wave comes.'

'Keep them at work.'

Deep down inside himself DaSilva knew that Schmidt was right. Every pound of ice they could lever overboard between inundations gave the ship a little longer to float, to live, to move forward to what might be safety, or a kind of safety. They had to get clear of the black frost or die.

So for sixteen hours they changed the work teams at even more frequent intervals, gave the men time to go below to dry out and warm up before they froze to death, and then after a short break they toiled up again, to start all over again, to get rid of a pitifully small amount of ice, to face the cold and the wind and the sea and the danger of ice spars flattening them against the bulkhead walls. Only a man like Schmidt could have subjected them to such an ordeal; only for a man like Schmidt would they have submitted to the ordeal. And Grayson and Langer took their turn with the rest while Gorov, the man who had brought them all to this, lay on his bunk seasick.

The break came suddenly, and DaSilva was the first to grasp what was happening. Down on the deck for the fourth time, levering at a slab of ice, he looked up and stared at the others. They were still working, still hacking at the ice, still unaware of any change. He threw his crowbar down a stairwell, ran to the ladder, climbed up to the bridge. 'It's lighter!' he shouted as he burst inside. 'We're through!'

'I do believe we are.'

There was no relief, no satisfaction in Schmidt's voice as he gazed through the rear window. It was simply a statement of fact.

The vessel was still tilted to port, there was still a small mountain of ice on that side, but the atmosphere was clearing and something like moonlight was bathing the deck in its pale wash. And the curtain of black frost was a distinct curtain, drifting away from them in all its horror many cable-lengths behind the stern.

It was 11 p.m. when Beaumont made his way slowly and painfully up the stairwell which led to the foredeck, wondering what the hell was going on. He had just seen a seaman running up the staircase ahead of him and out on deck, and above him he heard the excited clatter of other running feet. Nobody ran about a ship layered with ice unless he was very bothered indeed.

When he entered the bridge, Schmidt—in these weather conditions—had opened a window and was staring through his night-glasses. Beaumont glanced at the helmsman, at DaSilva, and decided not to ask any questions at this moment. Both men were standing in attitudes suggesting more than a little anxiety. The answer came to him unasked as he moved closer to the open window and heard a reedy lookout's voice travelling up to the bridge.

'Icebergs on the port bow! Icebergs on the starboard bow! Icebergs ahead!'

'No!' Tuchevsky exploded. 'I would ask to be relieved of my command before even thinking of giving such an order. In fact, I shall take action now. I shall order the radio-jamming to be stopped—until I have sent a signal to Moscow and had a reply. . . .'

'You can't!' Papanin's tone was matter of fact. 'You know we have a Special Security detachment aboard this ship—it has already taken control of the jamming section.'

It was very warm inside the large chart-room behind the bridge of the *Revolution* and the argument had been going on for ten minutes. Papanin was, in fact, wearing down this prig of a captain, a tactic he had known would be necessary the moment he set eyes on him. Tuchevsky protested again.

'When I took command of the *Revolution* it was to carry out research, oceanic research. . . .'

'Hypocrite! You have been tracking American satellites. This is research, of course—military research!'

'We also do oceanic research,' Tuchevsky snapped. 'Water temperatures, salinity. . . .'

'All of which vitally affects submarine operations! You make me sick, Tuchevsky! You know that all the data you collect goes to our military intelligence people—who decide what scraps they will hand on to the professors. . . .'

'I will not do it!' Tuchevsky shouted. 'I will not sink the American icebreaker. You must be mad—we could never get away with it. . . .'

'You are wrong again,' Papanin observed cynically. 'The *Elroy* is steaming south without radar—we know this from the helicopter which found her two hours ago. And she cannot communicate with anyone—the jamming barrage has completed her isolation.'

'She has a helicopter,' Tuchevsky said viciously. 'I suppose you'd overlooked that?'

'No.' Papanin went over to the chart table to hide his irritation. Tuchevsky had touched a tender nerve there; for hours the Siberian had tried to think of a way of immobilizing the *Elroy*'s Sikorsky. 'Gorov and the Catherine charts are on board that ship,' he explained patiently. 'If we cannot get them back we must destroy them. . . .'

'I will not do it.'

'I don't remember asking you to do anything. But these waters are littered with icebergs—and accidents can happen. And you should think of your family,' Papanin added casually.

'My family? What has this to do with my family?'

'Your wife, specifically,' the Siberian said woodenly. 'She is a Jewess. . . .'

'That is a lie!'

Papanin sighed. 'She is half-Jewish. Her mother was a Jew. You seem to have forgotten that one of my duties is to check on Jewish agitation in Leningrad. . . .'

'She has nothing to do with that. . . .'

'Tuchevsky! Please keep quiet! Have you forgotten the signal ordering you to carry out my instructions?' Papanin went on explaining patiently. 'If it was discovered that your wife is mixed up in certain anti-Soviet activities I could easily arrange for her to be sent to Israel. You would never see her again, would you?'

'You wouldn't dare. . . .'

'What would happen next? For a few years she would hope —hope you would come. Women are very strong on hope. Then she would realize it was all over, that she must live her own life. We might even arrange for a divorce if she requested it. . . .'

'You bastard. . . .'

'I have to be,' Papanin agreed calmly. 'It is one of the main qualifications for my job.'

'There must be some other way. . . .'

'If you think of it, let me know.'

'Your Sikorsky is on the way back, Beaumont,' Schmidt said without the trace of a smile.

Beaumont didn't reply as he stood on the *Elroy*'s bridge with Grayson and Langer. 'Your helicopter. . . .' It was Beaumont who had urged Schmidt to send up Quinn again to check what lay ahead of them—if Quinn was willing. The fact was that Quinn had been itching to take up his machine ever since they had emerged from the black frost. Not unnaturally, Schmidt was most concerned at the moment with the problems of navigation.

Icebergs surrounded them on all sides, icebergs only dimly visible in the heavy sea mist drifting over the suddenly calm ocean. Two hours ago the scarred and battered ship had been fighting for her life in forty-foot seas, and now she was cruising slowly forward over water like cold milk. But she was still listing heavily to port, she still carried the enormous burden of the great load of ice pressing against the port rail, and it was still diabolically cold.

One massive berg, over a hundred feet high, a jagged cliff of floating ice, drifted less than a quarter of a mile away on the port bow. Mist curled at her base, another belt of whiteness was wrapped round her waist, but her enormous peaked head loomed up clear in the moonlit night. A smaller berg, her summit fretted and turreted like a Spanish castle, floated the same distance from the ship to starboard. They seemed like mountainous islands from the bridge, appearing, vanishing, then reappearing.

Langer moved closer to Beaumont, whispered the words. 'You asked me to check with DaSilva whether there were explosives aboard. There are . . .'

'Later,' Beaumont murmured. He was worried about Quinn —he felt responsible for this latest flight and he wouldn't feel happy until the chopper was safely back on its pad. At his suggestion one of the powerful searchlights near the bows had been switched on and elevated almost vertically into the night. It was this beacon poking up through the mist which Quinn was homing back on from the south, as yet only a tiny blip in the distance where it was caught by moonlight. The mist drifted, the blip vanished.

Beaumont shifted his feet restlessly.

'I wonder whether he found those ships,' Grayson ruminated aloud.

'If they're still steaming north he probably has,' Beaumont guessed. 'He had seven vessels to look for—he should have spotted one of them. . . .'

'I don't give a damn where they are,' Schmidt growled as he looked to starboard. 'We're on the high seas—we'll steam straight past them.'

Behind the captain's back Beaumont caught DaSilva's glance, a very dubious glance. The acting mate did not share Schmidt's sublime confidence in the freedom of the seas, a doubt which Beaumont had detected earlier, which had encouraged him to ask Langer to talk to DaSilva about explosives. 'Find out if they have any on board,' Beaumont had suggested. 'It's likely they're carrying something to blast their way out of ice. You're an explosives expert, so he won't think the question funny.'

The ship throbbed its way slowly forward over the oily sea, a sea which was dark and shiny in the moonlight, which made it look very much like a lake of oil. The mist so far was patchy, clinging to the iceberg zone on either side, and at this time of the year the sea was often calm like this in these waters. Perhaps it was the great weight of the floating masses of ice which gave it stability. Faintly, they heard the beating of Quinn's chopper coming in, but they still couldn't see him.

Beaumont looked to starboard where a searchlight was playing on the nearest berg. Illuminated, it looked gigantic, more like a Spanish castle than ever as the light shone through windows high in the turrets, through holes which penetrated the ice to the atmosphere beyond. It was almost frightening in its proximity and vastness. 'Couldn't be a ghost berg, I suppose?' Grayson murmured.

'I hope not—they're liable to collapse if you shout a rude word at them.'

Which was literally true, Beaumont thought, incredible though it might seem to people with no knowledge of the Arctic —that an unguarded human voice could bring down a colossus weighing millions of tons. Eskimos knew this; in their kayaks they glided past a ghost berg, not even daring to whisper, so fragile were these floating giants on the verge of collapse.

Beaumont watched the light playing over the castled berg, hovering at its summit, then the summit burst.

One minute the peak was there, then it had gone, vanishing in a cascade of ice bursting outwards in all directions as the echo of its detonation reverberated across the ocean, echoing from berg to berg. Fragments of ice shot down the beam of the searchlight, vanished into the floe-littered sea. At least twenty feet of the summit had disintegrated. Schmidt gave a quick order, altering course a few degrees to port, away from the monolith.

'Not a ghost berg—an exploding berg,' Grayson commented. 'I don't want to meet any more of them.'

Quinn's Sikorsky came into view, was close enough now to see the rotor disc haloed by the moon, was less than a quarter of a mile away as it lost altitude and came down to two hundred feet, heading for the *Elroy* on a course which would take it over the summit of the huge berg to port. Schmidt gave a fresh order to slow the engines while Quinn landed. The mist round the berg's waist had drifted away, showing the immensity of the great cliff of ice rising sheer from the mist at its base.

'I hope he found the *Revolution*,' Langer said.

The vast berg exploded as Quinn flew over it, exploded like a gigantic bomb no longer able to contain the pressure inside. But this time it wasn't just the summit which disappeared—the whole berg blew up with a boom that thundered out across the ocean, deafening the men on deck below the bridge. The bridge itself shuddered under the shock wave. The face of the overhead compass shattered, showering glass over the helmsman. Schmidt grabbed at the wheel to keep them on course.

The roar went round and round among the bergs, and came back to the ship as a shattering echo. Foam and vapour where the berg had been shot five hundred feet up into the night, a massive geyser which rivalled Old Smoky. As the vapour column fell back to sea level it revealed nothing but boiling water. The berg had gone, the Sikorsky had gone, and Quinn had gone.

Beaumont went to Schmidt who had handed back the wheel to the helmsman and was standing close to the window, staring at the frothing lake of sea. 'He was right over the summit when it exploded. . . .'

'I know,' Schmidt replied quietly. 'Dear God . . . Quinn.' He squared his shoulders and spoke without looking at the man beside him. 'If you get any more bright ideas, Beaumont, you know what you can do with them.'

It wasn't so much the words as the quiet way he said them which expressed the bitterness. Beaumont walked away, nodded to Grayson and Langer, and they followed him off the bridge. He was appalled at the death of Quinn, but if possible he was even more appalled at the loss of the helicopter. The radar was gone, the wireless-jamming made it impossible to send or receive any signal, and now their last link with the outside world had been taken away from them. With Papanin to the south of them they were isolated.

One hour later the *Elroy* struck the berg.

Friday, 25 February

'ONE HUNDRED POUNDS of gelignite, timer mechanisms and a few hundred foot of cable. . . .'

'Where do they keep it, Horst?'

'You'd never guess—inside a cabin off the main deck.' Langer grinned at Beaumont. 'Strictly against the regulations, DaSilva says, but he also says that when he has to heave defective jelly overboard he doesn't want to carry it all the way up from the explosives store.'

'DaSilva has his head screwed on the right way,' Grayson said. 'Those people back in Washington who write out regulations never travel with the stuff.'

The three men were sitting inside Beaumont's cabin while they ate their lunch of clam chowder and cinnamon pie. The fact that the meal had been sent to the cabin suggested that once again their popularity had waned. 'We're in the doghouse,' Grayson observed as he put down his coffee cup. 'Anybody would think you sent Quinn out so he'd be blown up by that berg. . . .'

'Schmidt's more worried than he lets on,' Beaumont replied. 'He pretends he's concentrating on his navigation but I've an idea he's as worried as we are about those Russian vessels. It's the *Revolution* I'm bothered about—all sixteen thousand tons of her. The trawlers the *Elroy* could push out of the way. What's that, Horst?' The German was showing a key in the palm of his hand with a smug expression.

'Key to the explosives cabin. DaSilva doesn't see eye to eye with Schmidt on this "we're on the high seas so no one can touch us" business. And somehow that hundred pounds of gelignite has got itself tucked away inside a couple of shoulder-packs—just in case. . . .'

The cabin lurched under the massive blow, shuddered as though the bulkheads were on the verge of caving in. The cabin walls tilted to port, then to starboard and upright again. From under the ship came a terrible grinding sound as though its keel was being torn out and the grinding went on and on. 'Christ. . . .' Grayson hauled open the cabin door and they heard shouting, the thud of running feet, a terrible crash beyond the port bulkhead, then the vessel was still with its engines ticking over. The lights dimmed, almost went out, came back to full power reluctantly.

'We've struck,' Horst yelled.

'Unless the *Revolution* just hit us . . .' Grayson began.

'More like an iceberg!' Beaumont was dragging on his parka. 'Make for the bridge.'

Beaumont ran along the deserted companionway, paused at the bottom of the staircase to button his parka, to slip on mittens and gloves, and from the deck above he heard men's voices, voices with more than a hint of panic. He went up the staircase, opened the door, and the mist met him, cold clammy mist with silhouettes moving about inside. It was impossible to see what had happened, what was beyond the port rail. Beaumont couldn't even see the damned port rail as he felt his way towards the ladder leading up to the bridge. A large burly figure came out of the mist and cannoned against him. Borzoli.

'We've struck!' he gasped hoarsely.

'Going down?' Beaumont asked, feeling the core tube inside his parka pocket.

'God knows. . . .'

Beaumont went up the ladder to the bridge, had almost reached the top when the mist beyond the bows shifted. Something like a mountain appeared and then vanished, a mountain only yards away. He went on to the bridge cautiously as Grayson and Langer came up the ladder behind him. Schmidt was standing at the front of the bridge with a window open and the icy air was rapidly dispersing the warmth. The helmsman was still holding the wheel although they weren't going anywhere, and the floor was canted towards the stern. DaSilva was hanging out of another open window, staring to port. And the engines had stopped. Glancing over his shoulder, Schmidt saw Beaumont.

'Come over here a minute, Beaumont,' he called out. His tone was neutral, the mood of anger gone. 'It's the damnedest thing—we've ridden up on an iceberg.'

It took them an hour to assess the position, the extraordinary position they were now in. Steaming very slowly through thick mist, the *Elroy* had passed inside a small bay on the coast of a giant iceberg; in less than a minute it had crossed the bay and the bows had driven inside a wide, scooped-out gulley of ice eroded out of the side of the berg, a huge natural ramp tilting up out of the sea. At the first grinding scrape Schmidt had acted, but by then the bows, the forepart of the ship, were lifted out of the water like a ship in dry dock, while at the stern the screw was still in deep water.

Schmidt had stopped the engines but the 6,500-ton vessel was marooned, the bows and a third of the hull resting on the ice chute, the other two-thirds of the ship and its stern still in the bay. At the end of the trough the wall of the berg rose sheer in the mist, greenish and massive like a cliff in the searchlight's beam. To Schmidt it had seemed incredible, but to Beaumont it was only strange: a year ago a British trawler had endured a similar experience off Spitsbergen; in heavy fog she had driven her own bows deep inside a chute at the edge of the icefield. The captain had used his common sense, faced with this unique experience—he had simply reversed his engines and the screw had dragged the trawler back into the sea.

'Jesus!' DaSilva called out from the rear of the bridge. 'How the hell did we ever get inside here?'

They went to the rear window and Schmidt blinked. The mist had cleared a little for the moment and beyond the stern was a small bay with arms which curved out to flank a narrow entrance. It had been little short of a miracle that the *Elroy*, moving blind through the mist, had cleared both arms of the bay when she steamed direct inside. The mist drifted over, blotted out the arms of solid ice.

'With a little judgement, a lot of luck, we should be able to manage it,' Schmidt said thoughtfully. 'Most of the ship is still in the water so if I reverse the screw it should haul us off the ice chute.' He let out a deep breath. 'Isn't it the damnedest thing?'

'You know the ice went?' DaSilva asked Beaumont. 'It went as we hit the chute—you can see now.'

Beaumont looked down out of the port window where the mist had lifted off the chute. It wasn't surprising he hadn't been able to see the port rail when he came up on deck—the port rail hadn't been there to see. As the keel ground its way up inside the chute the mountain of ice they had tried to shift for so many back-breaking hours had left them, had taken the rail with it. Beyond the ship a vast mass of heaped-up ice lay on the chute floor with here and there a fragment of rail sticking up out of the heap. Fur-clad figures, the seamen Schmidt had sent down rope ladders to explore the berg, were moving like ghosts in the mist.

A head came up over the side where the rail was still intact close to the bows. Langer's. He scrambled up the ladder and joined them on the bridge.

'It's not a ghost berg, Keith, I'm sure. . . .'

'You're certain?'

'Dead certain. Sam and I climbed up as far as we could and it's solid—a cliff of ice. . . .'

'You can see it now,' Schmidt called out from the front of the bridge. The mist, swirling, in constant motion, had drifted away beyond the bows and for a few minutes the majesty of the berg they were marooned on was exposed. A hundred yards beyond the bows the ice sheered up vertically like the cliffs of Dover.

The mist drifted further and they saw the cliff sweeping away on both sides until it disappeared inside the drifting whiteness. They were marooned on a floating island of pure ice, on a leviathan of a berg which could easily be half a mile long, maybe longer.

'Recall the men,' Schmidt said crisply to DaSilva. 'Use the loud-hailers. We're getting out of here.'

'I suppose we have to leave the berg right away?' Beaumont asked quietly.

'As soon as we can make it. . . .' Schmidt stopped speaking and stared at Beaumont. 'Just for a second I thought you were coming up with another of your bright ideas.'

'It might be safer to stay where we are for the moment.'

'Stuck here? Getting nowhere? You want to get home some time, don't you?'

'We are getting somewhere,' Beaumont pointed out. 'I know we don't feel to be moving but both of us know we are. This huge berg is being carried south all the time by the Greenland Current—at a rough guess the berg is moving at a rate of twenty miles a day. . . .'

'Not exactly breaking nautical records, is she?' Schmidt observed dryly.

'Do we have to?' Beaumont persisted. 'A few hours ago Quinn reported that those Soviet trawlers were forty miles south of us, that the *Revolution* was only thirty miles away— they'll be much closer now. This berg is acting as a gigantic transporter for the *Elroy*. If we stay on her the berg will carry us past those vessels some time during the night.'

'We'd be stuck here—unable to manœuvre. . . .'

'Does it matter?' Beaumont rasped impatiently. 'If they don't see us? The *Revolution* carries the latest radar but what will her radar pick up when we're close to her? Only another iceberg!'

'The berg as a giant transporter!' DaSilva was excited. 'I like the idea. . . .'

'I don't!' Schmidt walked over to the voice-pipe to speak to the engine-room. When he had re-stoppered the tube he looked at DaSilva. 'Chiefy reports there's no structural damage to the engine-room. The glass on the gauges shattered, one man got steam-scalds, but he thinks the engines are O.K. And I think, Mr DaSilva, I asked you to recall the men on the ice. I'm starting up the engines to check them. . . .'

'That is inadvisable,' Beaumont said bluntly. 'The *Revolution*'s hydrophones will pick up the vibrations. . . .'

'And then,' Schmidt went on, ignoring Beaumont, 'we'll steam out backwards the way we came in.' He gave Beaumont the benefit of his attention. 'You are getting to be too much of a sea lawyer for my taste. And whether you like it or not this ship is disembarking off this berg in two hours' time!'

'The *Elroy* is very close to us—we have picked up her engine beat on the hydrophones!'

Kramer had run on to the bridge of the *Revolution* with the news, had hardly recovered his breath before he gasped out the words. The Siberian, who was standing next to a silent Tuchevsky, took his pipe out of his mouth and waved it at the Balt.

'Calm yourself, Kramer—and report to me every five minutes from now on.'

Tuchevsky stiffened his shoulders as Kramer left the bridge, turned to Papanin and spoke emphatically. 'So now I can start my engines again—I have warned you repeatedly that it is terribly dangerous to drift in these waters without power. . . .'

'You will do nothing of the sort! You have the most advanced radar in the world—use it! We must continue drifting to give our hydrophone operators the best possible chance—I want to locate the American icebreaker's exact position.'

Papanin put his little pipe back in his mouth and went to the bridge window, leaving Tuchevsky on his own. Beyond the clear-vision panel he saw a world of mist and sea. And somewhere out of sight were the icebergs. The radar operators were at this moment plotting the monsters' course as they drifted steadily south with the Greenland Current, their eyes constantly focused on the greenish glow inside the rubber hoods where the sweeps went round and round and the echoes never stopped, the echoes coming back from over a dozen enormous icebergs.

Everyone was aboard, the engines were ticking over steadily, the bridge was fully manned, lookouts had been posted, the *Elroy* was ready to disembark from the berg, to put to sea.

Schmidt, his hands clasped behind him, for once stood looking the wrong way—towards the stern through the rear window—as he waited to perform two dangerous manœuvres, taking his ship out of the chute, steering her backwards between the arms of the bay. Beaumont stood beside him, ignoring the chilly expression on the captain's face as he stared into the distance beyond the bay.

The mist had returned at just the wrong moment, was rolling like fog just beyond the two white peninsulas of ice which almost enclosed the bay. Towering above them, Beaumont stood between Schmidt and DaSilva, who stood with almost as bleak a look on his face as Schmidt's. He totally disagreed with the decision Schmidt had taken, but he couldn't say anything; still only acting mate, he couldn't say as much as Carlson might have done had he been standing in his place. The engines built up more power, they would soon be moving, stern first, into the water—if the screw managed to haul them out.

Grayson, who had been standing near the lookouts at the stern, burst into the bridge without ceremony, speaking with even less ceremony to a man whose word was almost life and death aboard his ship. 'You'd better wait! There's something out there—just inside the fog!'

'What?'

Schmidt's single-word question was explosive, betraying some of the inner tension he was labouring under, and he stared at Grayson with a look the crew knew and feared.

'I don't know . . . but there's something. . . .'

'I can see it myself,' Beaumont said grimly. 'You'd better not move this ship yet, Schmidt.'

'God, it's the *Revolution*. . . .' DaSilva muttered.

But it wasn't the *Revolution*, it was too big, infinitely too big even for a 16,000-ton ship, the thing which was coming slowly through the mist towards the exit from the bay. It sheered up like a ten-storey building, a moving ten-storey building, its invisible summit way above the height of the *Elroy's* masthead, lost in the mist. The stern lookouts were shouting now, shouting at the tops of their voices as Schmidt opened the window and leaned out into the night. Ice-cold air flooded in over them and they were hardly aware of it as they stared, hypnotized by the menace coming towards them. It looked like a towering head-land now, a headland of ice as it brushed aside the mist and came on, drifting straight for the bay. Even across the width of the bay it seemed to hang over them, above them, a colossus of an iceberg heading straight for the leviathan they were beached on.

Schmidt reacted very quickly to give warning. He hardly seemed to move and then he was talking into the tannoy system which would reach every corner of the ship. 'Hold on tight. Hold on tight. Major collision coming!'

DaSilva grabbed Beaumont's arm. 'Look! Inside the bay!'

'Underwater spar.'

A spur of ice projecting from the giant berg, a spur which could be up to fifty feet in diameter, was spearing across the bay after slipping inside the entrance, disturbing the moonlit water, water very palely lit by a shaft percolating through the mist.

Behind the leg, the body followed. The men on the bridge were gripping rails, bracing themselves for the coming impact, and below them the lookouts clung to the rails still intact. Beaumont's head moved slightly as something fell out of the sky, something huge, bigger than a mansion, something from the summit of the berg which hadn't even touched the opposing ice yet. The mansion, the enormous chunk of ice, hit the water just beyond the bay and sent up a great funnel of water.

'Christ!' Langer gasped. 'This is a ghost berg. . . .'

Which meant that the entire edifice, millions of tons of ice, could collapse at the moment of impact, bringing an avalanche down over the bay, over the ship, burying it. Like waxwork figures they waited for the impact. At the last moment Schmidt gave the order to stop the engines. The colossus floated out of the mist and showed them its enormity, then the spur reached the shore of the bay and the bergs met.

The impact sound was deafening, a sound like the end of the world. The shattering collision sent a tremor through the iceberg which had been struck, a tremor which shuddered the *Elroy*, shaking the hull, rattling the plates, hurling rivets on to the ice. The impact threw DaSilva clear across the bridge, shook a man off the catwalk above the engine-room and sent him to his death twenty feet below. It shattered crockery, wrist-watches, fractured the still-intact glass on the engine-room gauges, made compass needles spin. Then it was suddenly quiet, frighteningly quiet.

The engines had been stopped before the impact. No one spoke. For a short time no one moved. They were gazing at the exit from the bay, an exit which was no longer there. The ice cliff filled it, locked into the opening like a cork into a bottle. The bay had become a lagoon, a lake without an exit. They were trapped inside their giant transporter, an iceberg drifting with the Greenland Current at twenty miles a day. But the ghost berg hadn't collapsed yet despite the collision. Beaumont was the first to break the silence and everyone on the bridge stared at him as though it were strange to hear a human voice.

'Now we'll have to drift with the berg, Schmidt. No option.'

'No option,' Schmidt agreed grimly. 'And all the time we'll be waiting for that thing to fall on us.'

'Their engines have stopped!'

Kramer sounded alarmed, bewildered, and Papanin left the bridge with the Balt to go down and see the hydrophone section for himself. The seaman in vest and shorts who was listening to the instrument looked up as Papanin came in. 'Kramer tells me you can't hear them any more. Is your instrument defective?'

'No. Their engines have stopped. We are getting no echoes.'

'How far away?'

'A mile, maybe even closer. . . .'

'They were that distance ten minutes ago!' Papanin glared at Kramer. 'Listen to me! They were a mile away only ten minutes ago. Their engines continued beating until a few seconds ago. They are still a mile away. It's not possible! We are drifting—they are moving south under power. They must have moved closer!'

'It's true,' the seaman said.

'It cannot be true—it's technically impossible!' the Siberian stormed.

'It's been puzzling me. . . .' the seaman began.

'That's a hell of a lot of use!' Papanin folded his arms and stared at the seaman. 'If they were drifting with the current like we are, then it would be true—we would remain the same distance apart. But they're not drifting! You heard the sound of their bloody engines!'

'Very distinctly—until a minute ago.'

'How do you explain it?' Papanin gestured towards the hydrophone equipment. 'It's your job to explain things!'

'I can't. . . .'

The Siberian said nothing, standing with his arms folded while he mastered his frustrations. When he spoke again it was in such a reasonable tone that the seaman was frightened. 'Don't worry about it—just go on listening with those earplugs of yours.' He turned to Kramer. 'There is another way of checking—since they are so close—send up that helicopter. The pilot can't come back until he's found the *Elroy*.'

Perched aboard its giant transporter, hemmed in by the two coupled bergs, the *Elroy* continued to drift south with the current. It drifted for many hours, timeless hours, because for the men imprisoned inside the ice there was no longer any way of being sure of the time.

It had seemed incredible at first, so incredible that Schmidt had ordered a check on every timepiece aboard the ship, and when the check had been made the incredible was found to be true: every single clock and watch had stopped, stopped presumably by some freak tremor which had passed through the vessel at the moment of impact when the ghost berg struck. There was a frantic search for one clock or watch which was still going, and there wasn't one.

So they had to guess at the time and from then on the ship's log carried strangely imprecise entries. 'Approximately 19.00 hours. . . .' 'About 22.00 hours. . . .' Not knowing the time gradually got on men's nerves, the proximity of the ghost berg got on their nerves, the knowledge that at any second millions of tons of ice might simply topple, come down on them, flattening the ship and everyone inside her.

And there was nothing to do, nothing they dare do. All normal work ceased: they couldn't even occupy themselves with levering up and throwing overboard the remaining ice on deck—because they were afraid that some unguarded echo from the hammering of a tool might be just enough to bring the colossus crashing down on top of them. The atmosphere became far worse after Beaumont and Langer returned from an exploratory tour of their overhanging neighbour.

'It has all the appearance of a ghost berg,' Beaumont said when he proposed the tour to Schmidt, 'that huge piece of ice which came down from the summit was pretty significant, but I think we'd better check before we all go crazy. . . .'

It was a ghost berg, the biggest Beaumont had ever seen. The far side of the two hundred foot high cliff, the side facing away from the sea, was like something out of the Arabian Nights. To get there they crossed the great spar of ice sticking up out of the bay and made their way along a narrow ledge at the base of the cliff, and when they turned a corner they looked up in horror. Enormous alcoves and caves were hollowed out of what had seemed solid berg from the outside; great roofs of ice were precariously poised on frozen columns fifty to a hundred feet above them; and below where they had paused, a long way above sea level, was a gigantic hole at least three hundred yards in diameter, a hole which might have been gouged out by a meteorite. The hole was a lake of blackness and as they listened they heard the faint lapping of water, the splash of the Greenland Current against ice. The ghost berg, at least half a mile long, was hollow, a dangerous sham, like an enormous rock pinnacle eroded by termites. It was about as stable as sweating gelignite.

'Can't understand why it didn't come down when it hit us,' Langer whispered.

'They can take a lot of punishment and then they go suddenly,' Beaumont replied. 'We've seen enough. Let's get back.'

'God in heaven, look up there, Keith. . . .'

The mist had drifted away from a giant column of ice, exposing a good two hundred feet of ice tower, a tower whose summit was hidden. The tower was massive, at least a hundred feet wide, but there were huge windows cut out of the tower, windows which were holes in the ice, so many that Beaumont couldn't understand why it was still vertical. The mist cleared from higher up and Beaumont's expression tightened as he saw the tower was supporting a great overhang from the back of the cliff, was probably supporting the whole damned cliff.

'It won't last much longer,' he said. 'We'd better get back.'

Only a few men aboard the ship were told what they had found, but within an hour the grim report had spread through the *Elroy*'s grapevine. From then on the tension became appalling. If a man banged his elbow against a bulkhead his comrade glared at him; they found their appetites had gone, that they couldn't sleep, that they could do nothing but keep quiet and keep still, and the inactivity crucified their nerves. For seamen accustomed to the movement of the ship the lack of movement was another source of tension. The bergs were moving all the time, rotating slowly in the current, but there was no sensation of movement. Given time, just a little more time—the time they couldn't gauge—and they would become a bunch of screaming neurotics.

'Why are we so interested in explosives?' Grayson asked at one stage while they were sitting in Beaumont's cabin.

'If we ever get out of here we may need some kind of weapon to defend ourselves. I don't know how or where or when—but I don't share Schmidt's optimism. I'm thinking of some kind of floating mine—I've actually talked to DaSilva about it.'

'He wasn't worried—about Schmidt?' Langer inquired.

'DaSilva is in a mutinous frame of mind,' Beaumont told him. 'Normally he wouldn't be—it's the silence and the stillness that's getting him, getting us all,' he added with a bleak grin. 'The *Elroy* doesn't even creak any more.'

'You feel we might get out one day?' Grayson asked.

'If we do, it will be when the ghost berg is on the southern side of us—with the current tugging at it. There's just a chance that it might break loose again, drift away.'

'And you still think you heard a chopper while you were on the ghost berg?' Grayson asked. 'Schmidt didn't look as though he believed you.'

'That's because Horst didn't hear it. I not only heard it—I think I saw it for a second when the mist cleared for a few seconds.'

228

'Which means Papanin now knows where we are?'

'I fear so. Time—whatever it is—will tell, if that ghost berg cuts loose.'

The ghost berg broke loose some time on Friday, 25 February. 'Approximately 22.00 hours . . .' the log recorded. Its departure was not spectacular, there was no great rending of ice, no inundation of sea rushing in; there was simply one loud terrifying crack which stopped the pulse of every man aboard. From his post at the rear of the bridge DaSilva saw what had happened. The huge spar jammed inside the bay had snapped; the ghost berg, still intact, still not collapsing, moved away from the entrance to the bay while DaSilva watched it go. And something like a half-submerged monster, the huge severed spar, was following the mother berg into the current.

When Schmidt reached the bridge with Beaumont the view they had become used to—the land-locked lagoon with the towering cliff on the far side—was transformed. The exit was again open. Beyond it the colossus was only faintly visible in the gathering mist, disappearing even as they watched her go. Schmidt permitted himself a rare display of emotion: he let out a deep breath.

'That's it. We take off as soon as I can get the screw moving —whatever there is waiting for us out there.'

The developing situation in Iceberg Alley—so far as it was known—had been anxiously followed for days by Leonid Brezhnev in Moscow, still worried that something might happen which would cancel the American president's visit to the Russian capital in May. Then all communication with Col. Papanin ceased; the radio-jamming which was so effectively isolating the *Elroy* also cut off the *Revolution* from the outside world.

On Friday, 25 February, 1972—while the American ice-breaker was still drifting aboard its giant transporter—Brezhnev undoubtedly consulted Marshal Andrei Grechko, and the Soviet Minister of Defence decided that a diversion was necessary, something to distract certain journalists who were already checking rumours that something was happening in the Arctic. Whatever happened, there must be no reference to the crisis in the world's press, so something else happened— something close enough to Iceberg Alley to account for the rumours, but something far enough away to distract attention from the events taking place hundreds of miles further north.

The Times, published on Wednesday, 1 March, carried the first report, datelined Washington, 29 February.

A crippled Soviet submarine wallowing in a North Atlantic gale for the past four days, was taken in tow today by a Russian tug according to a United States Navy spokesman.

Rough seas . . . now subsiding, enabled the tug to get a line aboard the vessel six hundred miles north-east of Newfoundland.

The submarine of the 3,700-ton H2 'hotel' class has a crew of ninety. It was first spotted on Friday by reconnaissance aircraft from the American base at Keflavik, Iceland. . . .

The Soviet ships, the tanker *Liepaya*, and the fish factory trawler, *Ivan Chigrin*, have also entered the immediate area.

The cause of the Russian vessel's trouble was not known here.

Despite the fact that the world's newspapers were full of their accounts of the American president's return from his recent visit to Peking, the report of the near 'disaster' to the Soviet submarine appeared in many newspapers, together with aerial pictures showing the supposedly stricken vessel wallowing in fifty-foot waves under the lash of fifty-five-knot wind. And the diversion worked—not a line was written about the missing *Elroy*, which should have been well on its way to its home port of Milwaukee via the St Lawrence Seaway.

It must have been just about the time when American aircraft from Keflavik first spotted the Soviet submarine that the *Elroy* left the iceberg and steamed out into the fog-bound channel.

Friday, 25 February: the last hours

THE HUGE SCREW at the stern of the *Elroy* was revolving, churning water, slamming aside small floes as it whipped up a white froth. Schmidt gave the order and the icebreaker began moving backwards slowly, then it stopped and Schmidt increased the power. The screw thrashed, the engines throbbed as though they were coming up through the deck, and the *Elroy* moved again. She came down the chute very slowly, like a ship being launched the wrong way, and the noise was terrible as the keel ground over the ice under it, spitting out sparks, channelling deeper into the iron-hard ice.

The screw churned on, its dragging power greater now that more of the ship was in the water, heaving the *Elroy* back into the sea. There was an enormous splash as the bows went down, but the crew on deck behind Beaumont at the stern didn't make a sound as the vessel edged her way across the bay and out through the narrow exit. Beaumont left the stern, walked along the vibrating deck towards the bows.

They had chosen the moment for departure carefully. Above them the mist had cleared briefly and the moon shone down, reflecting off drifting floes, off the ice-coated starboard rail, but ahead of them as Schmidt turned his vessel slowly there was dense mist only half a mile away. 'I don't like it,' Grayson said as he stopped behind Beaumont close to the bows, 'I think we should have stayed on the berg. DaSilva thinks so, too. And why the hell do we have to come out like a flaming cruise liner?'

The simile was apt. On Schmidt's specific orders the *Elroy*'s lights were ablaze. Every possible light which could be lit was switched on, and her searchlights beamed out to port and starboard and over the bows. 'We'll be on the high seas,' Schmidt had repeated for the hundredth time. 'If I go down Iceberg Alley with my lights ablaze and the horn booming there's no possible excuse for a collision.'

'You think they need an excuse—with Gorov and the Catherine charts aboard?' Beaumont had demanded. 'When we're totally out of touch and can't even signal what may be happening?'

He had lost his argument—as he knew he would. And up to a point Schmidt had reason on his side: if they tried to slip south without lights and in silence Papanin could afterwards say that the collision had been the Americans' fault—how could they have seen them or heard them in the fog? As they headed south Beaumont raised his night-glasses and swept the water.

'See anything?' Langer asked anxiously in his ear.

'Just ocean. And mist.'

'See anything?'

It wasn't Langer who asked the question this time. DaSilva had come quietly down from the bridge and stood at Beaumont's left shoulder. 'With your eyes,' he added, 'you ought to be up top where you were before.'

Beaumont looked behind him, stared up at the eighty-foot mast where a seaman hung from the crosstree with a headset clamped under his fur hood. This was the lookout who would try to warn Schmidt of any obstacle in the *Elroy*'s path. 'No thanks,' he said. 'Not again. And I can't see anything out there—yet.'

'The Carley float is near the stern, starboard side,' DaSilva murmured. 'Near the cabin where the explosives are—and Langer has a key. If we need him, Borzoli will help us with the launch—he's on lookout duty near the float. Mind telling me what you have in mind—if something does happen?'

'I'll have to try and scare them off,' Beaumont replied vaguely.

'O.K., so play it close to the chest.' DaSilva paused, looking back at the bridge. 'Maybe it's better that way—considering Schmidt doesn't know a thing about it yet. I could end up as a clerk in a shipping office for this.'

'Better that than a skeleton floating at the bottom of Iceberg Alley,' Beaumont replied brutally.

'She's coming out,' Papanin said. 'That other berg we saw in the aerial shot must have broken away.'

On the bridge of the *Revolution* the Siberian bent over the radarscope hood, his head almost inside it, and the greenish glow from the scope bathed his smooth-skinned face, his close-shaven head and his hands, making him a green man.

'How long?' Kramer asked nervously.

Papanin looked up briefly from the hood, glanced across the bridge to where Tuchevsky was standing with his back to him, his hands clasped tightly behind him. 'You can start your engines now,' he called out. 'From now on we can track her by radar.' He put his eyes close to the hood again as he replied to Kramer's question. 'By midnight I would guess—by midnight it will all be over.'

The *Elroy* was steaming due south down Iceberg Alley, her engines ticking over at half power, the bows sliding through water like milk, her lights blazing. But now there was an added factor to pinpoint her position: her powerful foghorn was booming non-stop, a deep-throated, mournful sound which echoed back to them across the ocean—and the echoing was significant. Somewhere inside the mist there had to be walls off which the echoes were rebounding, walls of ice.

Four men stood at the bows, chilled and numbed with the bitter cold, moving about frequently with the lookout Schmidt had posted. Beaumont moved about less than any of them, was constantly staring through his night-glasses as he swept the sea ahead. Feet crunched behind them.

'Coffee for you guys. . . .'

DaSilva and Borzoli poured them mugs of steaming coffee from an insulated jug, but the coffee was still half-cold before they could swallow it. The acting mate sent Borzoli back to his post near the Carley float, sent the lookout away to check something imaginary on the port quarter before he spoke. 'Schmidt is feeling he took the right decision.'

233

'I'm glad somebody's happy,' Beaumont commented.

'It's looking good so far.'

Beaumont said nothing as he finished his coffee and raised his glasses again. His arms were weary with holding them, his eyes were sore with the cold, with the strain of staring into the lenses. There was a narrow channel of calm, moonlit sea ahead for almost a mile and then it was lost behind more mist. On the port side a huge berg was coming up, an ugly monster with a table-top summit. To starboard lay a great bank of mist, a dense pall rising at least two hundred feet above the ocean, and it stretched the full length of the channel they could see.

'Nothing over there,' DaSilva remarked as Beaumont swivelled his glasses on the bank. 'Just a load of mist.'

'Is the radio-jamming as strong as ever?' Beaumont inquired.

'Stronger. The worst yet.'

'Which means we're getting very close to the jamming source.'

The *Elroy* moved closer to the bottleneck formed by the monster berg to port and the mist bank to starboard, altering course a few degrees to pass down the middle. Ice crunched underfoot as Grayson moved his numbed feet. Langer banged his arms round his body to try and get some circulation back into his system. Behind them a door slammed high up as DaSilva returned to the bridge, and they were alone with the seaman on watch.

Langer watched Beaumont as the Englishman perched his elbows on the rail and stared through his glasses, sweeping them slowly to starboard. It was the huge bank of impenetrable mist which seemed to intrigue Beaumont, the bank which drifted less than a quarter of a mile away, the bank which would hem them in between itself and the iceberg once they entered the bottleneck.

'What's that? That thing in the mist well south to starboard?' Grayson called out.

Beaumont was already looking at the huge mass which had come out of the mist like a moving cliff. It was the ghost berg presenting its false face of rock-like stability. They were inside the bottleneck now with the table-topped monster coming up on the port bow. Beaumont glanced at the mist bank and stiffened. The bows of the *Revolution* broke the mist, bore down on them like a battleship.

'The American ship is heading due south—on a course at right-angles to us. . . .'

'You'd better get ready,' Papanin ordered Tuchevsky.

The mist was smothering the *Revolution*, drifting just beyond the bridge window as Tuchevsky bent lower over the radar-scope, watching the echoes which registered the *Elroy's* approach. It was going to need very careful timing—he had to bring his huge ship out of the mist at exactly the right moment, otherwise he would fail. 'Maintain present course,' he ordered the helmsman.

The *Revolution* was creeping forward at her lowest speed, her engine beats muffled by the mist, moving forward on inter-ception course. Tuchevsky stared at the echoes, his face gleam-ing with sweat, his beard moist. His calculations had to allow for the speed of the *Elroy*, his own speed, the distance which would separate them when they first saw each other. He sensed the presence of the Siberian behind him.

'I want you to hit her amidships. . . .'

The sweep inside the hood was pinging non-stop, tracking each fresh position of the *Elroy* as she approached the bottle-neck between mist bank and iceberg. Tuchevsky heard Papanin's boots stirring restlessly. 'Aren't we moving too slowly?'

'You want us to come out too soon?'

There were no lights showing aboard the *Revolution*, the ship was in complete darkness, but Papanin's eyes were accustomed to the gloom as the ship crept forward. He could just make out the bridge window frames and the faint blur beyond them, otherwise they might have been in a fogbound port, so smooth was the sea, so quiet the hum of the vessel's slow-beating engines.

'Maintain your present speed,' Tuchevsky droned.

'For how long?' the Siberian demanded.

'For as long as is necessary.'

Papanin fumed, remained silent, his nerves screaming with the tension. They had to destroy the American vessel first time. One annihilating blow out of the mist, steel smashing into steel, the bows of the *Revolution* grinding into the *Elroy's* starboard side, cutting clean through her. He imagined what it would be like—the Russian ship astride the American, driving her under, the broken stern to his left, the wrecked bows to his right. Which section, he wondered, would go down first?

'Papanin! Get to the back of the bridge! Hold on to the rail!'

The Siberian did as he was told, went back and held on to the rail with both hands as the helmsman, one of his own men, took a tighter grip on the wheel. Papanin was watching the mist beyond the bridge. When it lightened they would be coming out, they would see the *Elroy* under their bows. Why wasn't Tuchevsky increasing speed? The captain left the radarscope, took a firm grip on the telegraph handle, pressed it down to 'Half Speed', then ran back to the scope.

'Maintain present course!'

A flicker of pale light passed beyond the bridge window. The mist wavered as the engine beat increased enormously. It was very warm inside the bridge and Papanin wiped a hand quickly over his forehead to stop sweat dripping into his eyes. The mournful booming note of the *Elroy's* foghorn they had heard before became very loud, dead ahead. Tuchevsky was staring into the radarscope, praying, then they were through.

Moonlight flooded the bridge. The lights of the *Elroy* were a glare. Dead ahead. The *Revolution's* bow wave spread out to port and starboard with the increased speed. The hull of the icebreaker rushed towards them. Tuchevsky gripped both sides of the radarscope as he stared through the window. Never before had he concentrated on a scope with such intensity—and he had calculated exactly. Or had he? Increase speed! He prayed for the *Elroy's* captain to react in time, tried to will the order into the American's brain. Increase speed! Get out of the way! I gave you one chance, one warning—please, please, please!

The *Elroy* was moving faster already. The order had been given the instant the *Revolution* appeared out of the mist. Exhausted as he was, Schmidt had reacted with all the decision Tuchevsky had prayed for. The Russian continued on course, heading point-blank for its target, so it seemed to Papanin from the back of the bridge where he couldn't see clearly. The *Revolution* swept forward, the American ship's hull slid across at right-angles to the sweep, its mast towering above the Russian ship's bridge. Tuchevsky ran to the starboard side, looked down beyond his own ship's rail. He saw the *Elroy*'s screw churning the water and his own bows cut through the turbulence.

'You missed her!' Papanin's control went. 'Next time I will take command!'

In his blind fury he strode across the bridge and began swearing at Tuchevsky, standing over him. The little captain pushed him out of the way, caught him off balance and pushed him across the bridge. 'You stupid animal—we're going to hit the berg!' Papanin stared in horror as he looked to the front. The monster berg with the table-top summit had filled the window.

Beaumont was close to the stern of the *Elroy* when the bows of the *Revolution* plunged towards them. Collision seemed inevitable, the *Elroy* was presenting her midships to the 16,000-ton Russian ship as the bow wave came forward, as the huge bows reared above the ship's rail. At the last moment Beaumont was certain the bows would smash the *Elroy*'s screw, destroying her motive power. Then the Russian ship was sweeping past beyond their stern, missing its target by yards as it sped on towards the monster berg.

'She's going to hit the berg,' Grayson said.

'I hope to God she does. . . .'

Beaumont stayed near the stern, saw the frantic effort to bring the *Revolution* round in time, saw the great wake behind her which showed the extreme course she was taking to save herself, then he saw that she had saved herself. He gave very brief instructions to Grayson, Langer and Borzoli, and went straight to the bridge of the *Elroy*, his face grim, his boots thudding on the deck. When he reached the bridge Schmidt turned round from the rear window he had been gazing through.

'You were right, Beaumont,' he said tersely. 'She tried to sink us.'

'She'll try it again. You can't outrun her.'

'Outrun her? With my top speed sixteen knots?'

'So if possible she's got to be stopped. For the sake of your crew, for the sake of everyone on board. . . .'

'DaSilva is co-operating with you over the explosives?'

Beaumont stared at Schmidt who was nodding his head cynically.

'You think I don't know what's going on aboard my own ship, Mr Beaumont?'

'She's got to be stopped,' Beaumont repeated.

'This is something I may forget to put in the ship's log.' The captain looked across the bridge at Beaumont and spoke two words. 'Stop her.'

The Carley float, a raft for throwing overboard if the ship had to be abandoned, was packed with one hundred pounds of gelignite, was wired for detonation. The timer mechanisms were in place, the clocks had been set to trigger detonation in ten minutes' time, but they hadn't been activated. The float was now a potential mine.

Schmidt had to reduce speed considerably when they winched the launch over the side near the stern, and this was a nerve-racking decision because the *Revolution* was now coming up behind them, still a distance away, but she was overhauling the icebreaker. And the view ahead from the bridge was hardly more encouraging than the view beyond the stern. Heavy mist still drifted to starboard, half-obscuring the ghost berg which lay half a mile ahead. To port a whole column of icebergs had appeared, narrowing the channel of clear water, and in the distance dead ahead two massive bergs stood on either side of the channel, like sentries guarding a gateway. It was indeed an alley of icebergs Schmidt had to take his ship through.

'How long before she overtakes us?' Beaumont asked DaSilva.

'I'd say about ten minutes—and that's a guess.'

'Looks more like five minutes to me,' Grayson said grimly. He frowned and looked to starboard. 'Schmidt's changing course—he's moving closer to that line of icebergs.'

'I asked him to,' Beaumont snapped. 'He's going to leave a wider channel between the *Elroy* and the ghost berg.'

'So the *Revolution* can slip through on that side? He must be crazy. . . .'

'Then I'm crazy, too. We'd better get down in that launch.'

DaSilva followed him across the deck to where Borzoli and other seamen waited by the launch suspended from davit cables. 'Beaumont, I still haven't asked you what you're going to do—my guess would be you hope this blows up under the bows of the *Revolution*.'

'It wouldn't work—she's moving too fast. Now, lower us—and for Pete's sake watch that float when you send it down.'

The whole operation was diabolically tricky. The launch—with Beaumont, Langer and Grayson inside it—had to be winched down over the side of a moving vessel and then held there until the float joined them. The only thing working in their favour was the calmness of the sea. They hit the water with a heavy slap and then held on to the cables while they looked up.

The float was already on its way down to them.

While still on deck Langer had given DaSilva a little warning. 'Technically, if the float hits the side of the hull on its way down nothing will happen.' He had paused and smiled without humour. 'And heaven is full of demolition experts playing harps who said the same sort of thing.'

The airborne mine came down to them with a terrible slowness, suspended from ropes gripped by seamen high above them. Langer watched its descent with his hand gripped tightly round the winch cable. They only had to unbalance it, to let it slant downwards, and securely as the gelignite was lashed something devastating could happen. Then somebody let a rope slip. The large missile suspended above their heads canted at an angle and Langer drew in his breath with a hiss of fury and fear. 'They'll do Papanin's job for him,' he muttered.

The angled float swayed, bumped with a heavy thud against the ship's hull, a thud heavy enough to dislodge its cargo. Beaumont glanced towards the stern, suppressing his impatience; now the *Revolution* had changed course and she was heading fast for the open channel which would take her to starboard of the *Elroy*. For Christ's sake hurry it up! His prayer was answered—with unnerving speed. The float dropped and kept on dropping, coming down on their heads.

It jerked to a halt three feet above them, still canted at its dangerously unstable angle, then it was lowered more gently. Langer activated the clocks—the only clocks aboard which hadn't been put out of action because they hadn't been working when the ghost berg struck. The float was put over the stern, attached by ropes to the launch. Beaumont started the engine, took over the wheel, shouted up to DaSilva, the winch cables were released and they moved away from the *Elroy* at speed, dragging the float behind them.

'I think we're too late,' Langer shouted, looking back at the Russian ship.

Beaumont opened the throttle wide and the launch roared across the calm sea, heading direct for the ghost berg, following a course at right-angles to the receding *Elroy*, to the oncoming *Revolution*. The mist was parting now, drawing back to expose the towering wall of ice they were speeding towards. The berg reared up like the edge of some great continent, seemed even bigger than when they had moved across its treacherous surface behind the cliff wall.

As they came closer to a section of the cliff they hadn't seen earlier Beaumont saw that it was hollowed out at the base, arched into caves which disappeared inside the cliff. For the first time he realized how the ocean reached the lake they had found on the far side of the cliff; there were subterranean channels leading into the lake, channels under the arched caves. He took his decision almost without thinking.

'We're going in closer—we'll let the float go at the edge of the ice shelf,' he shouted.

'We'll never get back to the *Elroy*.' There was alarm in Grayson's shout. 'We'll never catch her up again.'

'We'll have to chance that. I'm going to get the float inside one of those channels—then it may detonate on the far side of the berg.'

Beaumont's plan was simple, a very long shot indeed. The ghost berg was on the verge of collapse, should have collapsed when it first struck the bay where the *Elroy* was marooned; even more it should have collapsed when it wrenched itself free from the other berg. But it was still intact and every hour it drifted brought it closer to final dissolution. It could be that the detonation of a large quantity of gelignite close to the ice would trigger off the catastrophe. Or it could no more than tickle the berg, blowing up a few pounds of ice.

And yet there were recorded cases where the unguarded shout of an Eskimo in his kayak had shattered one of these monsters, had brought it down into the ocean, falling like a mountain. Beaumont's plan—his faint hope—was to bring down the ghost berg ahead of the *Revolution*, filling the channel with minor bergs which would stop the Russian ship. It was a very long shot indeed.

'We are gaining on them! When the time comes I will take the wheel myself,' Papanin growled. He was staring through the clear-vision panel, watching the distant silhouette of the *Elroy* pass through a mist trail. 'You will take charge of the telegraph, control the speed,' he told Kramer.

'There will be no room for manœuvre,' Tuchevsky protested. Unlike the Siberian he was constantly switching his gaze from port to starboard and back again. And he was impressed by the enormous size of the great berg to starboard coming up, but he had no suspicion of its fragility as he stared at the towering wall. 'A launch has left the American vessel,' he said suddenly. 'It is crossing the channel ahead of us. . . .'

'Don't worry about that! Increase speed. . . .'

'It is dangerous—we are going too close to that berg. . . .'

'Full power!' Papanin shouted at Kramer. 'Full power. . . .'

*   *   *

The cliff rose vertically above their heads as the launch nosed its way through ice floes close to the shelf where ocean lapped the base of the ghost berg. Throttled back, the launch bobbed among the floes, a mere speck under the lee of the berg. Twenty yards to the south of them a great cave went inside the ice, the current flowed in under the berg. Beaumont could see the turn of the moonlit water as he shouted the order. 'Release the float!'

Grayson was ready with his knife. He slashed at the rope, holding it in one gloved hand while he sawed with the other, and it took him longer than he had anticipated to cut through the tough fibres. Behind him Beaumont and Langer suppressed their impatience with difficulty. Beaumont estimated they had about five minutes left before detonation—but without a working watch he couldn't be sure.

Grayson cut savagely at the frayed rope—the last few strands still held them to the float. Langer cursed, struggled to get his own knife out of the sheath under his parka. Beaumont watched helplessly, unable to leave the wheel. The arched opening drifted closer. Langer found his knife, hauled it out, cut at the rope Grayson was holding for him. The fibres parted. The float left them. Beaumont opened the throttle and the craft surged away from the ghost berg with a burst of power. The engine beats of the *Revolution* were much louder as he headed out diagonally down the channel, speeding after the *Elroy* he could hardly see.

In the stern Grayson clung to the gunwale, twisted round as he watched the Carley float bobbing in the current, sailing past the arched entry under the berg. At the last moment the float caught on the ice, hovered, then the current sucked it inside and sent it down the ice tunnel leading to the lake on the far side.

'It went in!' Grayson shouted.

The throttle was wide open, the launch was tearing down the dangerous, ice-strewn channel as Beaumont swung the wheel, avoided a large floe by inches, straightened up. More and more ice was appearing, small floes bobbing in the moonlight, large growlers drifting with the column of icebergs to port. Speed in such waters was excessively dangerous—and speed was vital.

The ghost berg still loomed to their right, stretched away beyond them to the south, went on for ever, it seemed, as Beaumont kept the throttle wide open and wrestled with the wheel.

A single light glowed at the *Elroy's* distant stern, the only light showing aboard the icebreaker since Schmidt had ordered all lights turned out, the light kept on to guide the launch back to the ship. The greyish spume of her vanishing wake showed to their left, the bitter air whipped at their faces, the launch zigzagged wildly to avoid more floes. And behind them the *Revolution* came on, was now moving alongside the ghost berg —because everyone had underestimated its speed.

'That gate's closing,' Langer said in Beaumont's ear. In the distance beyond the *Elroy's* silhouette the view was changing. It looked as though Schmidt was going to be too late. The two great bergs which flanked the exit from the channel were moving closer together, caught in a cross-current. By the time Schmidt reached them there would be no way out. As Langer had said, the gate was closing.

Beaumont swerved to avoid a large growler, an ice floe large enough to smash in the gunwale if they struck it, then he was swerving in the opposite direction to avoid a second one, using the launch like a powerboat. It was only a matter of time before they hit one of them, but the stern light of the *Elroy* was a little larger, was coming closer. When he glanced to starboard again he was surprised: they had moved past the end of the ghost berg, were speeding well beyond it.

'More power!' Papanin fumed. 'Overtake her!'

Tuchevsky said nothing. He was no longer in command of his own ship. Beyond the starboard window the huge iceberg reared up, towered over them, and for the first time Tuchevsky noticed the arched openings at her waterline.

Behind the ice cliff the Carley float had left the tunnel, had emerged into the dark lake beyond, was drifting round the edge, bumping up against the ice, covered with frost which had descended on it inside the tunnel. It caught a spur of ice and hovered. Above it the eroded ice tower sheered up, the tower which held up the overhang.

Close to exhaustion, Beaumont missed the floe, but the floe didn't miss the launch. The prow struck the ice spar floating underwater, leapt into the air, and the launch soared over it. As they went up, Beaumont's heart stopped—the screw was going to catch the ice, would be buckled, maybe even torn out of the craft. The launch continued its arc, the spar cracked under the pressure, went down as the screw flew over it intact and thrashed back into the sea. Behind the ice cliff the floating mine detonated.

The ice tower holding up the overhang began to collapse. The honeycombed pillar collapsed slowly, disintegrating chunk by chunk, dropping great masses of ice into the lake below, then it sagged, settled, broke. And as it broke, the enormous weight of ice above it came down, falling three hundred feet, shattering into thousands of pieces at the edge of the lake, sending an avalanche of ice over the brink. The tower was gone, the vast overhang above was gone, all support which had helped to hold up the ice cliff was gone. The ice cliff itself started to come down and one of nature's most terrifying spectacles unfolded.

The cliff fell inwards—away from the *Revolution*—and the sight from the bridge of the Russian ship stunned the men aboard. The entire cliff, which a moment earlier had climbed sheer above them, fell backwards. For a moment Papanin could hardly believe his eyes, then he saw the captain's petrified expression. 'It's a ghost berg. . . .' The continuing roar of its crash was still resounding when Tuchevsky took a grip on himself, turning on the tannoy system which would relay his message throughout the ship. 'There is no cause for alarm . . . no cause for alarm. . . .'

He was wrong, and Beaumont who knew Iceberg Alley as well as any man alive could have told him how terribly wrong he was. The tremendous spectacle the Russian had witnessed was a mere prelude to what was coming.

'The damned thing fell the wrong way!' Grayson shouted.

244

'Hang on!' Beaumont yelled.

The water was turbulent now, swelling with waves the iceberg had caused as it vibrated at the waterline. This didn't worry Beaumont: it was the tidal wave which haunted him as he desperately tried to coax more speed out of the roaring engine, the tidal wave which would come sweeping up behind them when the major catastrophe broke. If they didn't reach the ship in time they'd be overwhelmed.

The *Revolution* was still on course, moving past the wrecked berg, when the giant lost its equilibrium. The cliff which had reared up at one end of the berg was now gone, spread out over a vast area, so the immense platform which was left—half a mile long—began to turn turtle. The cliff which had stood above its surface had seemed vast, but this was nothing compared with the bulk which lurked beneath its surface, and this submerged cliff now came up out of the sea like some primeval upheaval when the very surface of the earth is transformed, dripping huge cascades of water which poured off it like a Niagara.

The sea itself began to boil, to churn as it felt what was coming up from the depths. Great dripping cliffs of ice began to tower, mounting high above the bridge of the *Revolution* where Papanin and Tuchevsky stared in horror. The Niagara of sea flooded down on the vessel. Chunks of ice larger than houses crashed down on the hull, tore away rails, left them like jagged rows of teeth. And still the berg continued to revolve, tens of millions of tons of ice on the move, mounting up as the berg continued turning its mass through a hundred and eighty degrees.

'God! It's like the earth coming up from the sea bottom!'

Grayson was staggered by the sight as the launch sped closer to the *Elroy* and Beaumont glanced back, glanced back only once and then concentrated his whole mind on reaching the *Elroy*. The tidal wave would be coming any second now. They had to reach the ship in time. Behind them the ghost berg overturned.

It swivelled, loomed above the *Revolution*, then millions of tons of ice descended, came down like the fall of an Alp. On the bridge of the Russian ship they saw it as an enormous shadow, a revolving shadow. Papanin was still on the bridge when the shadow struck, dropping a solid ice wall on top of the radar dome. The dome deflated, disappeared, the bridge was levelled to the deck, the deck was submerged. The bows went down, straight down, and the stern tilted up as though turning over an invisible fulcrum.

The stern went on climbing at an acute angle until it was vertical, with the screws still spinning like a helicopter's rotors. Two-thirds of the ship had vanished, buried under the falling cliff, but the stern paused with the screws turning more slowly as the power died. Grayson saw it hovering, like a ship about to plunge to the bottom, although the rest of the ship had already gone. Then another arm of the berg came down on it, hammered it down with one gigantic blow which drove it nine thousand feet to the bed of the Arctic. Then the wave came.

'Jump!' Beaumont shouted.

The launch had passed the *Elroy's* stern, throttled back, had drawn amidships and bumped the hull as Beaumont tried to keep pace with the slow-moving vessel. Schmidt had seen them coming a long way off, had reduced speed even before the destruction of the *Revolution*. Men peered over the rails above them, pointing to rope ladders slung over the ship's side. 'Jump!' Beaumont shouted again.

Langer grasped a dangling ladder, started climbing it while Grayson grabbed another swaying rope. Beaumont waited by the wheel, keeping the launch alongside the moving hull, and beyond the *Elroy's* stern the ocean was wild, turned in seconds from a milk-calm sea into a raging tumult. A fresh ladder thrown with skill by DaSilva slapped against Beaumont's chest. He let go of the wheel, grasped the ladder, felt the launch moving away under him, rammed his boots into swaying rungs. Above him by the rail DaSilva was screaming at him to hurry.

The tidal wave which was coming, about to pass the stern, was already twenty feet high and climbing every second. And it was composed not only of water—on its passage down the channel it had gathered up a collection of huge ice floes, floes which toppled at its crest, great rams of ice which could crush a man with one glancing blow. Langer was over the rail, followed by Grayson, when DaSilva shouted his last warning, knowing it was too late to do anything for the doomed man hanging from the side.

Half-way up the ladder Beaumont looked towards the stern, saw a foaming wall of green climbing above his head, saw the nose of a huge growler projecting through the froth. He was going to be mashed to a pulp, swept off the hull. The tidal wave hoisted the stern, lifted it high with an awful violence, and the bows went down. Beaumont clenched his gloved fingers round the rope, buried his elbows hard into his sides, squeezed his head between his forearms as he felt the stern going up like a lift.

An inundation of freezing water fell on him, a great weight pressing down on his shoulders, trying to rip him loose from the ladder. There was a roaring in his ears and then something slammed with immense force against the hull beside him. He shuddered with the impact, felt ice splinters shower against his face like a thousand tiny knives. The force of the water swept the ladder sideways, whipped him towards the bows where the launch had just been hurled and broken open.

Beaumont was frozen, the breath he held in his lungs bursting, petrified by the floe which had smashed so close to him, sodden with sea, scraped and swung up almost to the rail by the sway of the rope ladder. The roaring in his ears increased, he felt his strength going, his grip on the ladder weakening as the sea tugged and tore at him. Then the bows climbed and the ladder was swinging back in the other direction, banging his body brutally against the hull. Only extreme fear, a spark of self-survival, kept him conscious, aware that his numbed hands were still locked round the ladder. Then the sea dropped away and he felt himself falling, turning over and over. *It's your mind, you're still on the bloody ladder. . . .*

A long way off an American voice was shouting, shouting again and again. 'Hold on! We're hauling you up! Hold on!' Then he hit something very hard and hands were pawing him, fiddling with his hands, trying to unlock the fingers still clamped round the rope. He opened his eyes and saw a broken mast silhouetted against a moonlit sky, a mast whipping backwards and forwards. Something fell from it, came whirling down towards Beaumont's face and hit the deck with a horrible thud only two yards away. The lookout had fallen. Beaumont thought he was imagining things but there was a dead American seaman on the deck two yards away, his skull crushed in.

He was still unable to move as hands hauled his bruised and bloodstained body upright and started carrying him towards a staircase. He was muttering something as they carried him, and DaSilva had to ask him to repeat it before he understood. 'Grayson and Langer are safe,' the mate told him. 'We're O.K. We're on our way home.' It was not a sentiment shared by Commander Alfred Schmidt at this moment who was asking for full power at all costs. The icebreaker was heading for almost certain destruction.

Everywhere the icebergs were coming together, caught in the cross-currents, closing in on the *Elroy* as her engines beat faster. But it was the two huge bergs dead ahead that Schmidt was watching with great anxiety. The silhouettes of the bergs rose to port and starboard, castles of ice in the moonlight, castles converging on each other across the perilously narrow channel the *Elroy* was steaming down. Another five minutes and they would know whether they had made it. Another five minutes and they would be through the gate or crushed between the closing bergs.

'Full power. . . .'

DaSilva came on to the bridge as the commander repeated the order, something which he had never done before, something to drive home to the chief engineer below that this was a terrible emergency. In front of DaSilva, Schmidt's head was constantly swivelling on his neck as though supported by ball-bearings. Port, ahead, starboard. The view was always the same—icebergs, moving icebergs, and every time Schmidt looked they seemed to have moved closer. The bows thrust forward, brushing aside huge floes, pointing towards the ever-narrowing gate.

The repetition of the same order had communicated its

message to the engine-room, and without being told the men below guessed what was happening. The chief engineer stared at his bank of gauges but his mind was outside the ship, imagining cruel jaws of ice coming towards him. He sensed the tremendous impact when ice met steel, saw the hull coming in on him, first a spur of ice, followed instantly by an inundation of water. The engine-room crew watched him and he tried to maintain a bored look. They would never get out in time, of course. The engine-room was the ship's graveyard. As he had done on other occasions, he swore to himself that if he got out of this one he would never go to sea again.

The icebergs were on either quarter of the bows, so close it was like entering a deep cutting, like proceeding inside the Corinth Canal with rock walls towering on either side—but these were walls of ice, moving walls. Schmidt stared in front of him, refusing to look sideways any more, knowing that DaSilva, the helmsman and the officer of the watch were glancing at him in terror. Then he took out his handkerchief, mopped his forehead, and spoke in a casual voice. 'Getting a bit warm in here.' From the bridge window he could have thrown out a bottle and hit the iceberg on the port quarter. And no moonlight shone on the foredeck which was dark with the shadows of the icebergs. DaSilva, his hands clasped tightly behind his back, could have screamed with the tension, but Schmidt's erect figure, his recent remark, his refusal to look to port or starboard, kept him under control. Like the captain, the other men on the bridge stared stonily ahead.

'Take a look through the rear window, Mr DaSilva,' Schmidt suggested.

'We're through! We're through the gate!'

'Maintain your present course.'

Ahead there was a pale cold light in the distant sky, the sun returning to the Arctic, the sun whose palest glimmer had been blotted out by a heavy cloud bank for days. DaSilva looked back through the rear window. The gateway between the bergs was so narrow that even a launch could no longer have passed through. The silhouettes merged and across the ocean rang the appalling crack of collision, a terrible rumbling crack followed by a roar as the bergs ground up against each other. Then an echoing boom which went right out across the Arctic. DaSilva jumped when he heard Schmidt speaking.

'Clear water ahead, Mr DaSilva. We're going home.'

On Wednesday, 7 March, Beaumont went ashore at Quebec, limping as he moved down the gangway with the aid of a stick, and his face was so covered with bandages that only the eyes showed, eyes which were bleak and remote. Schmidt, Grayson and Langer leaned out of a bridge window to watch him go, but he didn't look back as he hobbled on to the dockside. Seamen lined the rails in silence, ready to wave, but he didn't even glance in their direction.

It was cold on that March day long ago, and ice drifted in the St Lawrence while snow glistened on the rooftops of the Château Frontenac as the sun came out. Lemuel Dawes and Adams were waiting for him, hurried forward, and then hesitated as the tall, heavily-built Englishman stared at them from between his mask of bandages. Beaumont shook hands formally and quickly. 'I have to get away,' he growled. 'Grayson can give you any details you need—and I've written you a report.'

He took the core tube out of his parka and gave it to Dawes. 'What you want is inside this core—take the top bit of rock out with a knife and you'll find it.' He paused as Dawes took the core. 'I hope it was worth it—a lot of men died.'

He hobbled away before Dawes could reply, hobbled past the official car and got into a taxi. 'Airport,' he told the driver. He was silent for most of the drive, staring out of the window without taking in anything he was passing. As they came close to the airport he asked a question. 'Any idea when the next flight for Miami takes off?'

Aftermath. May—July 1972

THE ICE ISLAND, Target-5, continued its drift south into Iceberg Alley—into destruction. On 7 March, the day Beaumont went ashore at Quebec, a C.130 transport landed safely on the airstrip, stopping a few yards from the burnt-out wreck of its predecessor. It was in no danger of repeating the earlier aircraft's suicidal performance because the rocks had disappeared off the airstrip.

The men who came out of this plane hurried to take on board the crated equipment—nervous about the island's nearness to the sea and worried because the fog was closing in again. When they found Matthew Conway's body under the wrecked Sno-Cat they assumed he had driven off the ramp in the fog; they hurried to put the body aboard the plane and later it was flown to Cincinnatti for burial.

What did puzzle these anxious men was that they could find no trace of Rickard, the wireless operator, or Sondeborg, the gravity specialist. Their disappearance became a mystery.

In May the American president visited Moscow and among the many agreements concluded was one which promised there would be no more close-shadowing—which might result in collision—of American vessels by Soviet ships and vice versa. No one outside government circles wondered why this particular moment was chosen to make this pact when near-collisions between American and Soviet vessels spying on each other—although rarely reported in the press—had been commonplace for years.

Also in May, Target-5, which had earlier broken into four pieces, further fragmented into eight separate slabs between Greenland and Iceland, and American planes from Keflavik kept a special watch on the slab supporting the huts. Then, while it was hidden from them by dense mist, they lost it for two months.

In July, a Danish liner cruising off Frederikshaab on the west coast of Greenland, reported sighting an ice floe which carried buildings. Police boats were sent out from the port and passengers on board the liner watched from the rails as the police entered the still-intact huts. It was an Inspector Gustaffson who went inside the research hut and examined it thoroughly. When he lifted the floorboards covering the hole where the core drill had once been lowered, a four-month-old mystery was solved.

Jeff Rickard and Harvey Sondeborg were lying frozen on the lower platform of floorboards, the platform which covered the hole going down into the Arctic. An autopsy was carried out and it was concluded that Rickard had probably been murdered by Sondeborg, who was still clutching an ice pick when the bodies were found.

Gustaffson then suggested—he had no proof—that Sondeborg had killed his fellow-American and had tried to hide the body inside the hole.

In Gustaffson's opinion Sondeborg had intended dropping the corpse below the second platform into the Arctic, but he slipped and fell himself, dying beside his victim from injuries received during his fall.

In Washington, Gustaffson's report was disbelieved and filed. Probably no one will ever know positively how these two men died.

It was in July that a shipping correspondent in London made a routine inquiry at the Soviet Embassy in Kensington Palace Gardens.

Looking for a copy for a projected article on modern ships, he asked for information as to the present whereabouts of the *Revolution*, nursing a faint hope that one day he might be shown over this showpiece vessel. The Soviet official he met consulted a more senior official, then told him that the *Revolution* had returned to a Black Sea port for an extensive refit. Apparently she had collided with an iceberg while undertaking research in Arctic waters.

And it was in July 1972 that the Fischer-Spassky world chess contest opened at Reykjavik in Iceland, the contest a certain Igor Papanin was to have attended, officially as one of Spassky's chess advisers, unofficially as chief of security for the duration of the contest. Another man, less qualified in both fields, quietly took his place.